MURDER AT THE OFFICE

I headed to the back of the giant room. Halfway there, a man dressed in a janitor's outfit stepped out from behind a partition, scaring the daylights out of me. "Help you?"

I told him I was looking for the offices and he pointed to a dimly lit corner of the room. I thanked him and headed that way. I pushed the door leading to the corridor open and paused. "Hello? Horatio? It's Violet Mooney."

Silence. Shoot. I bet he'd gotten tired of waiting for me, although I was only about fifteen minutes late. Still, I bet most people didn't make Horatio Hale wait. I moved down the hall, peering into doors as I went, and finally saw a gleam of light, like from a cell phone, emanating from the last office on the right. I went to the door and peered inside. He must have had his headphones in and couldn't hear me.

And I stopped just short of tripping over something on the floor. I focused. And screamed.

I'd found Horatio. On the floor, the obstacle I'd nearly tripped over. His cell phone lay on the floor next to him, shadowy figures moving around on the screen. It did indeed look like he had been watching a video. But my eyes were glued to his chest. And the really sharp pickaxe embedded in the middle of it . . .

Books by Cate Conte

WITCH HUNT

WITCH TRIAL

WITCH WAY OUT

Published by Kensington Publishing Corp.

Witch Way Out

A Full Moon Mystery

CATE CONTE

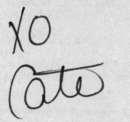

XO
Cate

www.kensingtonbooks.com

KENSINGTON BOOKS are published by

Kensington Publishing Corp.
119 West 40th Street
New York, NY 10018

All Kensington titles, imprints, and distributed lines are available at special quantity discounts for bulk purchases for sales promotion, premiums, fund-raising, educational, or institutional use.

Special book excerpts or customized printings can also be created to fit specific needs. For details, write or phone the office of the Kensington Sales Manager: Attn.: Sales Department. Kensington Publishing Corp., 119 West 40th Street, New York, NY 10018. Phone: 1-800-221-2647.

The K and Teapot logo is a trademark of Kensington Publishing Corp.

First Printing: April 2023
ISBN: 978-1-4967-3271-2

ISBN: 978-1-4967-3272-9 (ebook)

10 9 8 7 6 5 4 3 2 1

Printed in the United States of America

For Dacia

ACKNOWLEDGMENTS

First, thank you to everyone who reads my books and who wrote to me to say they love this series. It's been a delight to write and I'm so happy that people have enjoyed it.

Thank you to the Kensington Books team—especially my editor John Scognamiglio, publicist Larissa Ackerman, and the amazing designer who captures the feeling of these books so well—for everything you do to bring these books to life. And of course my agent, John Talbot, for all your support for these books.

Thank you so much to Jason Allen-Forrest, my beta reader who is the absolute best—he truly makes every book better. Thank you to Jessie Crockett, my fellow Wicked, who always can help me untangle a plot in five minutes or less. You and the rest of the Wickeds—Barb Ross, Sherry Harris, Julie Hennrikus, and Edith Maxwell—are the best friends and writing confidants a girl could have.

Special thanks to Jen McKee, my assistant and friend, who keeps me on track, makes sure I'm showing up, and always makes me laugh.

And Riham, thanks for motivating me, reading my books, and always having something lovely to say about them. You are an amazing friend.

I dedicated this book to Dacia, a dear friend

who we lost way too soon. A writer herself, she's one of my biggest inspirations to keep going even when the writing gets tough, and I know she's still sending me inspo to this day. Thanks, girl. Miss you always.

CHAPTER ONE

Saturday
Eight days before the full moon

If it wasn't for the puddle of slime waiting for us, things would've probably turned out a lot differently that night.

Sadly, this wasn't the first time a puddle of slime had greatly influenced my life. I'm still working through the repercussions of the previous puddle of slime from two months ago, which, admittedly, led me here to this one, on this night, in a leprechaun private investigator's office with a hot, sexy witch lawyer and my current liar of a boyfriend by my side.

Maybe I should explain. My name is Violet Mooney, and I recently discovered I was a witch. Not just any witch, but a combination of a Ravenstar and Moonstone witch, which, according to pretty much everyone I talk to who knows about stuff like this, is a big deal.

I know what you're thinking. Most people don't simply stumble upon the fact that they're a witch at age thirty-two. I would tend to agree with that. In my case, it's kind of a long story. Suffice it to say my long-lost mother, queen of the Ravenstar clan, showed up one day out of the blue—well, actually in a cloud of purple smoke and glitter—when I was in big trouble. Turned out my dad, who was half witch, and my grandma Abby, who was literally the high priestess of the Moonstone family, had been keeping me from my mother per my dad's wishes via a spellbound necklace that wouldn't allow her to locate me as long as I was wearing it. On the day I'd accidentally broken the necklace, my mother had found me. And she'd brought along my half-sister Zoe. They'd both appeared in a swirl of sparkles at the police station, where I was being questioned for murder. And no, I wasn't doing any drugs that day.

I'd been a little wary—okay, a lot wary—of letting my mother into my life, especially since I didn't understand why she'd been gone for twenty-seven years. But since my dad and Grandma Abby had both passed away, I had no one else that was an actual blood relation. Plus Fiona—that's my mother— does not take kindly to the word *no*. So we became a family. Kind of. And I became a witch. Or, as Fiona would put it, I stepped into my rightful heritage. Which meant the seat on the Magickal Council I'd inherited from my Grandma Abby, just waiting for me to claim it; powers to learn about and hone; a very complicated life in the mortal realm where I still had my crystal shop, The Full Moon; and, apparently, a bounty on my head from people who did not want to see the next in line on either the Moonstone or Ravenstar families take any position of power and perpetuate the current governing structure.

So that's my new year so far. And that's without the other bit involving Todd, my current boyfriend, and Blake, the sexy lawyer, both of whom stood next to me. Trust me, that's another story altogether.

Blake had gone into full-on alert mode when we'd arrived at Mac Finnegan's office for a debrief and instead found . . . this. Mac Finnegan was a leprechaun PI and yes, that's really a thing. The awaiting slime led Blake and me to believe that Mac had been the second magickal being in less than two months to have been genied. Todd, meanwhile, had gone into shock, unless he was just a really good actor. I figured he would pass out any moment now.

This whole thing was a mess. I mean, I was already mad at Blake for this little stunt. Now I was facing another genieing because he'd dragged me here. It had been less than five minutes ago that I'd been standing on a street in my quaint little town of North Harbor with Todd and Blake. Blake had pulled us away from a double date with my best friends Sydney and Pete—their first date, I might add—promising me that a lot of the questions bubbling up about my life, my grandma Abby, and Todd and his family were about to be revealed. By Mac.

But Mac didn't appear to be in a very talkative state at the moment.

I focused on the putrid-smelling puddle of slime, trying to tamp down my horror, not to mention my nausea. Unlike with Mazzy Diamond, the first being I knew who had been genied, this time I knew what I was looking at. And that it wasn't good. I saw a few red hairs in the puddle that hadn't disintegrated yet, but other than that, there were no identifying features left. I finally looked at Blake, trying not to breathe in the smell. "Please tell me that's not Mac."

Blake didn't respond. He was staring too, and judging from his expression, the confident, always-got-the-answer guy had left the building.

By the looks of things, nothing was getting revealed tonight.

Unless that was the case all along, and this had been nothing more than a clever ruse to get me to let my guard down. But by whom? Mac himself? Blake? Had I been the intended victim tonight and something had gone awry?

I tried to push those thoughts away. I hated to be so suspicious of everyone—it was not my nature—but recent events had definitely skewed my perceptions of, well, all beings.

See, I'd recently learned that not only was Todd from the Sageblood family of witches, but so was Blake. The Sagebloods were the third most powerful family in this realm, after the Ravenstars and Moonstones, and the ones who practiced the darkest magic. As a collective, they also hated both my family lines. Todd had kept this from me the whole time we'd been dating. When I'd found out

Blake was also related, I'd felt betrayed, although Fiona swore on her powers that Blake was the family outcast and nothing like them. The circumstances were not black and white in either case, but it still made me very edgy.

"Stand back." Blake finally spoke. He lifted his hand and waved it in my direction, a quick motion that I might not have even noticed if an invisible wall hadn't suddenly come up, stopping me from getting any closer.

"Hey!" I protested.

He turned to, I presume, do the same to Todd, but stopped short. We both stared at the empty space where Todd had stood a moment ago.

Gone. Not even passed out on the floor.

Blake muttered something that sounded like a particularly offensive mortal curse word. "Stay here." He did a quick sweep of the office we were in and the one next door. Upon his return, he grabbed my hand and pulled me away, out the back door and into the alley behind the building. It was a cold night, dark and quiet out here under a sky full of glittering stars. I had no idea how late it was or if time even worked the same way in the witch world.

I was getting freaked out now. "Blake, what is going on here? Where is Todd?"

"I don't know, Violet." He looked grim. "I'm guessing someone snapped him up and got him out of here."

"Like who? Someone from his family? Well, your family," I said pointedly.

He gave me a look that said he wasn't in the mood. "Probably."

"Well, what did Mac want to tell us?"

"I don't know. I wanted you to hear it with me, so I asked him to hold on to the information. Then I came and got you."

I narrowed my eyes at him. "Are you messing with me?"

The shock on his face was so raw that I instantly regretted my words. Maybe I was naive, but even though he was a witch I didn't think he was that good an actor. When he spoke, his voice was almost robotic. "No, Violet. I am not messing with you. If this is Mac, then this is bad. I'm sorry I brought you here to find . . . this."

"Blake—I'm sorry. I just—"

"Don't worry about it."

I was pretty sure I'd hurt him. Now I felt terrible. I didn't know what else to say, though, so I kept my mouth shut.

We both stood there quietly, absorbing the situation. "So what do we do now?" I glanced around nervously, worried that the genie who had gotten Mac was lurking in the shadows, waiting for the opportunity to get to us too. I'd been living with this constant, gnawing fear ever since someone had genied Mazzy, another witch, in my shop, an event that had put me under a microscope in my new community. And things had just gotten a thousand times worse.

"We need to call the police, right? Which ones?" I'd been introduced to a lot of different police forces in this new world, and I wasn't able to keep them all straight yet. We were in a specific district, which had its own police presence, yet the Magickal Police—the highest police force in the land—

were involved in the genie investigation, so it was probably them. And yes, it was all confusing to me. I'd grown up mortal and knew only the state and local police.

Blake didn't answer right away. He faced the building and closed his eyes. His lips were moving, but I couldn't hear what he was saying. Then he put his arms up in kind of an X shape in front of his face. I watched, fascinated, waiting for something to happen. I had no idea what because I wasn't really up on all the spells yet. But there was no lightning strike or other outward display of anything. Instead, there was complete silence. Then Blake turned to me.

"Come on," he said. "We need to get out of here." He grabbed my hand, and everything went black.

CHAPTER TWO

When I opened my eyes, we were standing in a fancy office, one that I'd never seen before. And it definitely did not belong to a rough-talking private investigator leprechaun. This office had class. Dare I even say it was fancy, with expensive-looking art and pristine, modern furniture. It looked like a suite of some sort, judging by how high up we were.

A coffee service hovered in the air next to the desk. If I hadn't been so freaked out, I would've totally demanded to know how I could get that at my shop, although I imagined it would be a little weird for Syd. Sydney Santangelo was my shop manager and best friend who didn't yet know I was a witch—another problem that needed addressing. On the immaculate desk, a laptop computer was typing on its own. When I went near it, it slammed shut, as if rebuking me for trying to get a peek at whatever confidential stuff it was doing.

From the way Blake moved into action and settled behind the desk, I assumed it was his office. Which meant we were at some kind of law firm.

"Sit," he said. "I need to call Bell, but first I want to alert my contact on the Squad."

By Bell, I assumed he meant Theonius Bell, the chief of the Magickal Police Force. And by the Squad, I assumed he meant the Stalker Squad. I'd recently learned about them. They were the special forces of the magickal police—although I kind of wondered why you needed special forces in a magickal police force. Weren't they all special?— and they investigated the worst crimes that magickal beings committed on each other. Since genieing was at the top of the list, not to mention a crime that, before Mazzy, hadn't been committed in a century, they had been brought into Mazzy's case. With a second one, they'd be all over this. There was only one problem with the Squad— they'd been investigating *me*. And yet I'd never met any of them, which gave me pause about how this investigating was occurring.

"Wait! They're already looking at me because someone sketchy put them up to it. Won't this make it worse?"

"No. Dewin can be trusted."

"Dewin?"

Blake nodded. "Dewin Mallor. He's one of the top-ranking investigators in the Squad, but he's the real deal. No politics, no bull—just truth and justice. There aren't a lot of guys like him nowadays. He's running his own investigation on the side."

"Is he a witch?"

"He's more like a sorcerer," Blake said. "A little more powerful than us."

I didn't even want to know what that meant.

"Anyway, Bell can make the formal announcement to his colleague over there after I tell him, but it won't hurt to have Dewin in the know first. Give me a minute." The phone receiver lifted and hovered next to Blake's ear. I could see the buttons lighting up, dialing a number, then Blake spoke.

"Dewin. It's Blake Alexander." A pause. "I'm not so great at the moment. I have to call Bell but wanted to speak to you first. There's been a second genieing. And I'm afraid it's Mac Finnegan." Another pause. "It was his office, he was the only one I was meeting. I don't know for certain, but almost positive." Blake's eyes were on me even as he spoke to the person on the other end, and his steady gaze made me squirm.

I was still working out what I felt for Blake. He was kind of my witchy life coach, a position to which my mother had appointed him, and one he had embraced wholeheartedly, if not with some amusement, at least until things like this had started happening. All I knew for sure was that he was hot, he was kind, and he'd been really good to me over the past few weeks, despite the whole not-telling-me-who-his-family-was thing. I believed him when he said it was because he didn't want me to think he was like them, or aligned with them in any way. In a place where I wasn't sure whom to trust, Blake seemed to be one of the good ones, his family ties aside.

But that was something I was still unpacking.

"I found him. I didn't touch anything. I put a protective spell on the whole building so no one else can go in. I had Violet Moonstone and Todd Langston—aka Sageblood—with me. Yeah, that Violet Moonstone. I know, Dewin. Trust me, it's definitely got something to do with her. I'm telling you that so you have the whole story, but I don't want it getting out that she was there." He listened, then said, "Okay, thanks," and hung up.

I gaped at him. "You told him Mac's genieing had something to do with me!"

"It does," he said calmly.

I stood, almost knocking my chair over. "Are you kidding? I was with you the whole time!"

"Not like that," he said impatiently. "Of course he knows you personally didn't have something to do with it. But it's because Mac was looking into this case, which is related to you. Better to just put that out there so they don't spin their wheels looking through everything else he had going on."

"How can you just know that?" I asked, incredulous.

He tilted his head in a *Seriously?* gesture.

I sat back down, my heart suddenly heavy. "So it's my fault this happened to Mac." I thought of the little man who'd appeared in my shop a week or so ago. While his size jibed with how I'd always imagined leprechauns, the rest of him was nothing like the caricatures we'd grown up with. For one thing, Mac was surly. There was no green sequined jacket, striped pants, and happy pot of gold for this leprechaun. Mac dressed all in black and spoke in a deep, husky voice that hadn't really fit his appearance. He'd had two of his leprechaun counterparts, Goldie and Shiloh, with him. They all dressed the same and basically had the same demeanor. At first I hadn't liked him much. He wasn't friendly or forthcoming. But Blake had convinced me that he was the best. I knew Fiona trusted him too. And it seemed like he got stuff done. No nonsense, no games. He just wasn't much for friendly conversation. Or someone telling him how to do his job.

What would happen to his firm now? Would Goldie and Shiloh be able to keep going? My mother was going to lose it. She'd hired Mac. And now this had happened because of me. I already felt guilty enough about Mazzy. She was a journalist, both in the witch realm and here in the mortal world. We'd met when she was doing a story on fraudulent psychic practitioners and had tried to put me in that category. Needless to say, we hadn't hit it off well. At the time of her genieing, we'd come to a truce—but she'd clearly made someone else angry. Angry enough to commit the worst magickal felony ever, and in my store no less.

"Violet, of course it's not your fault. Stop blaming yourself," Blake said. "That's not what I was getting at. I wanted Dewin to know what Mac was working on. That's all. If he doesn't know this, his team could possibly walk into something bad. They will need to be super careful. But Dewin is the only one I'm telling that you were there, okay? I'm not even telling Chief Bell. Which means you can't tell anyone either. Violet." He waited until I focused on him. "This is very important. You cannot tell anyone you were with me there. Do you understand?"

"Yeah. I understand." I had a million questions about why he wasn't telling Bell, but I wasn't even sure I wanted to hear the answer at this point. I dropped my head back into my hands, rubbing my temples. "But what about Todd?"

Blake's lips thinned. "I'll handle Todd. Once I find him." He reached over the desk and lifted my chin so my eyes were level with his. "It's not your fault," he repeated. "And we'll get Mac back. Don't worry. Now I have to call Chief Bell, okay? Just hang tight."

I tried to smile and nod, but inside I was devastated. And terrified.

What was going to happen to all of us before this was over?

CHAPTER THREE

Saturday/Sunday

Part of the reason my new life could be so disconcerting was the stark contrast to the normalcy that existed in my mortal life. Upon my return to my cozy apartment from my eventful evening with Blake, our slimed leprechaun, and an incredibly distraught Chief Bell, I realized I'd missed a bunch of phone calls and texts. For a moment I had a paranoid thought that someone else had been genied, then realized if that was the case other witches wouldn't be sending me text messages about it; they'd probably just show up in a poof of smoke or a shower of glitter to give me the news.

The texts were from Josie Cook, my part-time employee, lifelong friend, and also fellow witch. I scanned them while I listened to the voicemails, which were also from Josie. Finally, after a bunch of urgent *Call me now* and *I have amazing news* messages, Josie finally got to the point in the last voicemail.

"Violet. I have no idea where you are but you need to call me! We got a call from Horatio Hale tonight. They had a last-minute cancellation for booth space at the Spring Equinox Fair. The flower essence vendor put the wrong flower in one of her essences and ended up in the hospital. Anyway, we got a booth! We need to be there by seven tomorrow morning to set up. I'll meet you there. I left Syd a message too. We should have her working the shop while you and I handle the fair. Call me!"

I let out a squeal that woke my orange cat, Monty, who was sound asleep on my bed. His head snapped up and he glared at me before returning to his curled-up position, tail landing over his eyes. "Sorry," I said. "But this is a huge deal! Do you know how long I've wanted to be part of the Equinox Fairs? And Horatio Hale?" I nearly swooned. "He's a legend!"

Monty ignored me. Clearly, he didn't know about the prestige of being invited to one of the two major fairs on the circuit. Spring and Autumn Equinox fairs were legendary within our alternative healing community. And Horatio Hale was a huge name. He was a champion for ethical sourcing in the crystal world and aside from being one of the most reputable sellers, he'd also made a name for himself as an activist, speaking on every available platform he could find to educate people about ethics in our industry. I'd been following his work for years, sometimes watching his YouTube videos to the point where I could recite them verbatim. I'd followed his exposés on sourcing in the Congo and Myanmar, and watched his takedown of a consortium in the US that was hiding severe environmental damage at a Texas mine. Not only had he built a business on crystals, he had done it by uncovering and buying only from the vendors who went through rigorous sourcing protocols. Crystals—like anything else, I supposed—had a dark side to them. Many of the stones came from countries without any kind of regulation, not to mention lax or even nonexistent labor laws. Some came from the United States, but from mines that caused extreme pollution and contamination to the earth. Many sellers cared about these things and were careful about where they bought crystals. Others saw the stones as purely a money-making opportunity and tossed aside any care for human rights, the environment, or even the violence and conflict that came from fighting over mines and land from which the crystals were sourced.

As someone who believed wholeheartedly in the healing power of crystals, it seemed quite counterintuitive to purchase them from dark origins. How could something help you heal if it had bad energy attached to it? I only used a few vendors whom I trusted completely, and that was in large part due to what I'd learned from following Horatio. To get him as a supplier was really hard—he had a wait list. I'd been on it for years. So the fact that *he* had called *my store* was . . . well, I was having a fangirl moment.

But Monty didn't care, and Xander, my other cat, was nowhere in sight. Xander was a magickal cat. He was sleek and black and moved through both worlds like a ninja. He'd shown up in my life right before I met my mother. It had definitely not been an accident. And he'd saved my butt a few times already. I guessed in technical terms he was my familiar, although I didn't want Monty to feel shortchanged by that title so I never used it out loud. I figured Josie would be a better option with whom to celebrate, so I called her back.

"Jeez, took you long enough. Were you out with Todd this long?" Josie demanded without so much as a hello.

I did not want to get into anything about this evening. I couldn't anyway. News would be out soon enough, but I didn't need to be the one breaking it. "Sorry. I ended up, uh, running into Blake. Just got home." It wasn't totally a lie.

"Blake, huh? I thought tonight was your double date with Syd and Pete. And Todd."

"Yeah, it was. But hey, it's late. Let's focus on the matter at hand, shall we? Horatio? I'm dying over here. This is amazing news!" News I did not want to ruin by reminders of my train wreck of a relationship and the genieing of an innocent.

"It really is. Horatio was very complimentary of our shop. He knew about us. He sent me the floor plan of the space. We have a good spot, Vi! It's a little pricey, but they're giving us a discount since it's so last minute."

"That is so exciting! I don't care how much it costs. This is such great exposure. We're gonna need to be up at the crack of dawn to pack up," I said.

"Already figured. I packed a few boxes tonight."

"You did?" I asked, impressed.

"Vi," Josie said with amusement. "I'm a witch. It's pretty easy."

I burst out laughing. I really needed to remember to use my powers more to make my life easier. "Good point."

After I made arrangements to meet Josie at the store at six thirty tomorrow morning, I changed into shorts and a T-shirt and made a cup of tea. I couldn't stop smiling, momentarily forgetting the oppressive worries bearing down on me. My shop was going to be on display at the Spring Equinox Fair. This would catapult my business to the next level.

The fairs moved around the northeast, and this year the spring fair was taking place right here in North Harbor. Part of the reason they chose us was the indoor amphitheater that had been built across town a few years back. The town used it for everything from local theater to winter farmer's markets to other types of fairs and gatherings. The space could be adjusted based on the setup they wanted, so it was the perfect place. The fair would run all week, from Sunday through Saturday, including a big St. Patrick's Day parade on Wednesday and an equinox celebration on the final night.

Being asked to participate as a vendor was a dream come true. I'd put my shop's name in the lottery to get a booth. There were a few vendors—big names—who were guaranteed a spot every year and the others were picked from a lottery. Once locations were announced at the prior year's fair, all vendors were invited to submit their requests and a certain number were chosen. Honestly, it was a long shot because so many people wanted to exhibit. The total number of vendors was about sixty. They probably got five hundred applications.

I felt sorry for the flower essence lady who'd had to give up her spot, but reasoned that if she was able to poison herself, people probably didn't want to be buying her goods. I went to bed feeling like I was floating on a cloud.

But despite my good mood, I had a hard time falling asleep. I woke up every couple of hours convinced that someone was skulking around my apartment waiting to turn me into a puddle of slime. I woke up at six Sunday morning feeling more exhausted than when I went to bed.

Monty and Xander were snuggled up next to me, one on either side. Monty saw me awake and knew it meant breakfast time, so he hopped off the bed and rushed to the kitchen to be first in line. Xander remained splayed on the bed, tail swishing as he regarded me with those bright yellow eyes.

"I know, you'll eat on your own terms." I threw the covers off and got up, feeling cranky and out of sorts already. I needed coffee. Which made me think of Pete, which reminded me that I'd vanished in the middle of the double date last night. I cringed. Pete was a witch and he knew a little about what was going on, but I needed to see how he'd handled my disappearance with Syd. Still, thoughts of the fair cheered me. I figured once I had some coffee I would be in tiptop shape.

I was halfway to the kitchen before I remembered that I didn't need to actually go to the kitchen like the mere mortal I was two months ago. I could simply wave a hand and have a cup of coffee appear—which in my mind was probably the best part about being a witch. Next to teleporting, it was the spell I'd been spending the most time perfecting, which my mother found extremely annoying. In her view, there were way more important things to learn, like manipulating time, conjuring up the elements, and dressing yourself.

Still, I practiced conjuring my coffee as I walked, taking an enormous amount of pleasure in the perfectly filled mug that appeared in my hand. The first sip was enough to get me into a semi-better mood. We all had different priorities.

I fed Monty and left food out for Xander in case he wanted anything, then took a quick shower. I ran my fingers through my hair, drying it with a touch, then got dressed in my power outfit—a short purple velvet dress with rhinestones, sparkly black tights, a denim jacket, and my purple combat boots. And of course my giant winter coat, because it was freezing in North Harbor right now. I drained my coffee and hurried out the door, grimacing when the frigid air hit my face. Despite the looming spring equinox, it did not feel like spring was coming. I pulled my fluffy polka-dotted scarf up around my face, put my head down against the wind, and hurried down the street.

When I got to The Friendly Bean, Pete's coffee shop, he was just opening up. When he saw me, he grinned and opened the door wide. "Come on in, kiddo. How did it go last night?"

I really hated that question. I managed a grin. "That's my question for you." I avoided his eyes as I brushed past him. "But first, a latte?"

Chapter Four

"**C**ome on back." Pete led me inside and detoured around the counter to take his place at the espresso machine. His place was so cozy and homey, from the mason jars filled with twinkling lights in all the windows (which I'd discovered was a witch thing, a way to alert other witches to a like-minded place) to the gas fireplace he'd just installed last week. It gave the dining area that much more of a comfy, living-room-type feel. I came to Pete's probably too often. Part of it was the coffee, but mostly it was because I'd always felt at home here.

I guess now I knew why.

Pete fired up the machine and leaned on the counter. "What's up, Violet? Did something happen last night?"

"What? No. Nothing. Just need caffeine. I actually have good news. I got a last-minute invite to be a vendor in the Spring Equinox Fair!" I was a terrible liar and Pete wasn't fooled. I knew he could see right through me. But to his credit, he didn't push.

"That's terrific. I'm really happy for you. That's a great fair. Make sure you tell me your impressions now that you have a . . . different viewpoint." He reached over and squeezed my arm, then turned and got busy with the espresso machine. "Caramel mocha?" he asked over his shoulder.

"Perfect," I said. "What do you mean, a different viewpoint?"

"You know. Your newfound knowledge of your background. It'll definitely change things for you."

I thought about that. It hadn't even crossed my mind. "What do you mean? Like, there are . . ." I lowered my voice and glanced around. "People like us there?"

"Violet. Have we taught you nothing yet?" He turned around, shaking his head. "There are people like us everywhere. You just have to keep your eyes open and tune in."

I mulled that over and filed it away for later. I didn't really want to ask what he meant. Better if I didn't know everything right off the bat. "So? Don't keep me in suspense. How was the date?"

He grinned, flipping on the machine to steam the milk. "It was awesome. Syd is a lot of fun."

"I knew it!" I was truly delighted. Syd and Pete had been crushing on each other for ages and Pete had finally asked her out. "Was Syd mad that I, uh . . ."

"Vanished? Nah. After Blake unfroze time, she was a little disoriented. I told her you and Todd had to go sort things out."

"How does that work anyway?" I asked. "The time freezing thing? Do people feel, like, short-circuited or something?"

"No. If it's done right, everything is just as it was. But you left and she didn't have that recall of how or why. And she was asking about Blake. You know, she saw him come in and everything."

I winced. "She's always asking me about Blake."

"She thinks Blake likes you." He poured the latte and placed the cup on the counter in front of me. "I don't."

I stared at him, my heart plummeting somewhere down into my stomach. I could always count on Pete to be painfully honest, and I guessed I hadn't realized how much I'd been hoping the opposite of that assessment about Blake's feelings was true. "You . . . you don't?"

"Nope." He set the coffee cup down on the counter in front of me and regarded me with a serious face. "I know he does."

It took a second for that to register. Then I frowned, swatting at him over the counter. "Oh, stop." His words gave me a thrill, but I didn't want to admit it. Yet. "We're not talking about me and Blake. We're talking about you and Syd." I sipped the coffee. "Yum. Thank you. So are you going out again? Tell me everything!"

"Of course we are. Tonight, actually." Pete grinned. "I convinced her to let me take her to a comedy club."

"That's great!" I clapped my hands. "I'm sure she didn't need a lot of convincing, though."

"I guess not," Pete agreed. "It must be my wit and charm. So what happened after you and Blake left? Actually, come on." He came out from behind the counter and led me to a seat. "Let's talk."

"I can't, I have to meet Josie at six thirty," I protested, pointing to my watch. I had ten minutes.

"It'll be quick." His tone left no room for argument.

I let him lead me to the table in the far back and sat.

"So?" he prompted. "Blake? Todd? Don't leave me hanging, kid."

"Blake and I . . . went to talk. Blake said he had information for me."

Pete leaned forward. "About your grandmother?"

I took a long sip of my drink. "I don't know. It got derailed." I had promised Blake I wouldn't tell anyone I'd been at Mac's, but I hadn't promised not to tell a select few what I knew had happened. "Look. I'll tell you but you can't let on you know until it's out. Blake found out that there was another genieing."

Pete's entire face fell. "No way. Who?"

"He thinks Mac."

This stunned Pete. "No. It can't be. Mac Finnegan?" He sat back. "Are you serious?"

"That's what he told me. I know, it's terrible." I slumped in my chair and drank more coffee. I couldn't really say much more or it would be kind of obvious that I'd been there.

"Wow." Pete rubbed his forehead. He looked genuinely distraught. "Mac is the best in the business. No one takes Mac by surprise."

"Well, something bad happened. Blake was pretty freaked out. He called the Stalker Squad. I mean, that's what he told me," I added hastily. "Said he wanted to make sure the right message got to the right person. Which makes me think that things are kind of corrupt, even if no one is admitting it."

"It's good that Blake called them," Pete said carefully, sidestepping my disguised question. "Who did he talk to?"

"Darren, Dirwin, something like that?"

"Dewin. Good. He's the right guy." Pete nodded. "I'm sure they'll get all their resources focused on this."

"Great," I said, although I didn't know what that meant. No one seemed to know what they were doing in the law enforcement realm over there, but I didn't say that.

"What about Todd? What happened to him?" Pete asked.

"He . . . took off." Again, not a lie. "And I haven't heard from him at all. Which I suppose I shouldn't care about after everything he did, but . . ." I shook my head. I dwelled on things too much. I needed to learn to let stuff go. "Plus, there are way more important things to worry about after this." My chest felt heavy with the weight of it all.

"Vi. Listen. It's gonna be okay," Pete said, reaching over and resting his hand on my forearm. "Mac is beloved. Not that Mazzy isn't important too," he rushed to add when he saw my face darken. "I'm sure they were working really hard already to solve this. But with Mac in the mix, no one's gonna let them get away with this. Plus it symbolizes a potentially bigger problem that will have everyone on high alert."

"I know," I murmured, thinking of Sulamith, the genie Blake had taken me to for insights—and also to show me that not all genies were bad. She had given me quite the history lesson on genies and their role in past magickal wars. It had actually scared me. Of course, they weren't all bad and the bad ones had ultimately been defeated, but there were some who were determined to rule again. But they couldn't operate unless someone called on them.

Pete watched me intently. "So promise you won't worry, okay? The right people will be all over this. Whoever is doing this doesn't stand a chance."

"I really hope that's true," I said. "Because honestly? I wouldn't be surprised if they were coming after me next."

CHAPTER FIVE

"It's not possible." Fiona Ravenstar held up a hand, as if to ward off Blake's words. "Mac wouldn't allow himself to become someone's prey."

"Fiona, I don't want to believe it's true either." Blake spread his hands wide on his desk. "But it was his office and we were meeting him. It was late. And if it wasn't him, he would've reached out to me by now. Or you." Blake knew he wouldn't tell Violet he'd confided in Fiona about last night, but he had to. Fiona needed to be just as much on alert as Violet did. And Fiona could help protect her daughter like no one else could.

"Not if he didn't want anyone to know he'd evaded them." Fiona, who had yet to sit, strode around the office. Little flashes of electricity were coming off of her body, a sure sign of stress. They lit up the room in the early Sunday morning haze like a passing storm.

They were in Blake's office, which he'd put a soundproofing spell on before they'd begun talking. He didn't trust anyone right now, and he knew Fiona felt the same. Usually they met on her terms, but today she'd allowed him to summon her here with no questions asked.

Fiona, for her part, had known it had to be serious. Blake didn't usually do that unless he had a very good reason. And from what she was hearing, she'd been right. "Have you tried getting in touch with him?" she asked.

Blake gave her a *Come on* look. "Of course."

"Well, I have a special line." Fiona jabbed her finger, adorned by an amethyst ring that spanned almost the entire length of it, at Blake's phone. It immediately started ringing somewhere in the universe. But no one answered.

Fiona cursed under her breath, drumming her long nails on the desk in front of her. She jabbed her finger again and the ringing abruptly stopped. "Who did you talk to?"

"Dewin Mallor."

"Do you trust him?" Fiona rose again and circled the room, her long skirt brushing the floor.

"I do."

"And Bell?"

"I had to tell him. You know that. But I didn't tell him everything. Like that Violet was there. I forbade her from telling anyone she was there either."

"I don't trust Bell." Fiona turned a fiery gaze on Blake. "I wouldn't put it past any of those *normal* police." She should know. She'd been in her position for a very long time, both as head of the Magickal Council and a leading lady in one of the most prominent families in their realm. She'd seen a lot of bad behavior from the magickal police forces, both Bell's police force and the regional ones, but mostly it was one or two bad apples and things were always sorted out. But when power and politics blurred together, as was happening now with a vengeance, no one could be trusted. And clearly, no one was safe. Especially her first-born, who was right in the middle of all this insanity.

For Fiona, when it came to her family, there was no leaving anything to chance. She was going to have to take this on herself. Enough pussyfooting around, attempting to let other people handle it. Mac Finnegan was one of the only people she'd trust with anything, and even he couldn't withstand this crisis. Things were getting worse, more dangerous. And there was a lot at stake.

"Fiona?" Blake was staring at her.

"What?" she snapped.

"Are you okay?"

"I'm fine. So what is Dewin doing?"

"I don't know details. He'll tell me as much as he can, when he can."

"That's not acceptable."

"I don't know what to tell you, Fiona. I don't have control over it." Blake's frustration was evident, but Fiona didn't care. "I want to know what the plan is just as much as you do. But I'm not part of special forces." He picked up a paperweight and threw it across the room in a move so fast and precise that Fiona barely even noticed him do it. He stopped it the second before it crashed through the glass in the floor-to-ceiling window, returning it to its place on the desk.

"It's not half as much fun when you don't let it actually break something," Fiona said with a slight lift of her lips.

Blake didn't smile. Fiona didn't blame him. She wasn't in much of a mood for jokes either, but honestly, Blake's lack of restraint perpetuated the unease she already felt. Fiona wasn't used to being in this position—total lack of control. And she hated it.

"You know we have to take our own action, right? We can't just sit around and wait for these incompetents to get through all of their red tape and machinations to get anywhere. Especially if someone is paying them off to stall their progress." She finally dropped into the chair. "We know Mac was quite close to proving the Fernsbys are involved. That's enough to get a target on his back. Does anyone else know that he was on to them?"

"I certainly didn't tell anyone after you told me," Blake said. "Aside from Violet, who knows enough not to say anything. She doesn't know a Fernsby from a Ravenstar anyway. But no—that name would be enough to send the entire world into a panic."

Fiona nodded. "I know Mac didn't tell anyone. Not even his team. He wanted to make sure that he could pinpoint whom, exactly, in the family. And he didn't believe in putting others in potential danger. He knew how dangerous these people can be."

"And you know for a fact he didn't bring anyone else in on this."

"I know he didn't share with anyone on his team," Fiona repeated. "But he may have been working this case from a different angle. For a different client." She let that sink in.

"He was working with law enforcement," Blake said. "The Squad?"

"I'm not sure, but I would guess. He told me they still want to assess her shop. Especially now."

"That's right. They haven't been there yet," Blake mused. "Dewin didn't mention it to me." He steepled his fingers and looked at her over them. "But who do you think is in bed with . . . whoever is doing this? Someone on the Squad? Seems highly unlikely."

"I don't know them," Fiona said. "I can't say. But this is a cross-organizational effort now. If Mac did work for them, it meant they would've shared it with others."

"You're thinking Bell? He doesn't seem smart enough to be playing both sides of the fence."

"He's not. We all know he's only where he is because of family connections. Which means he could be ousted at any time if he's perceived as being in the way. But if he makes a calculated play to align with the side he thinks will ultimately prevail, he's guaranteed a place at the table."

Blake leaned back. "Not sure I buy it."

Fiona felt a flare of anger. "I don't care if you buy it. Until we find out otherwise, everyone is treated like an enemy. You need to talk to that man of yours in the Squad. Find out who knew what."

Blake acknowledged that with a tilt of his head. "I'll call him today."

"Good."

"I'm still worried about Violet," he said. "Even more now that Todd knows she's on to him. Which I'm sure means he told his family."

Fiona's heart almost stopped. "He knows?"

Blake nodded slowly. "She called him out. There was a bit of an altercation last night. He knows the jig is up. But we didn't totally get into it because I had to take her to meet Mac. I brought him along, actually. I got the sense he needed to hear it too. But he vanished from the scene. I figured he's hiding out with his parents."

She wanted to rage at him but she knew it wasn't his fault. Her eldest child, despite the years of distance and no contact, was a lot like her. Violet could be impulsive, righteous, and a bit of a fatalist. She was also compassionate, forgiving, and empathetic. If she'd found out who Todd was, the swirl of emotions likely would've been too much for her to hold in for very long.

If Violet had only come to her . . . but she didn't trust her enough yet. Fiona knew this, and on some level had almost accepted it. She could spend her time raging against Abigail, but what was the use? Abigail had done what she'd done out of love for Violet, and Fiona couldn't argue that. Plus, Violet's allegiance was still with her dead grandmother. She knew that too. And she just had to keep working at repairing the relationship.

In the meantime, Todd had to be silenced.

"Fiona?" Blake was waiting for her to react. Probably waiting for her to throw something at him, or put some kind of spell on him. He looked weary, though, as if he wouldn't try to fight it either way.

"So he knows Violet was there."

Blake nodded. "He does. I'm sorry. I've been trying to pin him down, but I can't get a bead on him. Once I do, I'll pay him a visit."

"I can't believe she confronted him." Fiona dropped into a chair.

"Yes, well. Violet is a bit headstrong," Blake said. "Believe me, I would've preferred she didn't. But I couldn't stop her."

Fiona shook her head slowly. "I don't blame you, Blake. My daughter can be foolish. We all know that. Now we just need to make sure she's safe. I'm going to have her stay with me for the time being."

Blake raised an eyebrow. "You think she'll go for that? I'm just saying," he said, holding up a hand to ward off any potential retaliatory response.

"I don't care," Fiona said calmly. "She's got no choice in the matter. Now, I have something to do. I'll talk to you later." And with a flick of her wrist, she disappeared, leaving a puddle of glitter in the chair she'd occupied.

CHAPTER SIX

The morning rush started to invade Pete's. I thanked him for the coffee and headed up the street to my shop. I loved my neighborhood—my apartment building, my shop, a sushi place, Pete's, and a yoga studio were all within a block of each other. Before all this witch and genie stuff, my most complicated days were those when my preferred yoga class overlapped with a client appointment and I had no time to get coffee. I'd been blissfully unaware that any other realm existed, much less one with magickal criminals who were out to get some faction of my family.

I kind of wished I could go back to those days.

The sight of Josie out front loading boxes into her little hatchback cheered me considerably. Josie saw me coming and grinned, standing up straight. Even with sneakers on, she towered over me. She'd recently cut off a lot of her dark blond hair, and now it swept casually over her forehead, the rest of it tucked into a purple bandanna. She wore jeans and a Batman T-shirt that had holes in it.

"That's how you dress for Spring Equinox?" I teased her as I walked up.

"Nah, I'm going to change when we get there. Didn't want to rip my fancy skirts hauling boxes." Josie wrapped me in a hug. "How you doing, sweetie? You look gorgeous."

"I'm fine. What else do we need to grab?"

"We'll talk later," Josie said. "You're not getting off that easily."

"Getting off of what?" I asked innocently, heading into the store. Josie, bless her, already had the rest of the boxes packed up. "Hey, do we have the scarves for the tables?"

"Already in the car," she said. "I brought the new druzy hearts, okay? And the latest batch of incense. And the bracelets we got in last week."

"Perfect," I said. "Do we need two cars?"

"Nope. We can get this all in mine."

I scooped up a box and headed back outside to the car. "This is so exciting. I hope we do well."

"It's a great opportunity for us for sure," Josie agreed, hefting her own box. "The hardcore fair followers are more than sixty percent likely to be repeat customers if they find a vendor they like."

"You've been doing your homework," I said, impressed.

She loaded her box into the car and turned to take mine. "I remember when it first started. It was tiny. They had the first one in Northampton in the high school gym." She smiled a little at the memory. "Thankfully all the incense overpowered the scent of smelly teenagers. And they got way more attendees than they imagined. That's when they started thinking bigger."

"Were you a vendor?" I'd met Josie when we first moved here from New York and I'd found the crystal shop she'd been managing. She'd taught me pretty much everything I knew about crystals.

"I was." Josie smiled. "The shop where I met you had been part of it from the beginning. When they closed, I lost my contacts so I never could pull any strings for us here."

"I wasn't asking for that reason. I wanted to hear about the early days." I locked up the shop and slid into the passenger seat.

"So much fun. A lot different than now. Not that it's bad, just a lot more structured. Has to be, I guess, since it's so big." Josie put the car in gear. We headed down the street and over the bridge toward the town hall.

"Did you ever cross paths with Horatio?" I asked. "I know he only started with the fair recently, but from a seller perspective?"

Josie shook her head. "No. He's had a pretty exclusive client list all along."

"Maybe we'll wow him this week and he'll be thrilled to sell us stuff."

"Maybe," Josie agreed. "So how was the date with Todd?"

I stifled a sigh. I figured she wouldn't rest until we discussed this. "It was cut short. I had something else come up. Pete and Syd did great, though. They're going out again tonight."

"I know. I offered to watch Presley but she's visiting with her grandfather," Josie said. Presley was

Syd's four-year-old daughter. In addition to work-ing part-time with me, Josie also nannied for Syd and worked a few other jobs around town. She liked variety in her life these days.

"Well, that's nice," I said. "I'm really happy for them."

"Yeah, me too. And I really want to know if I should be happy for you."

"Why?"

"What was the something else that came up? Blake showing up at the restaurant last night? Did he ask you out? Did you and Todd officially break up?"

I narrowed my eyes at her. "How do you know Blake showed up?"

Josie rolled her eyes. "Syd told me, of course. Well, the part about you leaving with Blake. She wasn't really clear on what happened to Todd. She told me he must've slunk away when he realized he'd messed everything up with you and he didn't stand a chance any longer."

"Can we talk about this later?" I asked. "I really just want to focus on the fair today."

"Fine," Josie said, pulling into the town hall parking lot. "But don't think I'm going to forget about it."

"Believe me, I know better." I got out, downing the last of my coffee. "Let's go in first and check out the space before we bring the boxes."

By the looks of the parking lot, a lot of the ven-dors were already here and setting up. There were people totally decked out in fun outfits that re-minded me of some of the outfits I would see when I visited my other world. I wondered how many of

these people were . . . like me. Pete's words had
me on alert.

I turned to ask Josie if she knew the ratio of
witches to mortals, but she'd gotten sidetracked
talking to a guy sporting a black mohawk and
neon-blue balloon pants that were vaguely remi-
niscent of MC Hammer. I left her to it and headed
inside. A smiley woman at the door with a bouncy
ponytail pulled high on her head held a clipboard,
checking people in as they arrived. I had to wait
for her to get through a few other people before it
was my turn.

She made a notation on her sheet, then looked
up at me with the same bright smile she had for
everyone who'd come through her line. "Good
morning! I'm Avilyn, from the fair committee. Your
name please?"

I immediately loved her energy. And the vicious
purple eyeshadow she wore. "Violet Mooney. My
shop is The Full Moon. Your eyeshadow matches
my boots." I held up a foot.

Avilyn squealed. "Oh my *goddess*! I need those. I
am a purple person, through and through. You
have to tell me where you got them."

The guy behind me—who clearly wasn't a purple
person—cleared his throat impatiently. I thought
about temporarily removing his ability to speak,
but figured that wouldn't be a nice way to start the
fair. "I'll send you the link," I said.

"You're the best. You're at space twenty-three.
Right over there." She pointed to a prime space
near the front of the exhibit area. "Let me know if
you need anything." She patted my arm, then turned

her attention to the cranky guy. "And good morning, sir! How are you today?"

I had to give her credit. I wasn't that nice. I headed over to my spot to check it out and see how much room there was. Just as I reached it I heard a voice eerily close to my ear.

"Is this the famous Violet Mooney?"

I turned, startled, and then clapped my hands over my mouth. Horatio Hale stood there smiling in all his quirky glory—tall, lanky, curly gray hair sticking out every which way, making him look like he'd been on the wrong side of an electrical socket, tight pink and green striped pants, a billowy yellow shirt, and matching yellow platform sneakers with electric green laces. His oversized glasses matched his shirt and sneakers. A man stood next to him, dressed a little less ostentatiously in jeans and a black T-shirt. His straight brown hair reached his shoulders. His beard was neatly trimmed. He had a silver stud earring in one ear. He smiled when he saw my face light up. He had a nice smile.

I tried not to sound like a gushing schoolgirl. "Mr. Hale! It's such a pleasure to meet you," I exclaimed. "Thank you so much for this opportunity. I've been wanting to exhibit here for so long." Ugh. I sounded like a starstruck teenager.

"Hey, you won the lottery, fair and square. And please, it's Horatio." He reached over and drew the other man closer. "This is Rand Gallagher. The real brains behind the fair."

"Lovely to meet you, Rand," I said.

Rand smiled. "I'm just a co-chair, like Horatio." I detected a slight southern accent when he spoke.

"Oh, you. So modest." Horatio took off his glasses to polish them with the bottom of his shirt. A gray curl fell over one brilliant blue eye. His gaze was intense, like he could see right through to my brain. "Now then, I trust this space is acceptable?"

"It's perfect. Thank you." I resisted the urge to read his aura. Auras were my specialty, but I tried not to do it without people's permission. Although inside I was dying to see what kind of aura a hero like Horatio had.

"Excellent," Horatio said.

"We are grateful to you for filling the spot," Rand said. "It's always distressing when we lose someone at the last minute. We have everything so carefully planned and then, poof." He flicked his closed hand open with a touch of drama. "And now all is well, because you're here."

"Rand," Horatio cut in, before I could respond. "May I have a moment with Ms. Mooney?"

Rand's smile stayed in place, but his eyes narrowed slightly. His tone was pleasant, though, when he responded. "Of course. See you, Violet." He gave me a little wave, turned, and hurried off.

Horatio waited until he was out of earshot. "I have heard great things about your store, Violet. I look forward to some crystal conversations over the next week. I brought quite a few of my own gems in my traveling crystal trailer. I would love to show you at some point before the end of the fair."

A traveling crystal trailer? That he wanted to show *me*? "Sure," I said. "I'd love to."

"Excellent. Perhaps tomorrow, then." Without waiting for an answer, he replaced his glasses on his face, smiled, and glided away.

I watched him go, still grinning like a fangirl until a fully transformed Josie walked up and waved her hand in front of my face. She now wore a lacy white skirt, heels that made her look like a giant, and a sequined black top. "Hello? What are you staring at?"

"I just met Horatio," I said, still grinning. "He's amazing."

"You've already got two guys vying for your attention. You don't need to add a third to the mix." Josie winked at me.

I grimaced. "Thanks for that buzz killer. Let's go get the boxes."

CHAPTER SEVEN

J osie and I were putting the finishing touches on
our table when a cheery voice I assumed was
Avilyn's came over the sound system. "Greetings,
Spring Equinox Fair team! We have five minutes
until we open the doors! On behalf of the entire
team, we want to wish you a blessed and successful
experience this year. May this week be memorable
and your hearts and spirits be filled to overflowing.
May the God and Goddess watch over you and may
we all share in the abundance of the spring sea-
son!"

Everyone cheered. My heart was certainly filled
to overflowing at just being part of this. That is, if I
didn't think too much about Mac, or Mazzy, or
Todd, or anything else. I really needed to stay in the
moment. And not just stay in it, but enjoy it. I
went back to rearranging the bracelets on my little
bracelet trees, making sure they caught just the

right amount of shimmer from the salt lamp we'd set up on the table.

"It looks great. Stop fretting," Josie said.

"I know. I want it to be perfect."

"It is," she assured me. "I'm going to go find us some snacks."

"That would be great." I realized with a jolt how hungry I was. I'd skipped breakfast in favor of coffee and then had kind of lost my appetite after my conversation with Pete. Not his fault, of course.

Josie left to wander the floor. That was one of the best parts of the fair too—not only selling my own wares and educating more people about the healing benefits of crystals, but being exposed to even more healing modalities. I was a holistic and spiritual junkie and craved learning more and more about this incredible way of life. There were already so many things I'd seen that I wanted to learn more about. Like the lady teaching oracle charm casting, and the man putting the finishing touches on his space for Tai Chi demonstrations. There was food and tons of crystals and jewelry and a tarot booth next to us—all the things that made me feel like I was in my own personal version of heaven.

A minute later, people started flooding in. Today would be one of the busiest days. The fair ran from ten to seven. Then on the weekdays it would run from noon to seven, and Saturday would be the longest day—nine to seven, immediately followed by the celebration. It would be a long week, but so worth it—not to mention that it was bringing tremendous business to town overall. The restaurants and local shops would see a huge boost from all the people coming in from out of town and spending their money here. The town tourism bureau was basically in heaven right now.

Before Josie even returned I'd completed three sales and given a group of teenagers a "crystals 101" lesson. They had been enthralled with the stones and their properties. One in particular reminded me of my own teenage self, on a search for something that had meaning when I hadn't yet been able to find much of it in my life. I gave them each a tumbled stone of their choice as a thank-you gift for stopping by.

They were walking away, chattering excitedly and comparing their stones, when Josie returned with a bag and two drinks.

"What'd you get?" I asked, nearly bouncing off my chair in excitement.

"There is so much good stuff here." She set the drinks down. "Green juice with ginger shots, and I got us . . ." she paused for dramatic effect as she opened the bag with a flourish, "tofu scramble wraps and gluten-free pumpkin donuts for dessert!"

"Ooh, yum." I took a big slurp of the juice and dug into my scramble, hoping to get a few bites in before the next customer showed up. And also hoping I wouldn't have spinach in my teeth when they did.

"Any sales yet?" Josie asked, coming around the table to sit next to me.

I nodded. "Three," I said once I'd swallowed. "And those girls will be back." I nodded to the teenagers, who were debating on who was getting the first tarot reading at the table next to us.

"Ah." Josie smiled. "I love watching teenagers find their paths."

"Me too." I set my wrap down as a woman approached the table. As she browsed the jewelry selection, asking me periodic questions, I took a moment to scan the floor. In addition to the vendors, all dressed in varying degrees of what could've been costumes but maybe weren't, there were people moving around the floor who were clearly part of the fair. My attention was drawn to a group of three children dressed like leprechauns. I knew that was a big theme, given the St. Patrick's Day celebration right in the middle of the week—they even had a pot of gold raffle going on—but something about their presence kept gnawing at me. Maybe I was just too caught up in the whole Mac thing. It reminded me that I needed to check in with Blake and see what was going on.

And it also reminded me that I needed to text Todd. If he or his slimy family had anything to do with what had happened . . . I felt a rush of anger, and it took me a moment to realize the woman browsing was speaking to me.

"Yes, I'm sorry." I rang up her purchases—two bracelets and a necklace with a moonstone pendant—and handed her my card. "My shop is right downtown. We have a lot more of everything there," I said.

"You have beautiful things," she said. "I'm sure I'll be back." With a wave, she headed to the next booth.

I turned back to where the leprechauns had been, but they were gone.

"What's wrong?" Josie asked.

"Nothing." I sank back into my chair and finished my tofu scramble. "I'm going to check in with Syd." I pulled out my phone and texted her, asking how it was going. Then, on impulse, I texted Todd.

Don't you have anything to say for yourself? I can't believe you were faking it all along. How could you?????? And where did you GO last night??

I waited a few seconds for the little dots to appear, signifying him texting back, but nothing. Syd responded with a simple thumbs up, but nothing from Todd.

"Violet."

My head snapped up at the familiar voice, but not before a little glitter sprinkled the table in front of me. What on earth was Fiona doing here?

"Mother. Hi." I stood. "I didn't know you knew about the fair." She was certainly dressed to fit in, though. Although Fiona would've been dressed this way, fair or not. She wore a forest-green velvet dress with black lace sleeves, and her matching heels had to be six inches high. Her hair was platinum today, tipped with the same green as her dress, pin-straight and brushing her shoulders. My mother was stunning, if nothing else.

She smiled. "I make it my business to know where you are, my dear. Josie. Hello." She nodded at Josie.

"Great to see you here, Fiona," Josie said.

"What are you doing on your phone? Shouldn't you be interacting with people?" Fiona asked.

"I am. Just checking on the shop." I stuck the phone in my pocket.

"Hmmm," Fiona said. "You're not worried about

that boyfriend of yours, are you?" She said the word *boyfriend* like one would say *cockroach*.

"Todd? Of course not. Why would you think that?" I asked. I was a terrible liar and I'm sure Fiona could see right through me. Even if she wasn't a witch.

"Well, you shouldn't be worried, if you are. These things have a way of working out, my darling." She gave me a lazy smile, but there was a sharp edge to it.

I started to get a bad feeling. "What do you—"

"Now," she interrupted, brushing off my unfinished question. "I wanted to invite you to a little slumber party."

"A . . . slumber party?" I repeated. A young couple came up to my table to browse. Thankful for their interruption, I started to talk to them, but Josie jumped in, leaving me no choice but to finish with Fiona. "What do you mean, a slumber party?"

"You, me, Zoe, the cats. Yes, even the non-magickal fat one."

"Monty's not fat!" I said indignantly. "He's big-boned."

"Yes, well. We're all going to stay at our place together for the next little while. So tonight, when you're done, pack them up and come over. I'll have dinner waiting."

"Tonight? I can't just—"

"I'll see you later, my darling. Don't make me come get you." With a wink and another dusting of glitter, she swept away, blending right in with the rest of the crowd.

I studied the glitter on the table. It actually added a nice touch to the crystals and I should have thought

of it myself. I picked up my doughnut and mind-
lessly bit into it, not tasting it at all. Why on earth
did I need to go stay with Fiona? She wouldn't take
no for an answer now that she'd handed down this
decision. But aside from the fact that I didn't really
want to move in with her, even temporarily, the
reason for her request made me nervous. She
must've heard about what happened. And she must
be scared. Fiona didn't get scared, so that in and
of itself was unnerving. But it wasn't just that she
was scared. It was that she clearly didn't want me to
be alone.

Which meant she must think I was next on the
hit list.

CHAPTER EIGHT

Thankfully, an endless stream of customers at the table helped me block out my obsessive thoughts about Fiona's motives and my potential endangerment for the rest of the morning. At lunchtime, Josie turned to me. "Why don't you take a break, walk around, grab some food?" she suggested. "Then when you come back, I'll go to the shop and stock up on merch. We're running low on a few things. And we've totally sold out of the druzy moons. Do we have more?"

"I think I have a whole other box in the back room," I said.

"Okay. I'll go when you come back. But take your time."

"Thanks, Josie." I was grateful for the break. I waded into the sea of activity, not sure where to start. But I was drawn to the tarot card reader in the space next to me. She was an interesting looking woman—green hair streaked with blond, hanging long on one side and shaved short on the other, a hoop ring through one nostril, and fabulous red lipstick. I thought there was something familiar about her. It took me a second, then it dawned on me.

She was a witch. I wasn't sure how I knew, but I knew it. But that wasn't all. She looked like someone, but I couldn't put my finger on who it was.

She was doing a reading, so I lurked on the sidelines looking at the materials on her desk. Her name was Calliope—one name only—and she was a tarot reader based in Hampton, which was on the other side of the state near the Rhode Island border. I ventured in a bit closer to pick up one of her pamphlets and caught some of the conversation.

"Sweetie—it's Lila, right?" The woman sitting in front of her nodded, and she went on. "It's time to move on. That's what this card means." She tapped the card in front of her, which I couldn't see. "He's no good for you. And you're not doing yourself any favors by hanging on."

The woman frowned. "Do tarot cards really say those things?"

I stifled a smile and risked a glance over at them. The woman receiving the reading looked like a mortal. She wore jeans and a North Face fleece, and her curly brown hair was piled on top of her head in a wild ponytail. She wore cool glasses—bright red with cat-eye frames.

"They all have a specific meaning, but I'm using my intuition to interpret," Calliope explained. "This man. You've been divorced for a while?"

The woman shrugged. "Six months."

Calliope cocked her head.

The woman sighed. "A year. Maybe a little longer," she amended.

"I thought so." Calliope nodded. "You've gotta let go, girl. You're better than this."

They wrapped up the reading a few minutes later. Lila didn't look thrilled, but she thanked Calliope and wandered off. I caught her dabbing at her eyes behind her glasses and felt kind of sorry for her.

"Hey, girl." Calliope waved at me. "Here for a reading?"

"Hi. If you have time, sure. I'm in the booth there." I waved at where Josie was talking to two different customers at the same time and doing a perfect job of making them both feel special.

"I know. Your stuff looks awesome. I definitely need to do some shopping before I leave. I'm Cali. Calliope, but that's only my tarot name. Not the name I use for friends . . . or kindred spirits." She winked at me.

I felt outed and slid into the chair. "You recognized me?"

"Of course. I know a fellow witch when I see one. Come on, I'll do a reading. On the house."

I grinned. "Thanks. I'm Violet."

"I know."

"You do?"

"Course I do. Violet Mooney. You're famous." She winked at me.

I tried to smile. It was a weird feeling to be known by so many people I didn't know. I was getting kind of used to it in the witch world, but it was still jarring.

"First time on the Equinox circuit?" Cali asked.

I nodded. "It's amazing."

"It is. This is my second one. I did the fall one too." Cali shuffled her cards while she talked. "My boyfriend is actually the one who got me into it. He runs them these days. Well, with someone else, but he's really the brains, you know?"

"Runs it? Your boyfriend is—"

"Horatio Hale," she said. "You know him?"

My eyes widened. "Get out! He's like my hero. I am super into sustainable and ethical sourcing for the crystals I buy. . . ." I trailed off at her grin. "Sorry. I'm kind of a geek about that stuff."

"Not at all. I'm kind of an expert on the topic myself these days, just by osmosis. Okay, here we go. I'll do a three-card spread. Past, present, future." She flipped over the card in the "past" position. We both peered at it. The Tower.

Cali tapped it. "Had any life-changing revelations lately?"

I studied her. I couldn't tell if she was messing with me or not, but chances are, if she was a witch, she knew all about my recent life-changing revelations. "You could say that," I said.

"Okay. Let's see what else we've got. She flipped the second card, indicating the present. Three of swords.

Gee, this was a fun reading so far.

"Heartbreak?" she asked after studying it for a moment.

I thought about that. I probably hadn't fully

processed the Todd thing yet, but it certainly could be considered a heartbreak. "Sort of," I said. "Definitely a betrayal."

Cali nodded, and flipped the third card, for the future: Ten of swords.

I slunk lower in my seat. This was not boding well.

"Wow," she said. "More upheaval coming your way, if this is any indication." She studied all three cards, then looked up at me. "Well. You certainly have some things going on, huh?"

She had no idea. And I didn't want to get into it. "Yeah. Sheesh. Guess I need to go get a giant selenite wand and clear myself. Which I will do as soon as I find some coffee."

"Look on the bright side," she said. "Usually a reading like this indicates a huge, sweeping change, which wipes out all the old garbage and puts you on the right path. Let's think of it that way, yeah? I mean, knowing your story, your reading is definitely on point, don't you think?"

I wondered exactly how much of my story she knew, but didn't want to invite more conversation about it. "Yeah. Sure. Anyway." I desperately wanted to forget about this reading, but didn't want to make it super obvious. "Forget about me. How did you and Horatio meet? How long have you been dating?" She seemed a lot younger than he was, but I didn't want to point that out.

Cali picked up my cards and shuffled them back into her deck. "Well, that's kind of the funny part. He came to me for a reading. When he was divorcing his last wife." She leaned in closer and whispered, "That woman who was just here? That was her."

My eyes widened. "You're kidding." Was that ethical?

"Nope. She's obsessed. Girlfriend just can't get over it. I mean, he's a cool guy and all, but I think no matter how cool someone is we need to keep our dignity, you know? If someone doesn't want me, it's *boy, bye.* Anyway, we met at a reading and kind of kept in touch, but we didn't start seeing each other until last fall. We're keeping it pretty quiet. He doesn't want a lot of people here to know." Cali took one last glance at the cards, then swept them back into the deck. "I should clear these," she said, almost to herself.

"Does she know . . . who you are?"

"Not a clue," Cali said. "You think she'd be coming for a reading if she did? Then again, I am a witch, so I could arrange it so she never knows."

"And she definitely isn't. A witch, I mean."

Cali laughed out loud. "How could you tell?"

I grinned back. "Is Horatio . . ."

"No. But he's special." She smiled. "But you know this already."

"I only just met him, but I kind of hope I get to pick his brain a little before the end of the fair," I said. "Hey, you look super familiar to me. I'm not sure why. I haven't actually been in the witch world for very long—long story—but wondering if I've seen you around somewhere."

"My last name is Diamond."

She said it so casually, like it was nothing at all, but I felt my heart pretty much stop. I tried to form words, but they weren't coming out. She couldn't possibly be . . . there had to be a million people with that last name. She couldn't be related to Mazzy. Could she? Is that why I'd thought she looked familiar? "I'm sorry. I have to ask. Are you . . ."

Cali sighed. "Yep. I need to change my damn name. That girl is always causing me some kind of drama. Yeah, Mazzy Diamond, the first genieing victim in like a million years, is my first cousin. Her dad and my dad are brothers. And we're both only children so she's like my sister. She's a pain in my butt." Then her tone softened and she glanced down at the table. "But I do still hold out hope that she'll be okay."

"Yeah," I said faintly. "I do too. I had nothing to do with it," I added. "I didn't even know I was a witch then. I swear. And I'm trying to help her."

Cali stared at me for a few seconds, then to my surprise she burst out laughing. "Of course you didn't have anything to do with it. Are you kidding? Anyone who understands politics at work knows that, Violet. Don't even give that a second thought."

"Oh." I felt faintly better. "Thank you. That's— I'm glad."

"Excuse me," a voice over my shoulder cut in. "How long is the wait for a reading?"

"I'm done," I said, jumping up. "She's all yours. Cali, it was great to meet you. I'll talk to you again, okay?" Without waiting for an answer, I slipped away into the crowd.

CHAPTER NINE

I moved away from Cali's booth and waded into the rest of the fair, pausing to buy a turmeric wellness shot from a juice vendor to calm my nerves. Mazzy Diamond's cousin, my neighbor. Talk about the potential for being uncomfortable. Although Cali seemed cool, unless she was a great actress.

Still, it was quite the coincidence.

I stopped at a booth where a woman was giving a tutorial on crystal singing bowls. I loved sound healing and spent a few minutes there listening to her explain the different bowls, the sounds they made, and the places in your body the vibrations were healing.

"Fascinating, right?"

I turned to the smiling woman standing next to me. Her smile was infectious, and before I knew it I was smiling back. "Definitely. I love the sounds."

She nodded vigorously. "I kind of want to take lessons. But until then I'll be happy to get her on my show." She stuck out a hand. Her long, oval nails were painted a hot pink that matched her dress. "Lorelai Lewis. I run the Healing Gem Podcast."

"Oh! Cool," I said. Her podcast was one of the most respected in crystal circles. She examined rocks from literally all angles, looking at meanings and healing properties, countries of origin, authors of books, speakers, sellers, buyers. "I listen sometimes when I'm out for a walk. Not that I've been out walking lately because, well, winter. I guess I have a lot of episodes to catch up on," I said, thinking about how long it had been since I'd really consumed any meaningful content. Or done anything except worry about genies and bad witches.

Lorelai laughed, a deep, robust sound. She tucked a black ringlet of hair behind her ears. Her sepia-brown skin was dusted with gold powder that reminded me of Fiona's sparkle preference. "Well, I'm glad you've heard of it. We'll have to find other opportunities for you to listen. What's your name?"

"Sorry. Violet Mooney. I own The Full Moon crystal shop."

"Aha!" Her eyes sparkled. "I went in there as soon as I got to town to check it out. It's perfect! One of the nicest shops I've been in recently."

"Wow. Thank you," I said. "That's so sweet."

"It's true. So it must be fate that I'm bumping into you because you were on my list to seek out.

Want to do an episode with me? I'm putting together my content calendar for the rest of the year and I'm doing a whole series on shops in small towns."

"Really? Yes! I'd love to." One of my New Year's resolutions—before my life was upended—was to work on a public relations plan for my shop. I did really well in the community, but I wanted to expand and possibly start selling online, especially after this fair. So I was committed to getting my name out there more often. Being on Lorelai's podcast would be a great opportunity.

"Awesome. Here's my card." Lorelai reached in her pocket and handed me a business card. "Let's sit down sometime this week. I'm set up in the back over there with my team." She waved vaguely at the back of the theater. "We're doing some live podcasting all week—you know, moment-in-time/man-on-the-street kind of thing—so I can get you on one of those too, but I'd really like to sit down and do some longer episodes. Since there are both shops and suppliers here, I'm thinking of doing a panel episode too. Maybe we can get Horatio to sit down with us. I've been stalking him." She grinned. "Anyway, I'll get with my content director and come back with some ideas. Does that work?"

"Sounds perfect," I said. "I'm up for anything."

"I love a sister who's up for anything. Now I'm going to stalk the crystal bowl lady." She winked at me and sauntered closer to the booth, where the woman was wrapping up her demo. "Amazing sounds! I'm Lorelai Lewis, a podcaster." I heard her start her pitch.

Still smiling, I put her card in the pocket of my denim jacket and checked my watch. I needed to get back so Josie could go run her errands. I turned and headed back to our booth.

CHAPTER TEN

By seven o'clock, we barely had anything left to sell, I'd run out of business cards, and I was grateful but exhausted. Josie, by contrast, looked exhilarated, like she could go another ten hours.

"What a phenomenal day," she exclaimed. "I mean, can you believe it?"

"I know. It was so great. So many new customers." I'd told her about Lorelai's offer to do some podcasting, and planned to tell Lorelai about her as well. Josie had been in the crystal world for a lot longer than me, and she'd be a great guest.

Josie studied me. "You're tired. And something else."

What I hadn't yet told her was that our neighbor was Mazzy's cousin. "Just tired. It's been a long weekend."

"Yeah. You've been through a lot the past few days. Come on. Let's get you home."

"I need to stop by the shop," I said. "I told Syd I'd check in when we wrapped up here."

"Sure, I'll drop you off," she said. "Sleep in tomorrow. I'll load up for the fair."

"Jose. I can't let you keep doing all this."

"Vi." She mimicked my tone. "I love it. I've wanted to exhibit at this fair again since, well, the last time I did it many moons ago. Take a break, okay?" She took a quick look around to see who was watching, then lifted an arm and waved it at the table. The remaining merchandise and all the decor obediently headed into the boxes she'd pulled out from underneath the table, arranging themselves neatly. "Let's go."

We piled into the car. "I can't believe that's all we have left," I said. "This is so cool."

"Isn't it?" Josie pulled out of the lot and headed toward the shop. "So are you going to Fiona's?"

"It didn't sound like I had much choice," I said, turning to look out the window.

"It'll be fine," she said, reaching over to pat my hand. "Fiona loves you, kiddo. She just wants you to be safe."

"Yeah," I said. "I know. I'm just worried about what I need to be safe from."

She squeezed my hand.

"The tarot girl next to us? Guess who it is," I said.

"Who?"

"Mazzy's cousin."

"Whoa. You're kidding."

"Nope. I wonder if she's going to try to offer me up to the genies in return for Mazzy." I sighed.

"Was she hostile?"

"Not at all. She was super nice. Which makes me worry."

Josie pulled up to the shop and looked over at me. "Maybe she doesn't blame you and you should give yourself a break."

"Maybe. She's also dating Horatio."

"Well. Small world," Josie said.

"It really is." I reached over and gave Josie a hug. "Thanks for the ride. I'll text you in the morning."

"Okay. Sleep late!" Josie waited until I stepped out and shut the door, then gunned it and took off down the street.

I headed to the door. Locked. Syd must've just closed up. I was too lazy to get my key out so I touched the lock, smiling a little when the door swung open. I heard voices inside. "Syd?"

"Hey, Vi! Out here!" she called from out back.

I followed her voice. Syd sat on the floor, surrounded by crystals and bubble wrap. Unpacking stock. "Who are you . . . oh."

Blake sat at my desk. He lifted his hand in a wave, a lazy smile spreading across his face.

"Hey there," he said. "Just stopped by to say hello."

"Cool. Hi," I said, then turned to Syd. "How was your day?"

"It was amazing! So busy! We got a ton of people who said they'd met you or Josie at the fair and that they wanted to check out the shop. It was so cool. Kept me hopping, let me tell you," she said. "I skipped lunch and everything."

I laughed. Syd loved lunch—she loved every meal, actually—so that was big. "I'm sorry. I should've gotten you some help."

She waved me off. "It was fun and everyone was patient. Let me show you what I sold."

I glanced at Blake. "I'll wait," he said.

I followed Syd out front. "People love your store, Vi. You've really created something special here." She peered at me. "Why are you crying?"

"I'm not!" I blinked the tears away. "That was just a sweet thing to say, that's all." And coming from Syd, it meant that much more. Prior to a couple of months ago she'd only been in my store once, despite the fact that we were best friends and she'd lived here for a couple of years. She just wasn't the woo-woo type. She thought my stones were pretty but she never gave them a second thought until she'd gone through some tough personal stuff herself and had been desperate enough to try out a crystal regimen. Now she not only worked here, but she was a believer. I especially appreciated it because Syd had her own store to run. Her vintage clothing and accessory shop, Yesterday, was also one of the town's favorite places. However, she'd hit a snag a couple of months ago because of some town zoning issues. Syd ran her business out of a tiny house that she had parked in a local businessman's parking lot—completely with permission. Charlie Klein adored Syd and was happy to let her use a portion of his barbershop's parking lot. The town, however, wasn't happy because they weren't getting paid taxes. The whole thing had come to a head recently and Syd's "house" was parked at Fiona's until it was all sorted out. She'd taken to running things online and by appointment. I was glad to help but it also kept me on edge because the more time she spent at Fiona's, the more chances I took that she'd see something suspect I'd end up having to explain.

"Well, it's true. And I need to buy these." She held up a handful of the bracelets I'd sold out of at the fair earlier. Thankfully I had a couple more boxes out back.

"Actually, you don't," I said.

Her face fell. "Oh. You need them for tomorrow. Sorry." She started back to the display to re-hang them.

"No, that's not what I meant," I said. "I meant you don't need to actually buy them. They're yours. Thank you for manning the shop today."

"Vi. You can't be giving stuff away for free."

"You work here," I reminded her. "It's a perk."

She hugged me. "You're the best. Now look. We sold almost all the big pyrites!" She led me around the store, pointing out holes where merchandise had been. I needed to put an order in. I'd come by in the morning to do that before heading over to the fair.

"This is great. And how is Presley's visit with her grandfather going?" Syd had reconnected with Presley's father's family here in North Harbor. Although her ex wasn't around—he was somewhere in Europe promoting world peace and railing against climate change—his father had expressed an interest in getting to know Presley, and they'd been building their relationship over the past couple of months. This week had been a big step for both of them, with Presley staying with him for a few days.

"She's loving it. They came by to visit me. He's a good man," she said.

"You sound surprised."

"Well, his wife and their kid haven't been the best role models," she said dryly. "Not to speak ill of the dead or anything." Presley's grandmother had died earlier this year.

"I hear that. Okay, let's get out of here. I'm exhausted."

She turned to me, thrusting her hands onto her hips. "No way. You're not getting off that easily."

"What do you mean?"

"What happened last night? Did you and Todd break up? Are you seeing Blake now?" She stage-whispered the last part, jerking her thumb toward the back room.

"No and no. Well, maybe yes to me and Todd breaking up, but it wasn't formalized yet." I thought about my unanswered text earlier. Where the heck was he? Had his crazy family handed him off to the genies because he'd failed on his mission to keep me from taking my rightful place in the witch world? I wouldn't put it past them from everything I'd heard. And the more I heard, the more my suspicions were growing that they were the ones behind all this insanity.

"What does that *mean*?" Syd demanded. "You're talking in riddles."

"Syd. Please. I promise I'll tell you everything once I get it figured out. Which I haven't yet. And right now, I'd rather talk about happy things like you and Pete. Please?"

She frowned at me, but finally relented. "Okay, fine. Yes, we had a great time. And we're going out—" We both swiveled around at the knock on the front door. "Now." She grinned at me. "I'm excited."

"Good for you. Now let him in or he'll think you changed your mind."

She scurried over to open the door at the same time Blake emerged from out back, grinning when he saw Pete. "Hey, man. How's it going?"

"Blake! Fancy meeting you here," Pete said with a sidelong look at me.

"Okay, you two. Go have fun," I said, turning them both toward the door. "Don't keep her out too late. She's in charge again tomorrow," I told Pete.

"I'll see you for coffee in the morning," Pete said, and it sounded more like an instruction than a question.

"You bet." I waved at them, then locked the door behind them, letting out a sigh of relief. "I wish everyone would stop freakin' asking me about last night."

"So I take it their date went well," Blake said. "But I bet ours was more exciting."

I frowned at him. "Seriously?"

He sighed. "I know. I'm just trying to lighten the mood."

"What are you doing here, anyway? Is there news?"

He shook his head. "Nothing definite. I've been putting out some feelers, though."

I sensed there was something he wasn't saying. "And?"

"Well. They might be narrowing in on the original genie who got Mazzy."

I felt my heart start to pound and my throat went dry. "Really? Who?"

"Well, we know Mac was tracking the Fernsbys." The Fernsbys were one of the original families responsible for the genie war. Learning this was one step closer, but we still needed the other piece of the puzzle—who had commissioned them. "But now they've narrowed it down to two possibilities, both in the most recent generation. Which is a little scary, because it could mean they're positioning for a revival."

A genie revival. That sounded terrifying, given what I knew. "Now it makes even more sense why he was a target," I said. "And you haven't heard anything from anyone close to him?"

"No."

"So it's looking . . ."

"Pretty grim."

We were both silent for a minute. I felt my stomach knot up again. "You'll never guess who I met today," I said.

"Who?"

"Calliope Diamond."

"I don't know her, but the name suggests she's related to . . ."

I nodded. "Mazzy's first cousin. She's the tarot reader with the booth next to mine at the fair."

"Of course she is," Blake said with an amused smile. "The universe is always at work. Does she know who you are?"

"Yes. We chatted. She said she doesn't blame me."

"Well, why would she? You didn't do anything. You're as much a victim as Mazzy."

"Yeah, well, I'm not stuck in a bottle for possibly all of eternity." I pressed my fingers to my suddenly aching temples. "I need to go home. Actually," I grimaced. "I need to go to Fiona's. Against my will. But I have to go get the cats first."

"I know. That's why I'm here. Thought you could use an escort."

"You did?" That was sweet. I was glad he was here. "Wait. How did you know I was going to Fiona's? For that matter, how did you know I was coming here after the fair?"

He shrugged. "I talked to Fiona today. And I know you. Figured you'd want to check in to see how the day went."

Scary that he did know me that well already. "Did you two cook up this idea together?"

"No. Actually I was going to offer to stay at your place with you instead. I figured you'd rather that than move in with Fiona. No offense to her," he added.

I stared at him. Again, no clue if he was serious or not. And if he was, well, he hadn't even kissed me yet! Now he wanted to move in? "Neither option is that appealing," I muttered.

"No offense taken," he said dryly.

I glared at him. "Let's just go."

CHAPTER ELEVEN

We went up the block to my apartment. I insisted on walking and using the front door like normal people, rather than teleporting. I just had this desire to feel like myself again, with only silly mortal issues to worry about. Outside, the air felt frigid against my face. I must not have been the only one who thought it was still too cold because the street was deserted, although the restaurants along both sides of the street looked packed. Residual effects from the fair crowds, I suspected.

When we got to my place, Monty and Xander were both lounging around. Monty was on my bed and Xander sprawled on the cat tree in the window. He looked like a normal cat, but I knew better.

"Hey, boys. We're going on a little adventure," I said. "To Grammy's." I could almost hear Fiona's indignant voice in my ear at being called Grammy. "Uncle Blake is coming too for a bit."

He started to laugh. "Uncle Blake? Grammy? Really?"

"Shut up." I went to grab an overnight bag, then paused. "Do I have to pack? Or can I just . . . imagine what I need?"

"Just grab a cat," he said. "The rest will take care of itself."

I went to pick up Monty while he grabbed Xander. In reality, though, Xander came and went as he pleased and I was certain he didn't need our help getting to Fiona's. As I reached for him, I noticed a feather on the floor next to my bed and cringed. "Xander, you better not be killing birds and bringing them in here." I checked under my bed, but luckily there was no carcass or anything disgusting. Just a lone, dark feather.

"What's that?" Blake called.

"Nothing." I turned to head back into the living area and as I did I moved past a mirror hanging on my living room wall.

And could've sworn I saw a shadow moving behind me.

With a gasp, I turned around. Nothing there.

"What is it?" Blake asked, poking his head around the screen that separated my living room from my bedroom.

"I . . . dropped something. I'm fine. I'll be right out."

He gave me a curious glance, but left me to it.

I risked another glance at the mirror. Still nothing. I was so tired, now I was seeing things. Still, I couldn't help feeling a little relieved to be heading to Fiona's, although I'd probably rather be genied than admit that.

I hung onto Monty extra tight as Blake and I teleported to Fiona's. Since he wasn't magickal like Xander, I was worried he'd try to get away from me and fall into some black hole in an alternate universe. No matter how many times people tried to tell me that didn't happen, I wasn't confident enough to risk it.

When we landed in Fiona's living room, I blinked and took a minute to take in my surroundings. It seemed like every time I came over here, Fiona had changed it a bit more. As a result, the home I used to share with Grandma Abby and my father looked less and less like the place I remembered. Despite the changes Fiona continued to make to the house—most of which I suspected were to push my buttons more than anything, because I still believed she was jealous of my grandmother raising me—she had kept Grandma Abby's favorite rocking chair and blanket, the place I always gravitated to when I came over. It made me feel like I was sitting with her drinking some of her lemon balm tea, which felt extremely comforting. Today, the walls were a different shade of purple— a soft lavender, which was preferable to the metallic purple she'd picked last time she'd felt the urge to redecorate—and one wall was stenciled with ravens, Fiona's family's witchy version of a coat of arms.

"You made it," she said, appearing in the door-way.

"We did." I let go of Monty, who was totally freaked out. He scrambled out of my arms and hid under the coffee table, watching Fiona suspiciously. I didn't blame him.

"Thank you for escorting," Fiona said to Blake.

"Yes, thank you," I added.

"Are you hungry?" she asked. "I've whipped up some dinner."

"I'm starving," Blake answered smoothly before I could say anything. "Let's eat."

I followed them both to the kitchen. Xander had also vanished. He was something else, that cat. If he was a cat at all.

As usual, Fiona had conjured up a spread for an army, with a little bit of everything she knew I liked. I realized as soon as I saw the food that I was pretty hungry. I hadn't eaten since lunchtime.

"Where's Zoe?" I asked, sliding into a chair and loading my plate with some lasagna.

"Out with that mortal of hers," Fiona said, her tone reeking of disdain. Zoe was dating Gabe Merlino, one of the local police officers. And Fiona wasn't a fan of witches dating mortals. As she put it, my father, who had been half a witch, hadn't worked out, so how could one expect a non-witch to work out?

To be honest, I was a little nervous about the pairing myself. Especially since it seemed inevitable that Gabe would have to find out at some point that Zoe—and by default, I—was a witch. Which could be problematic in our community.

"He's a nice guy," I said. "Don't worry."

Fiona sniffed. "He's a mortal. Case closed. Now. How was the rest of your fair? There were some interesting characters there."

"There were. It was great. Did you stay long?" I'd lost track of Fiona after she'd ordered me to her house after the event.

"I poked around a bit. The leprechauns are amazing. Did you see them?" she asked Blake. "They did a great job."

"Yeah, they were cute," I said, smiling at the memory of the kids dressed up like leprechauns. "I wonder how old they were."

Blake and Fiona exchanged a glance. I could see Blake trying to hide a smile.

"What?" I looked from one to the other.

"They were real leprechauns," Blake said.

"*What?*"

"Oh, darling. Don't be so dramatic," Fiona said. "You know there were multiple types of beings at the fair. You're not still that naive." She paused. "Are you?"

I looked at Blake. He shrugged.

"Were they . . . part of Mac's team?"

"Really, Violet? That's a bit bigoted, isn't it? Like assuming that every mortal who identifies as Italian is in the mob."

"How do *you* know about the mob?"

She shrugged. "Zoe's had me watching those Sopranos. Come to think of it, they remind me a bit of the Sagebloods."

I burst out laughing. "That, I can't picture. You, watching *The Sopranos*, I mean."

"To answer your question," Blake said to me, "the leprechauns were not part of Mac's organization, but they were there as security."

"Security?"

He nodded. "Everyone's on high alert. This was even before Mac. As much as you think they didn't take it as seriously as they could have after Mazzy, it's a big deal and they know it. But they had to dress the part of the leprechauns you all are used to because the fair organizers aren't all witches. It was a bit of a point of contention. Especially when someone asked them to do the Pot of Gold raffle." Blake smiled a bit at that.

"That's too bad," I said, not really sure how to respond to that. "Does that mean they think there could be like, a genie outbreak at the fair? Would they do that with a bunch of mortals walking around?"

"They're just making sure all bases are covered, that there's a presence in case of an emergency, and most importantly, that anything suspicious is being noted and reported on," Blake said.

My stomach was knotting up again. I pushed my plate away. "So what's going to happen?" I asked. I could hear my voice's unnaturally high pitch and cleared my throat.

"The news about Mac is starting to get out," Fiona said. "We've cleared any additional items on the council agenda for tomorrow night to discuss next steps. Chief Bell is going to report out." She rolled her eyes to show what she thought of Chief Bell and his report. "We need an emergency meeting of the subcommittee. Blake, we should do that after the council meeting. Can you make sure Ember and Alan know? I'll call Bell." She made a face.

Blake nodded. "On it."

Ugh. Tomorrow was shaping up to be a long day. In addition to being on the council, I, unfortunately, was also part of the subcommittee since I had the unfortunate status of being almost directly involved in the first genieing. "We can have all the meetings we want, but if we don't have a plan of action to save either Mac or Mazzy, what is the point?" I crumpled up my napkin and tossed it on my still-full plate.

"The point is to make a plan," Fiona said. "You're part of the *we*. So put on your thinking cap before tomorrow evening." And with a snap of her fingers, she left the table. I could see some extraneous glitter dusting the remaining food.

Guess we were done eating.

CHAPTER TWELVE

Monday
Six days before the full moon

After another rough night dreaming about sinister shadows in mirrors, genie slime and . . . Blake, I dragged myself out of bed. Early, despite my promise to Josie to sleep in. But even if I'd wanted to, it wasn't happening. Although I could've stayed snuggled up with Monty, who was right next to me. He had finally come out from under the bed in the middle of the night, but I got the sense he too was sleeping with one eye open. Xander was nowhere in sight. I wondered if he'd gone back to my apartment.

I stretched and looked around. It was so weird sleeping in my old room. At least Fiona hadn't redecorated it. I'd asked her to please leave it be, since she wasn't using it for anything. Luckily the house had four bedrooms, so she had the master bedroom and Zoe had one of the other rooms, leaving one guest room and my room. It still had some of my original crystals that my grandmother and her friends had introduced me to, as well as my old Nirvana posters. I often wondered if crystals could've helped Kurt Cobain.

I got up, went to the bathroom, then headed downstairs after peeking down the hall. Zoe's door was closed. Fiona's was open but she was nowhere in sight. In the kitchen, I envisioned the perfect cup of coffee in my hand, breathing a happy sigh when it showed up. One cup to get myself out the door, then I'd get my latte at Pete's since I'd promised him I'd stop by. On second thought, I "made" myself a plate of eggs and home fries too. I'd never finished my dinner last night and I was hungry. I conjured up a bowl of sardines for Monty and Xander.

After a quick shower, I imagined my ideal outfit for today's fair garb and murmured a quick spell to go along with it: *I look and feel my best, the universe takes care of the rest.*

I looked down and smiled at the lacy black skirt, purple T-shirt that matched my boots, and a short, black lace jacket, accessorized with a stylish tangle of silver and gold necklaces. I flipped my red hair over and sprayed some texturizing spray in the roots, added some eyeliner and mascara, and after a critical examination of the finished product in the mirror, added extra under-eye concealer. Sleep was hard to come by lately. I needed a good spell for that.

I went downstairs and outside before I realized

my car wasn't here. Duh. We'd teleported last night, and I hadn't even thought about the repercussions. And it was snowing. Just a little, enough to be pretty without being a nuisance, even though it was March and everybody mostly wanted winter to be over already. I went back inside so none of the neighbors would see me vanish into thin air and concentrated on ending up at Pete's. Bonus, I'd been able to sneak out without even having to see Fiona.

I landed in the alley behind the coffee shop. It was still early; the streets were quiet and still dusky with the remnants of the night. The fairy lights in the mason jars twinkled in the coffee shop windows. I stepped inside. There were only a couple of people at the tables. The fireplace made it extra warm and inviting. The air smelled like blueberry muffins.

"Morning, Casanova," I said when I'd reached the counter. "How was the date?"

Pete turned around, a smile lighting up his already handsome face. "Awesome. I really like her, Vi. I mean, we just kind of fit, you know?"

"That's so great, Pete." I'd never seen him so enthusiastic about anything, except maybe when he created a new latte special. "So when's the wedding?" I winked.

"Ha. If I could guarantee she'd say yes . . ."

I wasn't sure if he was joking, but it was sweet either way. I looked around to see if anyone was nearby. "So what do you think about . . . you know?"

He frowned. "About what?"

I sighed. "Our little secret? And having to eventually come clean with her?"

"Oh, that," he said casually. He could have been saying, *My guilty pleasure is watching Gilmore Girls re-runs* for the lack of angst in his tone. "Yeah, I don't know. I'm not going to worry about that at least until the third date. Which might be tonight." He winked at me.

"I'm glad you think it's funny. I don't. She's gonna be mad that I've kept this from her. I don't want her to be mad at you too."

He nodded. "I don't want that either. And if things keep going like this, I won't want to keep it from her for long, you know? I've been thinking about it, trust me. Working on how to tell her. You're a big part of this equation, so we'll probably need to figure that out together. If you're not ready, it's not going to be so smooth."

"Why did I have a feeling you were going to say that?"

"Because you know it's the right thing to do. United we stand, and all that. So think about it. Now, which latte do you want?"

"Surprise me."

He nodded. "Coming right up. Hey, any news?"

I knew he meant about Mac. I shook my head. "Council meeting tonight. And emergency sub-committee meeting." I was already dreading both of them. It undoubtedly meant another showdown with my arch enemy, Oscar Sageblood, who was already trying to pin Mazzy's genieing on me. Surely he would be raring to get me thrown in whatever witchy prison he could with the news about Mac.

"You worried? About the meetings I mean."

"Yeah. Oscar wants to take me down, clearly. I wish I knew more about this . . . family feud that seems to be dominating everything. Do you know about it?"

Pete turned on the milk frother. We both waited until it finished. Then he said, "I'm surprised you haven't asked yet."

I gave myself a mental head smack. Of course I should have asked Pete. He wasn't involved in politics or anything related to the witch world, but he'd been around long enough to know stuff. "I'm an idiot. What can I say?" I spread my hands wide. "Hit me."

Pete finished making my coffee, topping it off with a swirl of some yummy-looking syrup, and placed it on the counter. "Well, you know the Sagebloods are the third most powerful witch family already."

I nodded.

"Part of that equation is that all three of you—your Moonstones and Ravenstars, along with the Sagebloods—also have the longest witch lineages. The Sagebloods were in power once. Back when the genie uprising happened."

I sucked in a breath. "You're kidding. They were the ones who let that happen?" Fiona had left out a few details in her sporadic telling of these tales.

"They claim that they didn't. That they tried to fight it, but the genies had created such a strong base of power that they weren't able to. Most historians say that either the Sagebloods were behind the scenes fueling and funding the whole thing, or that they were just so incompetent and drunk on their own power that they didn't realize what was happening until it was too late. It's not a secret that a lot of people in politics who differ in opinion and approach from the Sagebloods believe they are not the best choices to govern our world. But they still have their base that believes in them."

"What do you think?"

Pete thought for a moment before answering. "I'm not a political analyst but if I had to guess, there were a couple of very bad apples and the rest looked the other way. I think it's irresponsible to classify an entire bloodline as evil. Although Blake might disagree with me."

"About that," I said. "He never talks about his family. Is he really that disconnected from them?"

"Oh yeah." Pete nodded. "Blake takes the law very seriously, in case you hadn't noticed. And when he realized what his family had been part of, he was livid. Not only did he disassociate from them, he also campaigned hard against them. He spent years in election and governance law making sure that there were no loopholes they could use to get back in power in a sketchy way. He's serious about it. As you may have guessed, they're a little bitter about that."

I thought about that. "Are his parents . . . bad Sagebloods too?"

"It's his mother's side of the family. She's a nice lady, but she wouldn't speak out against them. Her father is hardcore about the family. So Blake had to make a tough decision about his relationship with her. He speaks to his dad, but that's about it." He looked at me curiously. "You've never asked him?"

I shook my head, ashamed of myself. "No. I've clearly been too self-absorbed."

"Violet, stop. You've had a lot to deal with."

I waved him off. "Anyway. Go on."

He gave me a look, but continued. "To answer your earlier question, I think we've made better progress without them in a majority of power. In any event, the Magickal Council and the elders banded together to make sure that generation was removed from power and their seats were greatly reduced going forward so there would never be a Sageblood majority."

I sipped my coffee, absorbing the information. "Was it men or women in power? Back then, when the genie war happened?"

The door to the cafe banged open and two women came in, making a big display of shaking the snow off their shoulders and stamping their feet. Our conversation was over.

"They were men," Pete said, dropping his voice a notch. Whereas the Moonstones and Ravenstars always had matriarchs running the show." He gave me a crooked smile. "Some say this is why the Sage-blood reign never went very smoothly."

Amen to that. I raised my cup in a silent thank you, then headed out so he could attend to his customers.

CHAPTER THIRTEEN

I left Pete's and walked up the block to my shop. Aside from Mr. Quigley, who was out doing his morning search for cans, all was still quiet. He waved at me, but was clearly too busy to stop and talk. It was fine. I was still digesting Pete's download. I couldn't believe I'd never asked Pete about any of this stuff. It had just never crossed my mind. But he was clearly a wealth of knowledge of which I needed to take better advantage.

I went inside The Full Moon and locked the door behind me, then headed out back to grab the list I'd been compiling so I could put in an order. I took one more trip around the store to add in some of the things that had sold out yesterday, then went out back to my desk. I usually ordered my supplies from three main vendors. There were a few others that I was trying out, placing small orders to test them, but I stuck to the ones I knew more often than not. However, today I was kind of disappointed. I still couldn't get any moldavite, despite promises from two of my regular suppliers that they would be getting some in.

Moldavite was a highly coveted stone that was not easy to come by, at least for the real thing. It was often called the "Holy Grail" stone or the "Stone of Transformation" because its vibration was super high. It's actually glass, and the story is that it came from a meteorite that crashed millions of years ago in Eastern Europe. Today, it was found mainly in the Czech Republic and, according to the experts, was basically found at random—which made it very difficult to get. And since it had been getting a lot of attention these days, it was enough of a hot commodity to make it even harder to find. I picked up the phone and called my number one guy, Eduardo. It was early enough that he picked up himself.

"Hey, Ed. Violet Mooney."

"Violet! Good to hear from you. Hey, I heard you're exhibiting at the Spring Equinox Fair! Congrats."

"Thanks," I said. "It's been fun. And great for sales even just the first day."

"Awesome. So what can I do for you?"

"So I'm putting a new order in, and I still can't order moldavite. I thought you were getting some in?"

"Yeah, I know." Eduardo sounded like he was chewing on something. I suspected it was one of his cigars. Disgusting habit, especially so early in the morning. "Sorry about that. But I couldn't verify the source for the shipment I was supposed to get. You know me, kid. I can't take things when I don't know where they're coming from."

I bit back my frustrated sigh. He was right, of course. That's why I purchased from him. But darn, I wanted some moldavite. "Any ideas when you might have another go at it? I have customers looking for some."

"I'm working on it. Trust me. I'll call you as soon as I have an update."

"Okay. I'm putting the rest of my order in now."

"I'll be on the lookout," Eduardo promised.

I hung up and finished putting my order in, then saw movement out of the corner of my eye. I turned around and saw crystals flying into a cardboard box. I smiled. Josie was packing for the fair.

I texted her.

Should I get out of here before I get hit in the head with something?

She sent me a laugh emoji, but simultaneously I heard her voice. "Sorry. Didn't think you were in yet. Since I told you to sleep in." She frowned at me from the doorway, where she'd appeared. Josie, unlike the witches in my family, didn't really have a signature for her entrances and exits. She just showed up and left without a lot of fuss. Whereas I kind of liked Fiona's trail of sparkles and had adopted it for myself, although I probably needed to find a way to make it my own. Like using all purple glitter or something.

"Well, sleeping is tough lately. Let me help. We can do it the old-fashioned way," I suggested.

"Ooh, an old-fashioned girl. I like it. Let's pack."

Two hours later, we finished loading our boxes into Josie's car. Syd, who was in an incredibly good mood that I suspected had something to do with a certain barista, had arrived and customers were already filling the shop. I helped her out until we really had to go, then Josie and I hopped into her car. "Can we stop at Pete's on the way?" I asked. "I want to grab a snack." I didn't tell her I'd already been there today. Most people thought my coffee addiction had reached a problematic level, but hey, let them try walking in my shoes these days and then they could talk to me.

"Of course. I'd love a tea." Josie pulled up out front and I ran inside. Pete wasn't behind the counter, which must mean he was out back making muffins or something else yummy. I grabbed our drinks and chocolate chip muffins, then ran back out and hopped in the car just as the parking authority people pulled up behind Josie. She pulled away with an apologetic wave out her window.

I handed her one of the cups. She swooned a little. "Thank you. I've been craving tea all morning."

"Me too. Well, coffee." I sipped mine, wondering if there was a coffeeholics anonymous meeting nearby I should look into. "Got us chocolate chip muffins too."

When we arrived, I hefted one of the smaller boxes under my arm, piled the muffin bag on top, and grabbed my coffee in my free hand. Josie did the same. As we were heading inside, a man with a shaved head and a bright pink suit that rivaled anything Stanford Blatch wore in *Sex and the City* appeared in front of us, holding small paper cups and grinning like a deranged serial killer.

"Ladies! I'm so glad I caught you before you infused any more poison into those lovely bodies." His eyes were alert and focused behind his giant, square-framed glasses as he honed in.

"Uh—sorry?" I tried to tamp down my impatience. These types of things always happened at events like this. People who fancied themselves some kind of savior here to protect the masses from all the devilish things going on inside mystical fairs.

"The poison! That's coffee, right?" He indicated my cup. "I can't in good conscience let you drink that. You are much too lovely."

"Mine's not. Tea. Caffeine-free, too." Josie smiled sweetly and brushed past him, leaving me stranded with a crazy person.

"Thanks, wingman," I muttered under my breath, then tried to salvage the situation. "Mine's tea too, actually."

"Then where's your teabag?"

"I don't like it strong."

"Aha!" He swooped in, eyes bulging, his sudden shout startling me enough that the coffee cup slipped out of my hand. The lid popped off and it splattered all over the parking lot in front of me, not to mention my boots.

I briefly considered killing him, then figured it wouldn't be good for business. Instead I settled for a *"What do you think you're doing?"* through gritted teeth.

He peered at the puddle, then looked up at me.

But instead of an apology, he wagged a finger at me, still smiling brightly. "See what the poison does to you? Makes you *lie*."

"Oh. My. Goddess. What is wrong with you?" I started to brush past him, but he thrust one of the small paper cups at me.

"Drink this."

I glared at him. "No."

"You will love it. You'll be on the side of the angels. See, I channel my recipes straight from the heavens." He leaned back, arms extended, eyes closed, as if he were receiving divine intervention right now.

I resisted the urge to roll my eyes. After all, who was I to say he didn't have angels whispering recipes in his ear? How was that any different from Fiona showing up and telling me she was a witch and so was I?

He opened his eyes and went on with his sales pitch. "Two ounces of this herbal tincture per day is all you need. No more expensive coffees, no more rotting of your gut, no more afternoon caffeine crashes, no more *lies* or covering up your addiction. These blends are channeled directly from the angels." He raised his arms heavenward again, a silent *thank you*. "We have tinctures of all kinds, but my favorites for someone who has gone so astray—" he gave me a pointed look to suggest he meant me "—are the Archangel blends. Michael, Raphael, Gabriel, Uriel, and the rest of them. They're a steal at only $39.99 a bottle." He was still holding out the paper cups, and underneath the crazy there was a level of boyish charm to him. "These are Raphael's tinctures."

Channeling tinctures from the archangels? Now I'd heard everything. *No, you probably haven't,* a little voice reminded me. I tried to ignore it. "Fine, I'll try some," I said with a huge sigh, and snatched the cup, knocking back the drink in one gulp. It actually tasted sweet and very pleasant, with a touch of berry and something else I couldn't identify. "That's actually really good," I said, giving him my full attention for the first time. And did a double take. I could've sworn I saw angel wings floating behind him.

"See? I told you. Now wait ten minutes and tell me how you feel." He winked, then stuck out his hand. "Burton Jillette. Angel Tinctures is the name of my business. I'm hopeful you've heard of me."

I hadn't, but I didn't want to tell him that. I hesitated a second, then sighed and shook hands with him. "Violet Mooney. The Full Moon crystal shop." I started walking toward the doors. Burton fell into step beside me. "You have a booth inside?" I asked.

Burton grimaced. "No. I've had one for sixteen years, but this year that evil puppeteer blacklisted me."

I stopped and stared at him. "Who?"

"Horatio Hale." He nearly spit the words.

"That can't be," I said. "It's a lottery. I'm sure your name just didn't come up."

"No," he said. "I have been part of the vendor crew for so long I'm guaranteed a spot. Rand and I have worked this fair together for years. Then Mr. Hale rescinded the invitation under his new set of rules because I don't have the stupid certificate!"

He was getting louder now, and people walking around us to get to the doors were staring.

"Um, what certificate?" I really wanted to get inside, but I was worried now that he was unstable and would cause an even bigger scene.

"My organic certificate! For my herbs. Which are unquestionably organic, might I add. Everyone in the business knows that those certificates are just another way for our corrupt government to make money anyway. And when someone doesn't have enough money to pay for the certificate, this is what happens. It's not the first time either. He's pulled stunts like this on other people in the community. I'm trying to get that podcaster to look into that."

This guy sounded kind of unhinged. I hoped I hadn't just drunk poison or something from a madman posing as an organic herbalist. "Jeez. I'm sorry to hear that," I said. "That's not cool."

"It is not," he agreed. "And I think everyone should know that Horatio isn't the great guy everyone thinks he is. People who care about their fellow small business owners would never do that."

I wasn't sure what to say to that. I glanced helplessly at the doors, jerking my thumb toward them. "I have to go in. I'm really sorry. Hey, um, if you want to give me some business cards I'll put them on my table."

"Really! That's lovely of you." He reached into his pocket and pulled out a stack, pressing them into my hand. "Thank you, Violet Mooney. And here, take another sample." He handed me the other paper cup. "You'll need it in there with that bunch."

CHAPTER FOURTEEN

By the time I got inside, Josie had most of the table set up. "What the heck happened to you?" she asked.

"Well, you abandoned me with crazy tincture guy." I frowned at her. "But I tried one of the tinctures. I actually felt better."

She laughed. "He was an interesting character."

"You think?" His stuff seemed to work, though. I felt more energetic than a few minutes ago. I arranged Burton's cards on the edge of the table and started to unload a box.

"Violet Mooney."

I jumped at the voice in my ear and turned to find Horatio. Why did I never hear this guy coming? His gray curls flopped over the rims of his glasses as he studied our display, hands shoved deep in the pockets of yellow-and-green plaid pants, complete with suspenders, over a white button-down shirt. He wore black platform boots that made him even taller.

"Horatio, good morning," I said, automatically straightening as if I were at an inspection. Despite myself I thought of Burton's harsh words and wondered how much of his ranting was actually true.

"These are lovely amethysts," he said, picking up one of my larger raw pieces. "Where do you get your stock?"

"I have a few suppliers I typically use. Those are from DiMaisi's Gemstones in Boston."

"Ah, Eduardo," he said with a nod.

"Yes. Do you know him?"

"We have met at some shows," he said. "Good man. A lot of integrity."

"For sure. Always gets me what I need. Except moldavite. I haven't been able to get any moldavite." Why was I babbling like this? That stupid guy had made me all nervous, and now it was not only fangirl nerves; it was wondering-if-he-was-for-real nerves.

Horatio's eyes brightened. "You need moldavite?"

I nodded. "I've had some requests and would like to find some quality pieces."

"Well, you're in luck. I just got a shipment and I brought them with me, but I haven't put any out. I wanted to save them for the sellers who are serious about them. Maybe if you come see them, you'll give the rest of my stock a try." He winked. "So what do you say?"

I stared at him. "Really? You have moldavite?"

"I sure do. And you are more than welcome to first dibs on it. Happy to show you. All of us out-of-town vendors store our stuff in the other building right behind the theater. Come by after the fair is over." He leaned in suggestively. "I guarantee you will be delighted with my moldavite. And I would love to have a relationship with *the* Violet Mooney."

I wasn't sure where he was going with that comment, but the moldavite was tempting. I did resist pointing out the fact that I'd tried for years to get on his list to buy from him but never could. It made sense, though. He couldn't sell to every shop in the country, and I knew he was careful about his brand. He wouldn't want to sell to a virtual unknown. Here was my chance. However, tonight was the fun double feature of the Magickal Council and the genie subcommittee. "I wish I could. Tonight isn't good."

"Tomorrow morning, then. Before the fair opens. Promise me." He clasped my hand and brought it to his lips. "I am determined to say that my crystals are in the hottest shop in the county."

I felt that little fangirl tingle again at his words, despite the doubts Burton had successfully put in my head. Horatio Hale said my shop was the hottest in the county! Who would ever have imagined? "Sure. I would love to see it."

"Wonderful! Ten o'clock?"

"That works."

"Great. Go into the back building. There's a little corridor down the back that leads to some offices. I've commandeered one of them. See you then." He turned to go, but his eyes fell on Burton's stack of cards I'd placed at the front of my table. He tapped his finger on them reproachfully.

"This guy. Not to be trusted, Violet. His products are questionable." Before I could protest, he swept the stack of cards into his palm and walked away, dropping them into the trash can as he walked by. I frowned, then glanced to my right, feeling eyes on me. Cali was watching the interaction from her seat at the tarot table, her face carefully blank. When she saw me, she lifted one hand in a wave, then turned away.

As soon as the doors opened, customers streamed in and the flow didn't stop all day. Josie and I barely had time to talk to each other. But despite being too busy to do much outside of my little space, I couldn't help but see signs of my two worlds colliding. First, there were the leprechauns. Despite the outfits that were a lot closer to the leprechauns of legends, a closer look at their faces made it perfectly clear that they were not children. In fact, they reminded me so much of Mac and his team that it made my stomach hurt. Mortals who saw them would only see what they wanted—charming little men walking around with their pot of gold sweaters on—but I could definitely see their alert eyes and slightly forbidding expressions.

Second, there was definitely magic at work. At one point, I'd seen a woman trying to stealthily slip an extra snack into her pocket from the gluten-free bakery when the proprietor's back was turned. When the woman walked away, she mysteriously tripped over nothing. As she tried to save herself from falling, the wrapped brownie flew out of her coat pocket and back onto the table. The thief hurried away, obviously embarrassed at her clumsiness, while the bakery woman smiled just a little bit and turned to her next customer. I wondered if there was some kind of all-seeing security in place, or if it was just an individual witchy thing that mortals who behaved badly would be magically reprimanded.

I didn't get a chance to talk to Cali again. Her line was stacked all day long save for the twenty minutes she stepped away to get some lunch. I hoped she hadn't thought I was flirting with Horatio this morning, or that he had been flirting with me. First, despite my fangirl feelings, he was so not my type romantically. Second, I kept thinking about how he threw the herbalist's cards away. Even if he disagreed with the guy's business practices, he didn't have to be so mean. I'd thought that given his reputation for fairness and making sure people weren't being exploited, he'd show a bit more respect for a fellow practitioner. Burton, despite his quirky approach, was right about organic certifications often being meaningless and if he'd really been part of the fair for so long, he should have a bit of leeway. I was surprised Horatio was so black and white, although I guess in his line of work he had to be prescriptive.

But he had moldavite, I reminded myself. And I really wanted to hear about how he'd gotten it. He must have great sources. His reputation was stellar in the business, after all. I wondered if they were raw stones, or if he had jewelry too. I needed to bring the list my customers had given me tomorrow. Someone wanted a pendant, another person was looking for earrings. I figured even if he didn't have earrings, perhaps he had small enough pieces that I could get them made for her.

When we had a lull in the booth traffic, Josie and I took turns taking a break to get some fresh air or walk around a bit. Josie went first—she had that hangry look in her eyes that I knew all too well, and she'd had her eye on some mala beads at one of the booths that she was itching to get. Since I had no one browsing at the moment, I paused to do a few social media posts from the pictures I'd been taking of our display as well as just some of the overall experience—the room, the people walking by. The leprechauns.

"Busy day, huh?"

I glanced up from my phone. Cali lounged against my table, playing with a strand of purple hair. Today she had dressed all in black—a tight black jumpsuit with a black shirt and a long, lacy black jacket topping it off.

"Very," I said, putting my phone face down on the table. "You too."

"Yeah. These are the days when I wish I had an assistant tarot reader," she said with a smile.

"You don't have anyone to help?"

She shook her head. "I'm very particular about my brand. I read the cards a certain way, and that's that."

"I get that. It took me a while to let people help me too."

And then the conversation did this weird lapsing thing, where we both kind of looked at each other awkwardly. I got the sense Cali wanted to say something to me, but wasn't exactly sure how to, and that made me nervous.

"Can I ask you something?" she finally said.

"Of course."

"Since you found out about . . . your stuff. Have you, like, used it to help anyone over here?"

"You mean used my powers to help a mortal?" I asked.

She nodded.

I thought about how to answer that. Everything that happened just last week where my powers had helped point me in the right direction to figure out who had murdered two people was still fresh in my mind and could constitute a yes. But had I done something to directly affect someone's life with magic? I didn't think so.

"No," I said. "One of the first things my mother told me was that we weren't supposed to interfere in mortal lives. I guess I've always been one of those nerdy rule followers, especially if I don't know enough about what I'm doing yet to feel comfortable breaking the rules."

Cali nodded, her lips pursed together tightly. I got the sense this wasn't the answer she wanted. "I guess you're right," she said. "Thanks, Violet." She turned to go but I stopped her.

"Is everything okay?"

She twisted a silver ring in the shape of the infinity loop around and around on her finger. "Yeah. I mean, kind of. I just . . ." She looked around the room as she tried to find words. "Someone I care about—a mortal—is having a hard time. People are trying to wreck their reputation and they don't deserve it. I want to help, but the best I can come up with is to spell cast their mouths shut." She smiled a little, but I got the sense she wasn't kidding.

I was quiet for a moment thinking of Mazzy and the story she'd tried to publish, before her genieing, on fraudulent alternative healers. I understood how frustrating it was to have people saying false things about you. On the other hand, I did believe Fiona was right about this. Witchcraft may seem a simple way to fix things, but it could cause more problems than it was worth. "That must be tough," I said finally. "But getting involved could have unintended consequences. Have you, or your friend, tried talking to these people?"

Cali smiled a little, but there was no humor in it. "You know how it is once people make their minds up about something," she said. "There's no talking them out of it. Anyway, thanks for letting me pick your brain." She nodded at the woman hovering around her booth. "Better go get reading."

I watched her walk away on shiny black stiletto boots that looked like they could do some serious damage and wondered exactly who was talking smack about whom here in the mortal world. I wondered if it was Horatio, but I had a hard time thinking of him being the victim of anyone's smack talking. He seemed to know just how to put people in place.

CHAPTER FIFTEEN

J osie returned a few minutes later with a steaming cup of something and a bag of food. She also
had a new tiger's eye mala around her neck.

"Ooh, gorgeous!" I exclaimed, taking a step closer.
Mala beads were one thing I didn't carry and I had
been thinking about it for a while. "Where did you
get them?"

She handed me a card. "Already on it," she said
with a wink. "They're looking to place their stuff in
stores around the country, so we should look into
that."

"Nice." I stuck the card in my pocket and grabbed
my coat. "I'm going to go outside for a bit. I need
some air."

"Enjoy." She was already tearing into her food,
which looked delicious. "I would've brought you
something but figured you'd want to take a break
and explore."

"Absolutely." I didn't have the heart to tell her I wasn't hungry. I was dreading tonight, and that was enough to keep my appetite at bay. I headed out the side door to an area of the parking lot that, I hoped, was kind of deserted. I was on people overload right now. But when I pushed the door open the first thing I heard was an angry voice. A woman's voice, and its smoky tones sounded slightly familiar.

"I'm going public with what I know. I've already talked to the podcaster. Don't say I didn't give you a chance to explain yourself." The words were sharp and filled with emotion.

I froze, fully intending to slip back inside, but I was too late. I'd shoved the door just a smidge too hard when I opened it, and it flew back and crashed into the wall behind it. I cursed silently and tried to creep backward inside before they could see me, but a face appeared around the corner.

"Katia! Hey," I said, smiling weakly. I knew I'd recognized the voice. It belonged to Katia Leclerc, the second of my top three crystal suppliers. She was local, based in neighboring New Haven. Her place was close enough that I could go pick up my order if I needed it faster than it could be shipped. Like my other suppliers, she had a reputation for excellence. Also a tough-as-nails exterior and a no-nonsense business policy. I'd known her for years and we got along great. I considered her a friend as well as a business relationship. She was not only a supplier, but kind of a mentor—or at least she had been to me. On the other hand, her reputation in the business was pretty hardcore. She'd

been known to stop selling to shops for any number of perceived transgressions, which I guessed
kept her client list manageable. People were kind
of scared of her.

Right now, I was too. Her neck and face were
flushed an angry red, a stark contrast to her short
black hair. She shoved a huge pair of square-
rimmed glasses up on her nose and made a con-
scious effort to get herself under control. "Hello,
Violet."

"Sorry to interrupt. I just needed some air. I'll
see you later," I said, backing away.

But before I could get inside, her companion
appeared from around the corner too. My eyes
widened.

Horatio.

"Hello there! Not to worry, we were done." He
glanced at Katia with some disdain as he said it.
But he gave me a brilliant smile as he squeezed
past me, as if whatever unpleasantness had been
going on was forgotten. "Busy day! I need to get
back to my rounds."

Katia stared after him as he disappeared inside.

I stood there awkwardly, still holding the door,
wondering what the heck they had been fighting
about that sounded so nasty. "I'm sorry," I said
again, when the silence had stretched as thin as a
slice of hot mozzarella on a pizza.

She flipped a hand at me to say, *Forget it* and
started inside.

I knew I did not need to get in the middle of any
more drama—I had enough of my own, thank

you—but I couldn't resist. "Everything okay?" I held onto the door, kind of blocking her way.

"It's fine. Really." Katia smoothed the front of her dress, which was silky and billowy and looked hella cold to be out here right now with no coat. Then again, she'd seemed pretty hot a minute ago.

Her standoffishness was weird, though. She wasn't usually like this with me. "I just met Horatio yesterday," I said, to fill the awkward pause. "I'd been dying to for so long. I'm going to go see some of his stones tomorrow. I'd been hoping to get on his client list." It was none of my business, but I was really curious what her issue with Horatio was. If it was business, maybe she'd bite.

The dangling bait worked—that got her to pay attention. Katia turned to me with some alarm on her face. "Why?" she said.

I blinked. "Why not? You know I have multiple suppliers. Good business strategy, right? That's what you always told me. As long as they're vetted and I trust them."

"You really should stick with the people you have. You have me, you have Eduardo. We can get you everything you want." She reached out and put a hand on my arm. "I know how important ethics and quality are to you."

"Right," I said. "Of course they are. But I'm looking for moldavite specifically. Horatio has some."

Her eyes narrowed dangerously. "Violet. You want moldavite, you come to me." She stabbed her own chest with a thumb so hard I winced. "I have contacts. You know this."

Katia must not be remembering that I had gone to her for moldavite a couple of times, even as recently as last fall, just for that reason. Moldavite was obtained from the Czech Republic, very near where Katia had grown up. She had great contacts there—which was why I'd gone to her in the first place. I'd asked her a few times, and she hadn't come through.

"I did," I said. "I never heard . . ." At the look on her face, I cleared my throat. "Yes, of course. I completely forgot. I do need some, if you have any."

"I can get. I will be in touch." She marched inside, head and spine ramrod straight.

Sheesh. What was with her? I stepped outside, still looking for that breath of fresh air. I sincerely hoped their fight had been business-related. Horatio seemed to have enough women trouble without adding a third to the mix.

I took a brisk walk around the building, avoiding Burton when I got to the front, and hurried back inside. I made my way back to our booth, stopping when a pair of gorgeous dangly silver earrings with purple and black feathers caught my eye. I purchased them and slipped them into my ears while I walked. At our booth, Josie was wrapping up someone's purchase—one of my large crystals, from the size of the bag. I saw Horatio over at Cali's booth. He'd pulled a chair up next to her and was saying something close to her ear.

"Hey, nice earrings," Josie said when our customer walked away.

"Thanks." I gave one of them a little swing. "Cool, right?"

"Very. Where'd you go?"

"Well, I went outside to get some air. And I ran into Katia Leclerc and Horatio having some kind of argument." I kept my voice low so he couldn't hear. "I didn't hear much and he left when I showed up, but she doesn't seem to like him." I filled her in on Katia's reaction to me saying I wanted to purchase from him. "I'm supposed to go check out his stock tomorrow. He has moldavite. Now she's telling me she can get it and I shouldn't go to him."

"But she never got us any," Josie said.

"I know. When I reminded her of that I thought she was going to bite my head off."

"You still going to go?" Josie asked.

"I think so. I mean, whatever their issue is has nothing to do with me. Right?"

"Right. Maybe they had a professional dispute." Josie shrugged. "Happens."

"Maybe," I said. "But remember that guy who cornered us outside this morning? With the drinks?"

"Cornered you, you mean," Josie said with a grin.

"Yeah, yeah. Anyway, he was supposed to be a vendor but said Horatio kept him out. And Horatio threw his business cards away when he saw that I'd put them on the table. I thought it was kind of mean."

Josie studied me. "So what are you saying?"

"I don't know. I just . . . had this vision of this guy for all this time, you know? And not everyone seems to love him."

"He's human," Josie said. "I mean, he really is—

he's not a witch—but that aside, humans have issues and disagreements. He's an outspoken public
figure. It's really not strange that he'd have at least
a few enemies, right? Plus, you can't put anyone
on a pedestal like that, Vi. They'll just disappoint
you."

CHAPTER SIXTEEN

I saw Ginny Reinhardt making her way through the crowd and waved. Ginny was a local who worked at Todd's bar, Luck o' the Irish. She was also a witch, even though she didn't practice much. She waved back and made a beeline over. "Hey, Vi!" She reached over the table to engulf me in a huge bear hug. Ginny was a hugger. She hugged everyone, regardless of when she'd last seen you. I could bump into her in a half hour and she'd hug me again. It bugged some people, but I didn't mind.

"Hi, Ginny. Cool fair, huh?"

"It is. I can't believe you got in! *So* cool. Ohmigod," she said, staring at Cali. "It's Cali Diamond! Did you know . . ." she trailed off, giving me a questioning look.

"Yeah. We met. Do you know her well?" Ginny and Mazzy were good friends. If they spent a lot of time together, that might mean Ginny knew Cali too.

"I do. The three of us hung out all the time." She looked sad all of a sudden.

"She was really nice to me, even though she knows who I am. You think she's legit?" I asked.

"Oh yeah. Cali is sweet. She would never hold that against you. And why should she? It's not your fault."

"Okay. Just checking. I felt a little weird."

"Well, don't. I need to go talk to her. Hey, have you seen Todd at all?"

I felt my stomach drop a little. "No. Why?"

"I don't know. I just . . ." she leaned closer, her expression worried. "He didn't show up at the bar yesterday. And no one's heard from him. It's not like him to miss any big nights, you know? When's the last time you talked to him?"

"We went out Saturday night," I said. "Haven't seen him since. I'm sure he's fine, Ginny. Maybe he just took a night off."

"He took Saturday night off," she pointed out. "And he would've told someone. You know how he is with the bar. Especially with the fair being in town."

It was true. Todd loved that bar. Before I knew our whole relationship was a sham, I always felt like the bar was my competition. Now I knew with complete certainty he felt more for the bar than he'd ever felt for me. So she was right. For him to not show up was suspect. But knowing now how much of a worm he was, I was hard-pressed to worry and more inclined to think he was hiding out because he was embarrassed.

"I do know," I said finally. "Listen, Ginny. We kind of hit a rough patch and I don't know how Todd is dealing with it. So maybe that has something to do with it."

"Oh no! Vi, I'm so sorry." She hugged me again, this time almost knocking over my necklace display. "I wondered if you two were having problems. You're right, that totally explains it. Oh, the poor boo. He's heartbroken! And you must be too!" She looked genuinely distressed. "Are you going to work it out? I think you two are adorable together."

"Um, well, I'm not sure. And look, I have a customer." I nodded at the woman who had walked up to browse the table, so relieved I could kiss her. "I'll talk to you later, okay? Let me know if you hear from him."

Ginny promised and hurried off. I focused on my customer and the few that followed her. The afternoon flew by, and before I knew it I was once again out of bracelets and there were still a couple of hours left in the fair.

"These things are selling like hotcakes," I said to Josie, holding up the empty velvet bracelet display.

"They're really nice," Josie said. "Those are from the new place, right?"

I nodded. It was a supplier out of Denver. I'd met the owner at a crystal show out there last year and had been meaning to try his stuff. He sent me emails weekly with new offerings, and I'd finally given in and placed an order. His bracelets were definitely higher quality than the previous ones I'd been stocking. I'd even taken a couple home, like the eagle eye one I was wearing today. "I may have one more box at the shop. I'll text Syd."

As I pulled out my phone and started typing, a shadow fell over the table. I glanced up. Zoe stood there grinning at me. Her long black hair was pulled into two pigtails high on her head, and she wore a striped red-and-white shirt with a pair of jeans and her ever-present Converse sneakers. Today's pair was the same red as her shirt. She often reminded me of those Amy Brown fairies I used to obsess over when I was younger.

"Hey, sis."

"Hey. I didn't know you were a fairgoer." I hit send and put the phone down. "Or did you just come to visit me?"

"Are you kidding? I love these kinds of things. It's so much fun to try to pick out the for-reals and the Lulus, as Mother would call them."

When Fiona had first arrived, she'd brought her poor attitude toward mortals with her, often referring to them as Lulus—a jab at the sea of Lululemon attire that she felt was predominantly what mortals wore. I'd thought I had broken her of the habit, but it sounded like she still did it when I wasn't around.

"The for-reals?" I repeated.

Zoe nodded. "Yeah, the witches and other beings. Do you see that elf over there?" She pointed at a guy holding a bunch of dried lavender.

"Elf?" I repeated.

She nodded. "See his nose? It's pointy. I'm betting he's got elf ears that match. That's why he's wearing that hat."

The guy wore a black wool hat. "Huh," I said. "I

just thought he was cold." I studied the man more closely. His nose was a little pointy, but I didn't want to be judgy. What if she was messing with me? "Do all elves have the same features?"

"Mostly. Depends if they're full elf or part, how much elf blood they have, what other heritage they have. Did you really not notice his nose?"

I was getting used to feeling woefully behind in this realm, but it still felt bad. I was used to being in the top of my class. "No. Didn't even notice him, never mind the nose."

Zoe rolled her eyes. "Haven't you been mingling?"

"Uh, Zoe? I'm kind of running a booth here."

"Well, you'd be getting quite the education if you let yourself. I'm sure this event has a whole different look and feel than it did when you were just Violet."

"As opposed to who I am now?"

"You're crabby. Like, see that woman?" She pointed. I followed her gaze to a woman wearing a full-length black dress that looked witchy to me. An owl perched on her shoulder, making me think of Ember Wolfbane, one of my fellow Magickal Council members. Her hair, covered in glitter, was piled on top of her head in a complicated twist. "A witch or no?"

"A witch," I said after a couple of quick calculations. I couldn't help feeling like this was a test.

Zoe made a sound like a buzzer on a game show. "Nope. Trying too hard. You should go around and explore. You'll get better. Hey, I heard you're staying with us. Sorry I missed you last night, but I was out with Gabe. I was wondering why Monty was sitting in the window this morning. I'm trying to teach him some skills but he's a slow learner."

"Monty? You leave him alone. He's innocent!" I was horrified. "What did you do to him?"

"Jeez, relax. You're so uptight. There's enough of that going around with Mother. She's been a huge downer lately."

"Fiona? Come on. She's the life of the party."

"No. She's been in a terrible mood. Sulking around, hiding out in her room. And she keeps having all these hushed conversations with someone. Can't figure out who. Usually I can get around her spells and be nosy, but she's got things locked down right now."

Interesting. Maybe she was just working on the genieing stuff and didn't want Zoe to get dragged in. Speaking of. "Hey. Have you heard from Solomon?" Solomon was a guy—well, a witch—Zoe had hooked me up with. She'd introduced him as a kind of witchy information technologist who had access to the Witch Web and had been looking into the Mazzy situation. I got the sense he was a bit more than just a witchy IT guy.

"No. But don't worry, I know he's working on it. He'll be in touch when he has something." Zoe was completely distracted by all the goods surrounding her at the fair. "Can we talk about it later? Hey, are there clothes here?"

"Zoe—oh, never mind. Yeah, a whole bunch of cool stuff over that way." I pointed to the back left.

"Ooh, nice. I'll be back." She hurried off.

When she moved, I caught sight of a woman standing watching me. She looked vaguely familiar and she was heading my way. As she got closer I realized it was Lila, Horatio's ex-wife who'd been getting the tarot reading from Cali, Horatio's new girlfriend. Whom she didn't know was his new girlfriend.

"Excuse me," she said, walking up to my table. "Are you Violet Mooney?"

I nodded. "I am."

She leaned forward, eyes narrowed, slapping her hands onto the table. "Are you dating my ex-husband?"

CHAPTER SEVENTEEN

I stared at Lila in shock. "Excuse me?"

"Oh, don't play the innocent game with me," she snapped. "I know he's seeing someone here, and you look like his type."

"His type? I'm sorry, I have no idea what you're—"

"Lila. What are you doing here? You best not be bothering the vendors." Horatio's voice cut through the tension. Lila whirled around. Now that her laser gaze was off of me, I risked a glance at Cali. She was watching the whole thing out of the corner of her eye while she pretended to be engrossed in a customer's tarot cards.

"Oh, please," Lila spat at him. "The vendors. You mean your harem of floozies?"

"Hey," I interjected. "I'm not—"

"Shut up! I know what's going on here." Lila jabbed a finger in his face, her eyes blazing. She looked slightly deranged. "You were screwing around on me the whole time. Now you think you can just cast me aside, stop paying me, and carry on with your trophy girls?"

Horatio grabbed her arm and started pulling her toward the door. "If you don't leave, I'm going to have you removed," he said.

She pulled her arm away and screamed, "Help! This man is hurting me!"

For the first time, Horatio looked like he was about to lose his cool. His face turned red and I could see his fists clenching and unclenching at his sides. Out of the corner of my eye I saw a security guard—a mortal one, or at least not one of the leprechauns—heading over.

"What's going on?" he asked, looking from the woman to Horatio. "Sir, do you want me to remove this guest?"

"Remove *me*?" Lila screeched. "He put his hands on me!"

"Ma'am. Let's come over this way, out of the traffic." The security guard led her out of the main path of the exhibits, glancing at Horatio over his shoulder.

Cali looked at Horatio. Horatio looked at me. I had no idea where to look. My face must've matched my red hair at that point. I was mortified. I couldn't believe Lila thought it was me dating Horatio. Where on earth had she gotten that idea? And why hadn't Horatio set her straight? Although she probably wouldn't have listened anyway. She seemed like the type of crazy who wouldn't let it go, either. So now not only did I have to worry about bad genies coming for me, but also crazy exes.

Thankfully, Josie swooped over and wrapped an

arm around my shoulder. "What the heck was that about?"

"Nothing. That woman has me confused with someone else," I said.

"Jeez. Sounds like whoever it is is in for some fun. I need you for a second back here," she said. "Trying to figure out what we need to bring tomorrow."

I mumbled something in reply and let her lead me back behind the table. People started going back to their shopping. I ducked down behind the table, ostensibly to look through boxes but really to try to regain my composure.

After a minute, Josie ducked her head down too. "All okay down there?"

"No." I slumped down onto the floor. "That was Horatio's ex-wife. She thinks I'm seeing him. Why would she think that?"

"No idea," Josie said. "You said he's seeing Cali, right?"

"Yeah. She didn't look too eager to jump into the fray."

"Can you blame her?" Josie laughed. "I'm sure he'll set her straight, Vi. Don't worry about it."

"Excuse me!" A voice piped in from somewhere above us.

Josie poked her head out. "Yes, hello!"

"Hello there! I'm looking for a rhodonite for my daughter. Do you have any?"

"I certainly do." While she showed the woman our selection, I took a minute to regroup. I wished I'd learned how to stop time like Blake could. That would have been the best solution to that little altercation. Although I'd been so flustered I probably wouldn't have remembered in time that I could do it. And what would I have done after that anyway?

I pulled out my phone to check the time. Half an hour before the fair closed and I needed to be at the council meeting. Maybe I should duck out now so I could freshen up, grab coffee, mentally prepare myself. I checked my messages. Still nothing from Todd. I didn't think he'd been genied because no one had found the puddle of slime. And one of the big components of this crime, I was learning, was the fear factor behind making a very public deal out of it. So odds were that my first theory—that he was hiding like a little boy—was probably correct.

When Josie finished with the customer, I stood up and took a cautious look around. No deranged exes waiting to pounce on me. That was something at least. I turned to Josie. "Mind if I head out? I need a few minutes before the meeting."

"Go ahead. I'm just going to flick everything that's left into a box and lock it up in the car. Good luck tonight."

"Thanks." I gave her a hug. "You're the best."

I grabbed my coat and purse. I had to use the restroom before I left, so I detoured to the back of the room and ducked inside the thankfully empty bathroom. I was at the sink washing my hands when Cali came in. Our eyes met in the mirror.

"Hey," I said. "That was quite a show Lila put on."

"I know. I told you, she's obsessed." Cali reached for a stall door, about to disappear inside.

"Why would she think I was the one dating Horatio?" I asked.

"I have no idea."

I wasn't so sure I was buying that. There were hundreds of women at this fair. For her to single me out seemed really convenient. As convenient, perhaps, as Cali ending up next to my booth? "Is someone going to tell her the truth?" I asked. "Because I'd rather she didn't keep showing up to freak out on me."

Cali narrowed her eyes at me. "That's his deal, not mine. Look, I'm sorry she did that, but he needs to set her straight. It's not my job."

I bit back the nasty retort that was on the tip of my tongue and reminded myself that she was under stress. "That friend you asked me about yesterday. The one having a hard time. Was it Horatio?"

She looked away. "I really can't discuss someone else's private business."

I was about to push her on it when two women walked in, laughing and chatting loudly. They glanced at us, but continued their conversation as they went into separate stalls. Cali used the opportunity. "See you tomorrow," she said, and slipped into a stall.

I grabbed a paper towel and dried my hands. I wasn't sure what was going on with her and Horatio and Lila, but I didn't have a great feeling about it. I left the bathroom. As I emerged out of the corridor back into the fair space I saw Horatio and Lorelai Lewis, the podcaster, standing off to the side, talking. Lorelai had her microphone with her but it didn't look like she was using it. Horatio was speaking intently. Lorelai looked engrossed in whatever he was saying. I remember hearing Katia say she was going to the podcaster with whatever it was she was mad about. I wondered if Horatio was trying to talk her out of it.

I ducked my head and started to walk by, but Horatio saw me and called my name.

"We'll catch up about this later," I heard him say to her, then he hurried after me. "Don't worry. She's gone," he said when he reached me.

"Who?"

"Lila, of course. I had her removed from the fair."

"Great. Does she know you're dating Cali and not me?"

He stared at me. "How do you know that?"

"She told me."

"She did?" He looked surprised.

"Yes, why?"

"No reason. She was sensitive about it. Didn't want people to think she was getting special treatment because we were dating."

The exact opposite of what Cali had said. But I didn't need to care about that. Who they told or didn't tell was their business—unless it affected me. "Well, did you tell Lila?"

"She's not going to be a problem anymore," he said firmly. Not quite an answer, though his tone left no room for discussion. "I just wanted to make sure I'll still see you in the morning."

For a moment, I pondered bailing on him. This guy seemed to be full of drama and I had enough drama in my life right now. But on the other hand, I didn't need to get involved in people's personal lives to conduct business with them, right? Ugh. I was tired and I needed to go, not stand here and debate this. "Sure. Yes. I'll see you tomorrow."

"Excellent." He turned and headed off before I could change my mind.

I walked toward the front door, tugging my coat on as I went.

Outside, Burton Jillette still stood near the door, his tray filled with cups. When he saw me, he smiled and offered the tray. I grabbed two of the tiny paper cups, thanked him, and hurried off.

CHAPTER EIGHTEEN

I downed my tinctures and felt better right away. More energetic, less cranky. But I still thought I needed something to get me through this night. The archangels had better up their potency if they wanted me to stay away from coffee. I teleported myself to the Potions Cafe for a special brew. Blake had turned me onto Potions. It was kind of like Pete's coffee shop, only it offered specialty brews that helped with certain qualities. Coffee was the add-on here but the blends were fascinating, all tailored to help spur personal growth in a number of areas—wisdom, confidence, fear-fighting, empathy, self-awareness—the combinations were endless and the drinks were amazing. I wondered if Burton would approve or disapprove.

Plus, it was fascinating in here, from the colorful bottles all with their own unique shapes like the unique potions in each, to the magickal menu board hovering above the counter that was constantly updating itself to advertise different specials, to the magickal machines making and serving the drinks without any assistance. I really enjoyed the atmosphere. And tonight I was wondering if there was a concoction that encompassed all the blends, because I certainly felt like I needed an upgrade in pretty much every area of my being.

Melina, one of the baristas—I guess that's what you called them—saw me and grinned. "Whatcha in the mood for tonight, Violet?"

"A new life," I said with a cheery smile.

She leaned forward a bit. "What was that? Sorry, kind of loud in here."

"Nothing. Can I have the . . ." I scanned the menu board, "peace and calming brew, with an extra shot of emotional intelligence?"

"You got it, girl." She picked up a cup and flicked it into the air behind her, where a machine started to whir and spin. Two potion bottles flew off the rack on the wall, clicked together, and poured into the machine, showering bubbles into the air. When the machine finished mixing, the beautiful, seafoam-colored liquid poured into a cup, which floated over and landed in my hand.

I reached in my pocket for a couple of the coins that Fiona had given me. I was still learning the payment system over here. Fiona had told me a little about it and said that things were mostly done on family account—whatever that meant—but had given me some of these strange little coins for "incidentals." They were shaped like different magickal beings, some that I could recognize and some that were completely foreign to me. I pulled out what looked like a flying horse and handed it to her, but Melina shook her head.

"It's on the account."

"What account?" As far as I knew, Fiona didn't frequent this place.

"Blake's account."

I stared at her. "What do you mean?"

"Blake Alexander. You know, your lawyer friend?"

"I know who he is," I said, trying to turn my gritted teeth into a smile.

"Right. He has an account here. He asked that your purchases be charged to him."

"What?" I laughed out loud. Leave it to Blake. "That's not necessary." I tried to hand her the coin, but she refused.

"Do you know how mad he'll get if I don't? No way. He's too cute for me to annoy. Have a nice night!"

I had no idea why Blake was funding my potions, but arguing with her was clearly fruitless. I took my drink and went outside to sip and, hopefully, start to feel less anxious before I showed up at the meeting. It was a lovely night, and I sat down at one of the cafe tables. It struck me that not only were the tables empty, but the street was too. That seemed odd. Amethyst Street was usually hopping. There were a lot of businesses out here.

My drink was delicious, but instead of shoring up my confidence, I felt less and less like showing up for these meetings. I immediately felt guilty thinking that, what with all the history and prestige associated with this council seat, but that only made it worse. My grandmother had been such a presence, and someone with infinite knowledge about these matters. I knew nothing. How was I supposed to live up to the expectation that I would carry on her work? Right now, it felt like all I was doing was tainting her seat and her legacy.

A copy of the witchy newspaper, *Magickal Minute,* had been abandoned on the table. I picked it up. The evening edition. Which meant it was hot off the presses. I scanned the headlines, immediately sorry I had. The news about Mac had broken. But not only that—the news about *me* had broken. The above-the-fold headline read, *Private investigator missing.* The subhead read, *Second known genie attack this year involving Ravenstar/Moonstone heiress.*

My heart was pounding in my ears so loudly I couldn't hear anything else around me. I wondered why Fiona hadn't appeared in front of me screaming about this. She must not have seen it yet, but how could that be? She knew everything pretty much before it happened. I scanned the article, written by a reporter named Belinda Marvelle. It called Mac out by name, citing his reputation as one of the leading private investigators of the century with a well-respected firm, and noted that he had allegedly been investigating the Mazzy Diamond case. Since Mazzy had been a reporter for this newspaper—albeit freelance—they were keeping her story alive as much as possible. That was one silver lining—at least someone was.

But then Belinda went on to say that sources confirmed that Violet Moonstone, heir apparent of the recently deceased Abigail Moonstone and daughter of Magickal Council queen Fiona Ravenstar, was again tied to the scene of the crime, re-

portedly having been in the building and likely
called in the anonymous tip about the event. She
also reminded everyone that this was the second
genie attack in mere months after a century of
peace, and that the first one had been in my mortal crystal shop.

Other than that, the story didn't have a ton of
details. It said evidence found at Mac's office
pointed to him as a victim, and the Magickal Police were treating this as a very serious situation.
All beings were asked to stay inside as much as possible, and if they did have to go out, to stay alert
and notify authorities if they saw or heard anything that could potentially be tied to these cases.
No wonder the street was empty. People were scared.

She closed the story out with some color about
my much-anticipated return to the witch world,
stopping just short of saying I was responsible for
this madness.

I didn't know whether to be angry or devastated
by this. Immediately my mind went to Todd. Had
he outed me, then disappeared to save his own
skin? One last attempt to take me down? I was so
angry I couldn't see straight. It had to be him. The
only other people who knew I was there were
Blake and that Stalker Squad guy. I believed Blake
when he said he hadn't told anyone else. He had
proven himself trustworthy. No, my money was on
Todd. He better stay hidden because I was going
to kick his butt when I found him.

Then I realized, I should probably be very
afraid. Someone—or multiple someones—had it
in for me. And if they could get to someone like
Mac, I would be a piece of cake to attack.

I shivered, realizing I was nearly alone on this block right now. I didn't want to start being completely paranoid, but I was easy prey. I needed to get out of here. I picked up my cup, touched my finger to the pendant Grandma Abby had given me all those years ago, and vanished into the night.

CHAPTER NINETEEN

I landed in council chambers as I'd planned. I had a moment of pleasure when I opened my eyes and saw the cathedral ceilings and floor-to-ceiling etchings on the giant room's walls. Until I realized my chair was a lot softer than I remembered. And it smelled good. Like incense. My intention had been to end up in my seat, ready for business like everyone else always seemed to be. Instead, I found myself sitting on Blake's lap.

With a screech, I jumped up, spilling what remained of my precious potion all over Blake's fancy suit. Everyone in the room—the witches and their familiars—all turned and stared at me. For the second time that day, my face turned beet red. I heard a burst of laughter and a cheer.

"You go, girl!" Christobel, who seemed like one of the nicer council members, winked at me. She was probably close to my age and wore a lot of black makeup—lipstick, eye shadow. I'd also heard she was a distant relative of mine on Grandma Abby's side, though I'd not yet had a chance to speak to her privately.

I cleared my throat, rose, and straightened my skirt. "I'm so sorry," I said to Blake.

To his credit, he didn't even blink. "No problem," he said, and waved his fancy pen at his pants. They immediately dried, no stain remaining. Well, at least that was easily fixed. He looked like he wanted to say something to me, but all eyes had turned my way—including those of Oscar Sageblood, my archenemy, and my cousin Posey, who wore a look of complete disdain at my ineptitude. Even her rabbit was giving me the stink eye.

I tried not to cringe under Posey's schoolmarmy gaze and remember that I wasn't going to be perfect right out of the gate. I'd been a witch for like five minutes, while she'd been one her whole life. I'd been warned that Posey was totally jealous of me and couldn't stand my mother, mostly because of her status. She thought her own mother—and therefore she herself, by default—should have more power on the council and within the whole leadership sphere. I didn't fully understand the dynamics yet, but Fiona was the eldest sister and had done the most for the world at large, from what I'd heard, so it made sense to me that she was queen bee.

But what did I know?

Keeping my head high, I moved toward my seat, trying to look like I'd planned the entrance all along. I didn't even look in Fiona's direction. I could already anticipate her response. Inside, I was dying. But it was no surprise I'd messed up because my head was such a train wreck right now. I could see eyes following me—Ember's, Oscar's, Serenity's—and I could feel the disdain.

When I got to my seat I was cheered by the sight of Xander, curled up on the table on top of my agenda. He glanced at me, and I thought I could read amusement in his eyes, which seemed to say, *Don't sweat it, girl.*

"Welcome, Violet!" Hattie Blandon, our secretary, waved enthusiastically at me, clearly trying to move things along. She was sweet.

"Hi there," I said weakly.

But Posey wasn't about to let me off the hook. "Honestly, Violet. Must you make such an entrance every time? I mean, we're all well aware that you're here." Her tone dripped with condescension.

My face went as red as my hair. Before I could formulate a response, Blake said, "That was my error. I accidentally interrupted her entrance because I was summoning her at the same time. But thanks for the input, Posey." His dry tone suggested he wasn't thankful at all.

I was grateful he'd stepped in, but I couldn't let him take the blame. I opened my mouth to chime in but at the slight shake of his head, I closed it again. Posey, always one to get the last word in, muttered, "A better witch could've navigated it."

At that, Fiona sent her gavel down onto the table with a smash. "That's enough, Posey. I'm calling the meeting to order."

I could feel the tips of my ears still burning as I extracted my agenda out from under Xander, who flicked his tail at me. It was nice people were coming to my defense, but it made me look like I couldn't handle myself. I already felt out of place here. And if my own family was attacking me, I didn't have much hope for the rest of them.

"Shall I go through the agenda?" Hattie asked Fiona. "Although, we really only have one item. Mac Finnegan. And the corresponding report from Chief Bell." She nodded at the chief, who sat just outside of the council table, flanked by another member of the Magickal Police, Deputy Merriweather. There was another man with them I didn't recognize.

"I have a walk-on first." Fiona didn't even glance their way. She threw her hand in the air, and newspapers rained down on the tables in front of each of us. Most of the familiars accompanying the council members jumped at the sudden flurry of papers, although I was proud to see that Xander didn't even blink.

I glanced down at mine. The same *Magickal Minute* I'd been reading at the cafe.

"The word is out," Fiona said. "Everyone knows about Mac. People are panicking. And clearly there's an agenda at play here."

Across the table, Blake's face was stony. I wondered if he'd seen this prior to right now. He had to have. He was probably more in the know than any of us, since he had that friend on the Stalker Squad. I wished he had given me a head's up.

"Mariza Diamond was one thing," Fiona went on. "While unsettling, that could be written off as a fluke. But this?" She shook her head grimly. "This is not good. Especially since Mac is a seasoned professional."

"And Violet was an alleged witness in both . . . incidents," Oscar said, leaning back in his chair, a small smile of satisfaction playing over his lips.

"An after-the-fact-witness," Fiona corrected. "And while people may try to spin that to formulate a certain story, we all know that the reality suggests something much more insidious."

I held my breath. Was she really going to go there? I knew one of the reasons Fiona had Mac working on this was not just because of Mazzy being genied in my store. Fiona had suspected for a while that there was something suspicious about my Grandma Abby's death and that somehow all of this other stuff was connected. But why would she want to say that in front of all of these people, especially with no proof yet?

"Oh?" Oscar sat forward. "Do tell."

I risked a look at Blake. His face was blank, but his lips were pressed tightly together. Guess he was wondering the same thing.

Fiona shrugged. "It's obvious that someone is targeting Violet."

I let out a breath. Out of the corner of my eye, I saw Blake do the same.

Oscar waited for more. When Fiona didn't offer anything else, he laughed. "That's your theory? Convenient, I'll admit."

"I have a question," Ember Wolfbane spoke up. As usual, she wore all white, and her platinum hair was as close to white as it could get. Her familiar, a black owl, was the only source of color around her. Tonight he sat completely still on the back of her chair, giving the eerie illusion that she had two completely contrasting heads. She turned those icy eyes on me. "Was Mr. Finnegan working on your behalf?"

"And is that why you were there the night this unfortunate event occurred?" Oscar couldn't seem to keep his mouth shut, and he fixed his glare back on me. Ember looked annoyed that he'd jumped in on her question, but Blake cut them both off.

"None of that is relevant to our agenda topic tonight," he said. "Let's stay focused."

"Our topic is Mac Finnegan, so I could argue it's directly related," Oscar said. "And if you were there, Blake, then you've clearly been covering up that Violet was there. Why?"

A collective hush fell over the room. I got the strong sense that Oscar had just crossed a big line. And judging from the waves of anger coming off of Blake, he just might be in big trouble.

"Excuse me," Gordon Magnum said, holding up his hand to try to head off whatever was going to happen next. "Oscar, I agree with Blake—that is not where our focus should be tonight. We've had two of these attacks in a very short amount of time and our community is frightened. They are looking to us find out where this is coming from, not to place blame on someone new to the fold. I think we should hear from Chief Bell."

"Good idea," Fiona said. "Chief Bell, what do you have for the council?"

Chief Bell stood, clearing his throat, trying to ignore the eye daggers flying between Oscar and Blake. "Thank you for having me, Chairwoman Ravenstar. I've brought Captain Christian Graeme with me, our lead investigator on the Stalker Squad.

He's been assisting me in all aspects of this inquiry."

I studied Graeme. He looked kind of foreboding-
ing, with black hair that hung completely over one
side of his face. I could see a scar of some sort
snaking down his cheek under all that hair. I wondered if he'd gotten it fighting genies or something. He didn't look at the council so much as
glare at them, and I couldn't help but wonder
what Blake thought of this guy. If he hadn't called
him directly and he was the head of the Stalker
Squad, that would indicate that Blake either didn't
know him well or trust him. I tried to get a read on
Blake, but his face was blank.

Bell nudged Graeme. "Your report, Captain?"
he prompted.

Graeme raised his head. His eyes were as black
as his hair. In a robotic voice, he recapped their investigation so far, which seemed to concern only
Mac, not Mazzy. "We have reason to believe the
Fernsby family is involved in this incident," he said,
which elicited some gasps from some of the council members. Vivienne Dandy had gone white.
Ember reached over and squeezed her hand reas-
suringly. "We're in the process of tracking down
their associates," Graeme went on, oblivious to the
angst he'd just caused.

As if Oscar's attack wasn't enough for Blake. I
could see he was caught off guard by this. I didn't
think Graeme was supposed to say anything about
that here. I remembered Blake telling me that no
one could know about it, that the Fernsby name
was enough to send the entire world into a panic.

I jumped up. "What about Mazzy? Are they involved in her incident too? Because I know Mac is the focus here, but if we figure out who genied Mazzy that will likely lead us to Mac's captor. And we have less than a week to free Mazzy," I reminded them. "Sunday is the next full moon, the third since her genieing." That was the deadline. If a genieing victim wasn't rescued before the end of three moon cycles, they were lost for good.

But the entire room stared at me like I was speaking a different language. I slid back into my seat.

"We're aware," Graeme said. "We've got every investigator from every agency making this a top priority."

"Which brings me to our next order of business," Fiona said, rising from her chair. "Chief Bell, would you explain to the committee what we decided?"

Bell nodded. "So with that, we felt it best to disband the committee we put together. My time is best spent working with the other investigators. Especially with such a limited timeframe in which to work," he added, glancing at me.

"But we're the governing body. We put that subcommittee together to ensure we were informed and could also offer our input," Ember said.

"Yeah," Alan Black chimed in, in that blustery way he had. "We were handpicked for this committee because of our expertise. I would think you'd be needing that expertise right about now."

"I have to agree, Fiona," Vivienne said. Her kind face looked troubled. "I would've liked to have had this discussion first."

"I understand, but given current circumstances I've made the decision that we're not going to fragment the operations any further," Fiona said. "We need our police forces to be putting their energy into investigating, not sitting around in a room with us. They certainly don't need our investigative input. We also need to make sure information isn't in danger of getting out. Like the Fernsby connection." At this, she gave Bell a pointed look. He had the grace to blush. "And we need every security resource we have working together on this," she continued. "So the police forces, special squads, and defense teams will now have a full-time focus on this. I'll receive daily reports on their efforts, and a representative will join us at each meeting to give the council a full report." To emphasize this, she rapped her gavel on the table.

"We'll be back next week with an update," Bell added, looking around the room. And with that, Bell and Graeme vanished from chambers, leaving the rest of the council speechless.

CHAPTER TWENTY

After Bell and Graeme laid down the law and left chambers, the tension was palpable. I guessed that Fiona hadn't told anyone else about this, except probably Blake. The rest of them just looked stunned, and some, like Oscar and Ember, looked explosive.

It was Ember who dared to speak first. "Fiona. I demand an explanation," she said. "This is a council decision, not your decision."

I winced inwardly. Ember was about to get the full Fiona experience unleashed on her if she didn't watch out.

"Actually, Ember, you may want to brush up on the bylaws," Fiona said. She remained standing, a subtle reminder that she was in charge here. "In times of great distress, the council chairperson has the authority to make a command decision, especially in wartime."

"Wartime? We're going to war?" Posey this time, and for once, there was no attitude in her tone. She looked genuinely frightened at this thought.

Blake jumped in, as usual the voice of reason.

"Fiona has decided, with counsel, to deploy a precautionary wartime structure for our defense teams. In short, we need to be prepared," he said bluntly. "If the genies and whoever they're working with are ramping up right now, we have to be ready to defeat them. And luckily, we have leaders now who are not sitting around waiting for an uprising like we had a century ago." This, with a sidelong glance at Oscar, a not-so-subtle dig at the Sageblood legacy.

"Fiona, I don't need to tell you that we must be careful about leaks. Who is in charge of overseeing the police efforts?" Oscar asked.

"I am," Fiona said calmly. "And I've appointed a new head of day-to-day operations while they're working in this structure."

"Well, who?" Oscar demanded.

"Blake," Fiona said.

All eyes—including mine—turned toward him.

Oscar laughed out loud. "You're kidding, right? He's a lawyer, not a sorcerer of defense. Speaking of which, if we had someone in that role—"

"You are correct. Blake's law background is the reason for this appointment," Fiona said. "We need someone who can look at the work with eyes on the legal obligations and repercussions more than we need someone else with law enforcement technique. And not to worry, Oscar. Once this is over, we'll put our efforts back into filling the sorcerer of defense position. There's still time to put in your application." She sat back down and turned to Hattie. "Anything else on the agenda we need to cover?"

There wasn't, or else no one was in the mood, so Fiona adjourned the meeting.

I took my time gathering my things. Xander was visiting with Gordon's ferret and Posey's rabbit, which struck me as kind of funny. They could get along. Why couldn't we?

"Let's take a walk." Blake appeared next to me. He took my arm and led me out of the room.

We moved silently down the giant hallway that looked more like a museum than a governing building. I took in the grandeur around me—the marble floors, the gold accents on the walls, the photos lining the corridor that looked like it went on for miles. Above me, the ceiling looked like something out of an art book—dark blue background with silver depictions of planets and stars. It made the ceiling at Grand Central Station in New York look like a toddler had designed it.

This was the first time I'd ever been out of the council chambers and actually seeing the rest of this place. And once again I felt kind of disgusted with myself. Why hadn't I taken the time to walk through the halls, learn about the place, the history? Where in the geographical sphere was it even located? I had no clue. I had no clue about anything, really. I didn't even fully realize the extent of Fiona's power. Not just her magickal powers, but the power she had as the leader of this world.

And me? Well, with all the powers at my disposal, the only ones I'd tapped into, aside from harnessing my aura-reading power and tapping into my innate knowledge of healing by crystals, I'd learned only the most basic spells. I'd learned how to teleport out of necessity, and I'd been so rigid in my approach, so fearful of screwing up, that I took the most rudimentary approach possible—think of the two or three places that you can envision and get there. I'd displayed no curiosity, no willingness to veer off track. I'd been so focused on my own dramas and feeling sorry for myself that I'd been behaving like an overprivileged rich kid who had been given an amazing opportunity that many would kill for, and not even recognizing it.

When we were far enough away from the council chambers, Blake pulled me into an alcove where we couldn't be seen by anyone casually stepping out of the room and turned me to face him. "What are you beating yourself up about?"

"What makes you think I'm beating myself up?" I asked, but it was weak.

"I know you by now," he said with a tight smile. "When you're upset at yourself, your lips get all pinched and you bite them a lot." He reached out a finger, smoothing it over my bottom lip.

Despite my self-contempt (yes, he was right about that), my stomach did a little flip, like I was about to go down the steep curve of a rollercoaster.

"First, I'm so sorry. Oscar attacked you because of me."

"Violet, Oscar Sageblood is the least of my concerns," Blake said. "If I had a witch's coin for every time a member of my extended family took a swing at me, I could be the richest witch in the land. Truly."

I knew he was glossing over this a bit. I could tell he'd been shaken, but I didn't want to call more attention to it. "Okay, fine. But also, I didn't even know," I said.

"Know what?"

"That Fiona could . . . do that. That she really is the person this whole world depends on." I swept my hand around to encompass our surroundings. I'd never actually connected the idea that my mother was pretty much the equivalent of the president of the United States, but with a lot more power. "And I've caused all these issues for her." I shook my head. "She's probably regretting that she even bothered to come find me."

"Violet." He gave my shoulders a little shake. "Stop. Fiona loves you. Fiercely. Trust me. If she could trade any of the power and reputation she has to get back some of the years she didn't have you, she would."

"Oh, come on. She has bigger things to worry about. Like this whole world. Or country. Or planet. See, I'm so lame. I don't even know how to refer to a dimension that I'm standing in! I haven't done enough, Blake. I haven't tried to help her. I've fought her at every turn, and because of me, she's having to make decisions like the one she made in there, which made everyone mad. They're all going to turn on her because of me."

But he was shaking his head. "You can't know everything instantaneously, Violet. And this, everything that's happening, is not because of you. This is because some bad beings want to see people like your mother, and you, stripped of your rightful power. Because they are threatened by you. Because they understand that with women like you at the helm, our world will never be able to return to the screwed-up place it was when the legacy male witches were running things. And they're upping their game because they're scared. They know that they're running out of time. But she won't let them win. Believe that, Vi. Your mother is a force to be reckoned with, and so are you."

We stared at each other, him still holding me by the shoulders, until I broke the gaze. "Did you know? What she was going to do?"

He nodded. "We decided together that was the best course of action."

"So is this like a promotion for you?"

"No. It's a babysitting job. We need to check for leaks, and we need to be on our toes about who we can trust. Since at this point Fiona doesn't trust, well, anyone, I'm it."

I nodded slowly. That was a major compliment, to be the one person in whom Fiona was willing to put her trust. "Were they not supposed to tell everyone about the Fernsby thing?"

"No, they weren't. And I don't even know how they knew that, so that's my job for tomorrow—to figure out where they got that information."

"And how did that reporter know that I was there that night?"

"I don't know that either. Trust me, I was just as surprised as you were. I saw the paper right before we went into the meeting. Something else I'm worried about. I can't figure out where this leak is coming from. I'm going to go see Dewin after I leave here."

"Oh, come on." I crossed my arms over my chest. "That worm Todd must've told her. Or someone. I don't know where he vanished to, but if I find him first, I'm going to practice a spell on how to remove his tongue."

Blake stifled a laugh and ran a hand through his hair. He had great hair—dark, wavy, just long enough to hint that he was a rebel. He looked stressed tonight, though. I'd never seen him look that way before. Usually he took everything in stride.

"If that's true, I'll be right there to make sure you get it right. But," Blake paused, "I don't know if he'd be that stupid. Because it would be real easy to figure out he was the one who leaked it and then start questioning why he was there. And with the rumors already circulating about his family, it wouldn't look good. His father would kill him."

"Then who? Who on earth would not only know this but go to the newspapers about it?" I was startled to realize tears were spilling out of my eyes. I didn't even know I'd been crying.

Blake looked equally as startled, but he pulled me into his arms. "Vi, it's okay. We're going to solve this. I promise."

I let him hold me, burying my face against his chest. He smelled good. He always smelled faintly of incense smoke. I knew I was getting his fancy jacket wet but I didn't care. I didn't want to let go. I felt like I'd been holding myself up for so long, putting on a brave face, pretending I was okay, muddling through all the insanity that had seeped into my life over the past two months. Now I just wanted someone to hold me up for a change.

I don't know how long we stood there like that before we heard voices in the hallway. I immediately stepped back, not wanting anyone to see us. That wouldn't go over well. The rest of the committee was probably already mad enough at him for being Fiona's go-to. It would look bad if they thought some kind of romance with me was part of the equation.

But he still held on to me. "We're gonna figure all this out. Trust me." He kissed the top of my head, then stepped back and took my hand. The next thing I knew, I was in my bedroom at Grandma Abby's house. I hadn't even had the whole teleporting experience this time—I was just there one second and here the next. I had no idea you could just send people somewhere without sending yourself along. Yet another skill I needed to learn.

But at the moment, there was no place else I'd rather be than in my bed. I barely took the time to change into pajamas before I collapsed into bed and fell asleep.

CHAPTER TWENTY-ONE

Tuesday
Five days before the full moon

When I woke up the next morning, the clock that I'd programmed to hover over me read eight thirty-five. I had a moment of panic thinking I'd overslept. Then I remembered I didn't have to be at the shop, that Syd was covering because of the fair, and my first obligation was at ten a.m. to see Horatio's moldavite. Which I didn't even feel like doing, but in the interest of my shop, I would.

I dragged myself out of bed, muttering a spell to make me at least look amazing even if I didn't feel that way. When I looked in my full-length mirror I was pleasantly surprised. I wore a slim, silky purple slip dress with a long, black lace jacket over it. A giant amethyst necklace glittered at the perfect length against my chest. My red hair, which usually

hit my chin in a smooth, choppy cut, had grown a
bit—I hadn't noticed—and had some loose curls
in it. Dangly silver earrings brushed my shoulders.
Instead of my usual combat boots, black cowboy
booties with rhinestones completed the look.

My style was way better when I didn't think about
it so much.

I checked my phone, which I'd been avoiding.
No messages. Still nada from Todd. I headed
downstairs with Monty on my heels. Xander wasn't
around, but I figured he'd show up at some point.
I went into the kitchen to feed Monty, hesitating
only for a second when I heard Fiona's voice. I
wondered what kind of mood she'd be in today. I
took a deep breath, squared my shoulders, and
walked into the room.

Fiona and Zoe were sitting at the table. They
both looked up when I came in.

"Morning," I said, heading over to get Monty's
bowl.

"Violet!" Fiona jumped up and headed straight
for me. I winced, waiting for some kind of magickal slap to hit me upside the head. Instead, I was
surprised when she wrapped her arms around me.
I could see Zoe's face over her shoulder and she
looked equally as surprised.

Fiona stepped back and took my shoulders with
her heavily ringed hands, examining me closely.
"How are you this morning? I didn't have a chance
to speak to you after the meeting. I had some additional business to attend to."

"I'm fine. How are you?"

"I'm sure you're not fine," Fiona said. "I'm certainly not fine about what was done to you. I have

a mind to get that newspaper reporter fired. As it is, I'm going to speak to the editor today. We are going to get to the bottom of this. Have some coffee." She pointed to the table and a steaming mug appeared.

"I have to feed . . ." I faltered as I turned back to Monty's bowl. It was already full and he was munching happily.

"Wow. Okay, then. I guess I have time for a cup." I wasn't quite sure what was going on here, but this was not the reaction I expected. Fiona seemed almost . . . warm. And like she cared about how I was feeling right now.

"I saw the paper." Zoe tossed her long braid over her shoulder and leaned forward. Her eyes were outlined in dark purple, which made their intensity even more shocking as she gazed at me. "That's messed up. How do you think anyone knew?"

"I don't know," I said. Then I said, "I was wondering if it was Todd. Blake doesn't think so, but I can't think of how anyone else would know."

"That little—" Zoe muttered, but Fiona cut her off.

"Zoe. Violet doesn't need to worry about that. That little ogre will not come near you again."

I paused, coffee cup on its way to my lips. "What do you mean?" I asked suspiciously.

She sighed. "I'm sure he's gotten instructions from his family to stay away. He's caused more harm than anything at this point."

"So you don't think he told the newspaper?" I wasn't following.

"I don't know if he did that or not. What I do

know is that he failed on the mission his family sent him to do, so he's likely going to have to answer for that."

I didn't know what that meant, or if I even wanted to. "Do you know where he is?" I asked. "He hasn't been in touch at all since Saturday night."

"Please don't tell me you want to talk to him again," Fiona said.

"No, not like that. I just . . . I guess I wanted an explanation."

Fiona dismissed this with a wave of her hand. "Forget him. Now. Plans for the day?"

I recognized a closed door when I heard one. "The fair." I glanced at my phone to see what time it was. Almost ten. Shoot. I was going to be late for Horatio if I didn't leave now. "And, honestly, I was thinking of going to see that reporter myself."

Zoe and Fiona exchanged a look. "You're going to the fair?" Zoe asked at the same time Fiona said, "No reporters."

"Of course I am," I said, getting up and looking around for my coat. "Why wouldn't I be?"

Another look between them. "Can't Josie handle it today?" Fiona asked.

I looked up. "Why? What are you not telling me?"

"It's just . . ." Fiona paused.

I had never seen her trying to choose her words carefully. Fiona wasn't the beat-around-the-bush type. I turned to Zoe. "Can you fill in the blank here?"

"There could be some blowback," Fiona said before Zoe could open her mouth.

"Blowback?" I was confused. "About what?"

"The whole Mac thing."

"What do you mean?"

"I mean, whoever tipped off this reporter had one reason for doing so—and that was to cast suspicion on you. And they have succeeded," she added grimly.

I felt my stomach drop like I was on the precipice of a really high roller coaster. "What do you mean they've succeeded?"

"People are wondering if you really did have anything to do with it," Zoe filled in helpfully.

"But can't you tell them it's not true?" I turned to Fiona.

"Violet. Of course I've told everyone it's the most absurd thing I've ever heard. Most people know this, but as you know it only takes a few big mouths to sow the seeds of malcontent. That and our newspapers have turned into tabloids." She looked disgusted. "Anyway, not to worry. It will blow over but it might be better if you lie low until then."

"Lie low?" I couldn't believe what I was hearing. "You mean hide? I'm not hiding. I have a business to run. And a life outside of all . . . this." I waved my hands around, trying to encompass the whole world I'd been dropped into. "And I can't hide anyway! All these bad genies and witches can find me in a second, right? So what does it even matter? Plus, it's mostly mortals there." I wasn't sure if that was true, but I hoped so.

"You're safe here," she said quietly.

"Look, I'll stay out of sight in the witch realm if that's what you mean, but I can't hide here. This is my town. People around here—unless they're witches—don't know any of this." I paced around the tiny kitchen, frustration and fear warring inside of me.

"Right, but at this fair of yours, the two worlds collide. You never know what could happen," Fiona said. "I'm not trying to be a fatalist, Violet. Just practical. You're my daughter. I'm worried."

The words hung there until a knock at the door startled us all. I was closest, so I opened it. Gabe. Perfect timing. "Come on in," I told him. "I was just on my way out." I turned back to Fiona. "I get what you're saying, but I really do have to go." I hesitated, then went over and kissed her cheek before I hurried out.

CHAPTER TWENTY-TWO

I teleported to my car, hoping Gabe hadn't noticed my lack of a vehicle when he drove up.
Once inside with the heater blasting, I checked my
watch. My little powwow with Fiona and Zoe had
taken up more time than I'd planned. I was going
to be late. I roared out of the lot toward the amphitheater. It was harder for me to teleport there.
Despite the scores of magickal people, there were
just as many mortals and it could get messy.

Also I hadn't driven much lately and had forgotten how cathartic it could be to just floor it with
the windows open. Admittedly it was pretty cold to
have the windows open, but blasting the heat
helped. As I drove, I replayed the conversation at
Fiona's in my mind.

I couldn't believe how things had unfolded. Fiona
had sworn up and down that it would be good for
me to embrace this life, that I would be welcomed

with open arms. Instead, people weren't sure what to make of me. I clearly wasn't a skilled witch yet and I was sure my presence on the council rubbed people the wrong way. Here I was voting on things that had an impact on people's lives without even knowing anything. And now, it felt like the bad people—whoever they were—were already after me, and the people who thought *I* was one of the bad people were also out for my head.

I had no idea how to fix it, and I also had no idea how to stay safe. It was a no-win situation.

I was jolted out of my thoughts by the sound of a siren behind me. At first I thought an ambulance was coming so I started to pull over, then I realized it was a police car. With flashing lights. Right on my tail.

"You've got to be kidding me," I muttered, yanking my steering wheel and pulling over to the side of the road. I knew it wasn't Gabe, since I'd just left him at Fiona's. I didn't know anyone else on the force except for the two cops who'd wanted to arrest me for murder a couple of months ago. I surely hoped it wasn't either of them.

I rolled my window down and waited for the cop to get out of the car. Finally the door opened and a bald, slightly overweight guy got out, hiked up his pants and started over to me.

"Morning, ma'am," he said. "Do you know why I pulled you over?"

"I don't think so," I said, putting on my best smile. Liar, liar.

"You were going fifty-two in a thirty zone. License and registration please."

I kept my hands on the steering wheel and gave

him the brightest smile I could muster on a day like this. "Look, Officer . . ." I peered at his badge. "Hanlon. I'm sorry. I'm having a really crap day today and I'm late for an appointment. I'm a local and, well, do you think for just this once you could let it go?" I hated doing it but I forced myself to bat my eyelashes at him.

However, my smile mustn't have been up to snuff because Hanlon didn't blink, just waited for me to oblige.

I heaved a sigh and reached for my bag. But as I pulled out my license I suddenly thought, *you know what, screw it.* I'd been tiptoeing around both my lives, not wanting to bother anyone, let on about all my secrets, ruffle any feathers, whatever notions I had in my head about taking up space and letting people walk all over me. This guy wasn't giving me a ticket. If I was going to get stuck with all the insanity that came with being a witch, I was going to start using it to my advantage.

I took my time getting my license, all the while praying I wouldn't screw this up and get myself arrested. I had never tried anything like this before on a mortal. But I'd seen Blake, Fiona, and Zoe do enough shenanigans that I was hopeful I'd picked up something worthwhile. I turned back to him but instead of handing him the documents I focused on concentrating really hard to send him back to his car with complete amnesia about this whole interaction.

It partially worked. He flew backward like someone really strong had punched him in the stomach, but only a couple of steps. He caught himself, straightened up and sauntered back to my car with a small smile. "Nice try, Ms. Mooney. Make sure before you try any of your new powers you know who you're trying them on. For example, if a fellow seasoned witch can see it coming, we can counterpoint." He leaned into the car. "Now. That license and registration please?"

Fifteen minutes later I held a ticket in my hand, which Hanlon had presented with a triumphant flourish. I wasn't worried about the ticket. I was worried about being outed to Gabe. I needed to warn Zoe that there was a witch on the police force. A witch who knew who I was. I was already late, but what if Hanlon decided to go straight to Gabe as payback? I needed to talk to her ASAP. I figured I'd give summoning a shot. I closed my eyes and focused on her sitting next to me in the car. When I opened them again, she was.

"Oh, thank Goddess," I said with relief.

She looked around. "Jeez, Violet. You caught me off guard! What are you doing?"

I took a closer look at her. One side of her hair was in a braid, the other wasn't, and she wore black yoga pants and a T-shirt. And socks. "I thought you could tell if someone was summoning you somewhere? Especially if you're good at all this?"

"Yeah, well, I wasn't ready." She sniffed and began threading her hair in a braid on the unkempt side. "Where the heck are we, anyway?"

"On the side of the road. Was Gabe still at your house?"

She gave me a look. "You think I'd look like this if he was? No, he left and I just got out of the shower."

"Zoe, I have to tell you something."

"Well, I certainly hope you weren't doing this for kicks."

"There's a witch on the police force."

"Okay," she said, unfazed. "Do you have a hair tie?"

"No I don't have a hair tie! What's wrong with you?"

"For real, Violet? I can't be out like this!" She shook her head, murmured something, and swept her hand down her body, beginning at her head. As I watched, her hair braided itself and a hair tie neatly grasped it in place at the bottom. She now wore a fuzzy black coat and UGG boots over her casual outfit.

"Better," she said, tilting the rearview so she could see her hair. "Although who needs a coat when this car feels like a sauna?" She adjusted the air vents on her side, then put the mirror back in place and looked at me expectantly. "Okay, so what's the emergency?"

A car behind me drove by, giving me the evil eye as they passed because they had to veer into the other lane to get around me. I reached a hand up in an apologetic wave and took off. "Didn't you hear what I said?" I asked her.

"Yeah. Someone's a witch. Big deal. Do you know how many people are witches around here?"

"But this cop knows who I am. Which means he knows who you are too, I'm assuming."

Zoe continued to stare at me as if to say, *And your point?*

I wanted to pound the steering wheel with my fist. "What if he tells Gabe?"

"That's what you're worried about?" Zoe waved me off and sat back. "How did you find out he's a witch anyway?"

"Well. I kind of tried to use some powers."

"That doesn't sound good. Spill."

So I told her the whole story. The whole time, she was trying to keep a straight face. But when I got to the part about my hundred-dollar ticket, she couldn't hold it in any longer and burst out laughing. "You really tried to take out a cop?"

I turned to her, horrified. "I did not try to *take him out!* I was trying to send him back to his car and erase his memory. You know, so he'd forget he pulled me over."

"Oof." She shook her head.

I glared at her. "What?"

"Have you ever tried that before?"

"I knocked Oscar the Great over at a council meeting."

"Completely different," she said. "You were trying a turn-back-time move, but you did it all wrong. If he's a seasoned witch, he'd have seen it coming a mile away. I can teach you how to do it right. See, you can't do it in two steps. If you tried to send him back to his car and then erase his memory, it's the wrong order. Plus if you do it wrong you can erase too much memory. . . . What?" she asked, noticing the look on my face.

"Oh, nothing. I just can't believe you think this

is the best time to lecture me. What if Gabe finds out we're witches?"

"Vi." Zoe reached out and grabbed my hand. "Please don't worry about Gabe. I'll take care of it. What's this cop's name again?" She gave an evil, if not exaggerated, cackle.

"Don't even joke. If he finds out, better that you tell him."

She met my gaze, unflinching. We held the stare for a few seconds until she leaned back and sighed. "Look. Let's worry about that later, okay? You have a lot to deal with right now."

"Don't remind me." I closed my eyes and rubbed my temples. "I wish I could just go back to my old life."

"Aww. Don't say that. Then we wouldn't know each other and I kind of like having a big sister." Zoe reached over and squeezed my hand, the first really affectionate sisterly gesture she'd made since I'd met her.

I squeezed back. And my eye caught the clock on the dashboard. Ten twenty. "Crap. I'm so late right now. You need to go home."

She stared at me. "You brought me here."

"Well, now I'm asking you to leave. Shoo." I made a *go away* motion with my hand.

"You're a freak." She bared her teeth at me, then vanished from the car. I noticed with some amusement that she'd left a pile of hair ties on my seat, presumably for next time.

I drove as fast as I dared the rest of the way to the amphitheater, keeping one eye on the rear-

view for any cops. The storage wing was behind the
large building and the main entrance was all the
way around back. I pulled up to the curb in front
too fast and hit it. Great. All I needed was a flat tire
to top this morning off. Could things get any
worse?

I turned the car off, shoved the door open, and
rushed to the entrance door. It was quiet back
here. I guessed all the vendors had already hauled
their stuff over through the connected entrance,
or maybe it was too early. I pushed the door open
and stepped inside. Lights were on, but the place
was mostly empty. There were a few people collecting things from pods, and a couple of people talking here and there. I looked around, taking in the
pods and other portable storage units stacked up
around the giant space, each in their own little
area. Various equipment one might expect to find
in a warehouse littered the floor—dollies and lad-
ders, a small forklift parked in one corner.

I headed to the back of the giant room. Halfway
there, a man dressed in a janitor's outfit stepped
out from behind a partition, scaring the daylights
out of me. "Help you?"

I told him I was looking for the offices and he
pointed to a dimly lit corner of the room. I
thanked him and headed that way. I pushed the
door leading to the corridor open and paused.
"Hello? Horatio? It's Violet Mooney."

Silence. Shoot. I bet he'd gotten tired of waiting
for me. I bet most people didn't make Horatio
Hale wait. I moved down the hall, peering into
doors as I went. And finally saw a gleam of light,
like from a cell phone, emanating from the last

office on the right. I went to the door and peered inside. He must have had his headphones in and couldn't hear me.

And I stopped just short of tripping over something on the floor. I focused. And screamed.

I'd found Horatio. On the floor, the obstacle I'd nearly tripped over. His cell phone lay on the floor next to him, shadowy figures moving around on the screen. It did indeed look like he had been watching a video. But my eyes were glued to his chest. And the really sharp pickaxe embedded in the middle of it.

CHAPTER TWENTY-THREE

I could hear my scream echoing, bouncing off the walls of this giant space. When the janitor who'd directed me rushed in, I had a moment of panic that he'd done it and was coming to shut me up too. But when he saw Horatio on the floor, he immediately stopped dead in his tracks. Then rushed into another room and promptly threw up. I could hear other people making their way to the office area after hearing me and I knew I needed to keep them out.

The janitor appeared, his face white and hands shaking. "Come on," I said, and pulled him out of the suite. "Don't let anyone in there."

He nodded and reached for his keys. I made sure he locked the door, then hurried outside. As I pushed past the crowd, I scanned for any faces I knew, any guilty faces, anything that could give me a clue what had happened here. But everyone just looked confused and frightened.

I burst through the doors, gulping in air. I didn't want to admit it but I felt as nauseous as the janitor, and the cold air felt good. I fumbled in my bag for my cell phone as I worked on taking long, slow breaths, fervently wishing Officer Hanlon still lurked around. But he didn't. No one was outside. This parking lot was a ghost town, and there was a dead guy inside. I finally got my phone out of my bag and hit the emergency call button as I reached my car and slid inside it.

"Yes, hello, I'm at the amphitheater. In the back. There's a man. Dead. On the floor," I added, well aware I was rambling and sounded like an insane person. I hit the locks to make sure if the murderer was sneaking up on me they couldn't just open the door and grab me.

"Ma'am? You said there's a dead man at the North Harbor Amphitheater?" The man on the other end sounded way, way too calm for this event.

"Yes. In the storage building."

"Okay, thank you. And how do you know he's deceased?" he asked. I could hear computer keys clicking in the background.

"Because there's a pickaxe sticking out of his chest. And a lot of blood. It's a Truper," I added.

"It's a . . . excuse me?"

"A Truper. The pickaxe. It's got a yellow and black handle." I had no idea why I was focused on the tool, and no doubt the dispatcher found it odd as well. "Never mind. It doesn't matter. Just get someone here!" I disconnected, cutting him off when he tried to stop me.

When had he been killed? What if I hadn't been late? Maybe he'd still be alive right now. Another regret to add to the growing list. I pressed my fist into my mouth to hold back the sob and scrolled my contacts until I got to Gabe Merlino's. I pressed the call button.

He answered on the first ring. "Hey, Vi. What's going on?"

"Are you on duty yet?"

"In about five minutes. Why? Are you okay?"

"There's, um, I . . . I found . . ." I was having trouble getting the words out.

"Vi." Gabe's voice turned urgent. "What happened?"

"I had a meeting. He's dead."

"Who?"

"Horatio Hale. I found him when I came for our meeting. At the amphitheater."

"Are you in danger? Is anyone else in danger?"

"I don't think so. I'm outside. At the back building. That's where he is. I had the janitor lock the office suites. There are only a few people in here. The rest are probably all over at the main building setting up."

"Did you call 911?"

"Yeah."

"Hang tight. I'm on my way."

Gabe arrived right behind the cops who'd been dispatched to the scene, and right before the ambulance. He got into my car to wait with me while they went inside to check out the scene for themselves. The janitor and the other vendors had all

come outside too, probably not wanting to be anywhere near that horrible scene any longer.

"Are you cold?" Gabe asked.

I glanced down and realized I was shivering.
"Yeah."

"Shock, probably. I'll have the paramedics give
you a quick look."

"I'm fine," I said. "I don't want to see the paramedics."

"You want me to call someone? Your mother?"

"No! I mean, uh, no thanks." The last person I
wanted to see right now was Fiona. She'd have a
field day with this on top of everything else.

Gabe didn't seem too surprised by this. He wasn't
really sure what to think of my mother either, with
her wacky outfits and the glitter that she left everywhere she went. I think he thought she carried it
with her and threw it around. Once the woman
who owned the art store had gotten yelled at by
someone because they thought it was her glitter all
over the streets. Regardless, he usually tried to
steer clear of Fiona or at least fade into the background when she was around. He also probably
got the anti-mortal vibe she was giving off, although he probably just thought she didn't like
him.

And what was wrong with me that I was thinking
of all this right now when someone was dead?

"Vi?" Gabe stared at me, and I realized he'd
been asking me something.

"Sorry, what?" I refocused on him.

"I said, you're going to need to tell these guys
what happened." He nodded at his two colleagues

who approached the car. "Let me talk to them first." He hopped out and conferred with them.

I wondered if either of the other cops who'd arrived was also a witch. And how the magickal cops found each other.

Gabe returned. "Detective Briggs and I are going to get your statement while the other officer talks to the rest of them, okay?"

He led me over to the police SUV, which they'd left running. They let me sit in the warm backseat. I faced them, legs hanging outside the door while they stood in front of me.

Detective Briggs pulled out a notebook. He reminded a little bit of Jimmy Smits in *NYPD Blue*, but with a goatee. Yes, I watched a lot of cop show reruns. "Your name and address please, ma'am?"

I told him.

"And how did you happen to be here today?"

"I had an appointment. With Horatio. To see some of his stock."

"Horatio is the deceased?"

I nodded. "Horatio Hale. He was one of the fair organizers. He's a crystal supplier."

"Walk me through what happened."

I did, starting from how I arrived late. I left out my altercation with Hanlon as the reason I was late.

"Why did he ask you to come here instead of showing you his stuff at the fair?" Gabe asked.

"Because he kept a lot of it back here until he needed it." I thought of the numerous trips Josie and I had made to and from my shop to restock. "Plus if it's at the fair it's more stuff you have to keep an eye on. And the crystals he was going to show me are very much in demand. He wasn't just selling them."

"Expensive items?" Briggs asked.

"They can be, if they're the real thing. It's one of those stones that people try to fake and then pass off. But not, like Crown Jewels or anything."

"Did you see the stones?"

"He wasn't exactly up for show and tell by the time I arrived."

Briggs's eyebrows pulled together in the middle, a mini-frown. "So you don't know if they're missing. Could someone have tried to steal them? Maybe he caught them in the act?"

"I suppose it's possible," I said. "I have no idea."

"Who else was here?"

"The janitor. A few vendors. Just the people over there." I pointed to the small crowd around the other officer.

"None of them were around the victim?"

"No. He was in the office suite. Everyone else was out in the big room."

Briggs noted that. "How well did you know the deceased?"

"I didn't, really. I just met him Sunday when the fair started."

"But you said you knew of him."

I nodded. "He's—he was kind of a legend." I explained my business and why I was familiar with Horatio, and his reputation as an ethical crystal supplier.

"So Mr. Hale pushed for change," Briggs said.

I nodded.

"Fair to say he could've made some enemies from all of that speaking out?"

"I suppose, sure."

Briggs observed me for a moment. Then he said, "Did you notice anything strange at the fair? He have any disagreements with anyone?"

"He has an ex-wife who he doesn't seem to get along with. And a girlfriend. She's a vendor here." I gave him Lila's and Cali's names.

"Did he tell you he doesn't get along with his ex?"

"He didn't have to. There was a scene." I explained how Lila thought I was his girlfriend.

"Why would she think that?"

"I have no idea."

"But she didn't know who his real girlfriend was."

"Apparently not."

"Anyone else?"

I didn't want to throw Katia under the bus. She was my friend. But what if they found out anyway? Other people had to have seen them arguing. "It's probably nothing." I told them about the argument I'd witnessed between Katia and Horatio. "I don't know what it was about but she said she was going public with something. And when I told Katia I was meeting him about some crystals, she asked me not to."

Briggs and Gabe looked at each other. "She say why?" Briggs asked.

"No. Just said I should stick with the suppliers I have."

"So she was upset that you wanted to buy from him," Briggs summarized.

"I don't think it was because she was afraid of losing business. I got the sense it was something else," I said. I watched Briggs scribbling in his notebook.

"Do you know if she was losing business to him?" Gabe asked.

"I don't. But I don't think so. She has a very exclusive clientele and she keeps her list small. She was definitely not hurting for business."

Briggs looked up from his notes. "Any other issues that you've witnessed?"

"There's a guy. Burton Jillette. He was supposed to be a vendor but Horatio allegedly took his booth away because he didn't think his stuff was organic, or something. He's pretty mad about it and he's been hanging around the fair outside. But he doesn't . . . seem like a killer." I knew that sounded lame. I guess if he was going to murder Horatio, he wouldn't exactly advertise it ahead of time.

"Right," Briggs said. "They used to say that about Ted Bundy too."

Gabe shot him a look.

"Horatio's co-chair—Rand Gallagher—would know the details better than me. He and Burton are friendly I think. This is all just one side of the story, right? And you know what they say about the real story."

Briggs eyed me. "What do they say?"

"Well, you know. That there can be more than one version."

"Yes, I'm sure there can be." There was a trace of amusement in his voice, and I flushed. I was babbling now. "Thanks. This is helpful." He closed the notebook and nodded at Gabe. "If we need you we'll reach out." Briggs stepped aside. Gabe started walking me back to my car but Briggs called out. I turned back.

"How did you know what the weapon was?"

"Excuse me?"

"The weapon that Mr. Hale was killed with. You told the dispatcher what it was. Very specifically, he said."

I knew that was going to come back and bite me. "I'm familiar with some of the tools crystal miners use," I said. "From talking to suppliers and even some of Horatio's lectures. He would talk about the different effects certain tools had on the rocks and the surrounding area."

"How familiar?" he asked with interest. "Because I'm guessing you'd have to be pretty familiar to be able to identify one down to a brand name, especially when it's sticking out of someone's chest."

I wanted to explain how any crystal seller worth his or her salt learned not just about what they were selling but how they came to be in possession of those things. But I didn't. I said nothing.

"Briggs," Gabe said quietly.

Briggs glanced at Gabe, then back at me. "That's all. For now."

CHAPTER TWENTY-FOUR

Briggs rejoined his other colleague, pulling him away from the group of people. I could see them huddled together, Briggs gesturing as he talked. The other cop glanced over at me as Gabe walked me back to my car.

"He suspects me." My voice shook a little. I still had PTSD from a couple of months ago, during a similar situation when a local government official had been murdered and I was suspect number one because I'd been seen having an argument with her at Pete's right before she died. I could see the same thing happening here. It was just a matter of time.

"He doesn't. He's just being thorough," Gabe said. "It's what detectives do."

But something in his voice made me think he wasn't so sure either.

"I knew what kind of axe it was. That's not something normal people know." I shivered again, and not just because it was freezing out here.

"Look. Let me take you home," Gabe said. "This has been a stressful morning."

"No. I have to work the fair." And figure out who did this, I thought, but I didn't add that. That admission would likely cause a violent reaction.

"Violet. The fair might not even open today. They have a whole building of suspects to interview."

He was probably right, but I had to go see what was going on. And I needed to talk to Katia. And Cali. Someone needed to tell Cali. I wondered if she'd heard yet. I wondered who his next of kin was.

"Gabe. Thank you, but I'm not going home." I stood my ground. I didn't tell him it was because I didn't want to be alone in my apartment, nor did I want to go to Fiona's and have to explain all this. I thought about calling Blake, but pushed the thought away. He was probably up to his eyeballs in genies and special forces.

Gabe didn't look happy, but he opened my car door for me and waited until I turned the car on. "I'm sure you'll be over there too?" I asked, inclining my chin toward the building.

"I don't know. I'm going to go see where they need me. Either way, I'll check in with you later, okay?"

I nodded. "Thank you for coming."

"Of course." He nodded at me and closed the door.

I watched him walk over to join his colleagues. The flashing lights of the ambulance pulsed across their little group, casting strobes of light over them. For the first time I noticed a small crowd starting to gather across the parking lot near the amphitheater entrance and braced myself for what was to come.

Just as I was about to pull away, the paramedics came out pushing a gurney with a black bag on it. What was left of Horatio. I swallowed hard against the bile rising in my throat and fixed my eyes firmly forward. As I drove around the building, I could see the fair people gathered outside watching me curiously. Rand was at the front of the crowd. I could tell he recognized me because he started walking toward the front of the building behind my car.

By the time I parked, he was at my door. He must have jogged over because he seemed a little out of breath. Before I could open my door, he was hovering outside of it. Taking a deep breath, I pushed it open. "Hey, Rand."

"Violet. What is going on? They've blocked access to the storage area, and I can't get any answers. And I can't get in touch with Horatio, but he's going to be livid." He rubbed his hands anxiously together over and over as he talked. "Is he coming? Did you just finish your meeting?"

I hesitated. "How did you know I was meeting Horatio?"

"What? I don't know, I guess he told me. Why?"

I got out of the car and shut the door, holding on to it for a bit of extra strength. "Rand. I have some terrible news." I took a deep breath. "Horatio is dead."

Rand stared at me for a few seconds, his face completely blank. I swore I could see the color draining away bit by bit as he processed this. Finally he shook his head. "What are you talking about? That's a terrible thing to say, Violet."

"I'm sorry. It's true. I had a meeting with him this morning. When I got there he had . . . passed away." I didn't mention the axe.

"But how? Like, a heart attack? An aneurysm? What?" His voice had risen to an unnatural level, and I looked around to see if anyone was paying attention to us. Unfortunately, there were an inordinate number of people around because it was almost time for the fair to open, and people had a tendency to line up early to get in and have first dibs on all the new things. But judging by the police who had materialized in front of the door, they weren't getting in any time soon.

"The police will be here to talk to everyone," I said. "I can't tell you any more than that." I reached out and laid a hand on his forearm. "I'm sorry."

He pulled away from me and covered his face with his hands. I wasn't sure if he was crying or just trying to compose himself. After a moment, he dropped them and looked at me. His eyes were bloodshot and he looked like he'd aged in the few minutes we'd been standing here. "How can that be?" he asked. "How? What am I going to tell people? What do I tell the board?"

I assumed these were all rhetorical questions that I wasn't expected to answer. I shifted from one foot to the other uncomfortably. "I'm so sorry,"

I said again. I looked around, feeling eyes on us. People were starting to notice us talking. "We should go inside. Get out of the spotlight."

"Yes. Sure. Of course." He started walking robotically toward the door.

I beeped my car locked and hurried to catch up.

As we got closer I saw Burton Jillette leaning against the wall a bit away from the impatient line of people waiting to get into the fair. When he saw me coming, he waved.

"Hang on one second," I told Rand, and hurried over. I didn't want to miss this chance to talk to him before the cops found him and started grilling him about his issues with Horatio.

"Hey, Burton."

"Good morning." He absently held out his tray of tinctures as his eyes scanned the scene in front of him. I accepted one. "Big doings," he said. "What's that Horatio Hale gotten himself into this time?"

I paused, all my senses on alert. How did he know it had something to do with Horatio? "What do you mean?" I asked.

He shrugged. "The only person who could cause a ruckus like this is that guy. Probably a publicity stunt. So he can show all his followers how *great* he is and how much he *turned the fair around*." His voice reeked of disdain.

"What do you mean, turned the fair around?"

Burton made a face. "When he started working as co-chair. Made a big show of holding a press conference and telling everyone how he was going to rejuvenate a stale event, or some nonsense. Always thought he was better than everyone. That's what prompted this new list of rules and restrictions for vendors."

"Burton. This is important. Did you see him this morning?"

Burton shook his head. "He always goes in the back. Doesn't engage with the commoners out here."

I wasn't sure if I could believe him. Clearly his anger at Horatio was still raw. What if he had gotten tired of standing out in the cold every day trying to prove himself and decided to get back at the person who had made him feel less than? People had killed for less. And what did he mean about Horatio's plan to rejuvenate the event? No one had mentioned that it needed rejuvenating.

"When was the last time you saw or talked to Horatio?"

He peered at me curiously. "Sunday. When everyone was getting here. And I didn't really see him. He couldn't be bothered with someone as low class as me. Why?"

I swallowed the liquid from the paper cup and thanked Burton, ignoring his question, and headed back to where Rand waited impatiently at the door. Two cops stood in front of it, blocking access. Rand stepped up, conferred briefly with them, and pulled something out of his wallet to show them. One of them nodded while the other one stepped aside. Rand motioned for me to follow him. We walked past them, into the theater. They both stepped back in front of the door, closing ranks, as it shut behind us.

Inside there were more small clusters of people—vendors who had arrived early to set up, fair officials—talking intently, glancing over their shoulders at the cops who were crawling the place. They must have called out all their resources, given that there were a lot of people to interview.

Avilyn saw us and rushed over. "A detective wants to talk to you," she told Rand. "What is going on?"

"A detective?" Rand's head whipped in my direction. "Why would a detective need to talk to me? Is it about Horatio?"

I gave a slight nod.

"Where is he?" Rand asked tersely.

"I'll take you." She gave me a questioning look, then pulled him away.

I took a deep breath and headed over to our table. Cali wasn't at her booth yet, which was kind of a relief. Josie was here already though. "Hey," I said when I reached her.

"Hey." She straightened. "Where've you been?"

"Long story. When did you get here?" It was so weird to think all these people were here, so close to where Horatio's body was. And no one had a clue.

"Right when all hell was breaking loose, apparently." She glanced at me. "I heard someone died."

"Yeah. Horatio," I said grimly.

Josie's eyes almost popped out of her head. "*What?*"

I took a breath and told her what I'd found, the words spilling out clumsily, tripping over each other in my haste to get what I'd seen out of my head.

She stared at me in horror. "Oh, Vi. I'm so sorry. That's . . . that's horrible."

"Right?" I stashed my bag under the table. So many thoughts were running through my mind. Possible suspects. A more hopeful part of me wondered if Briggs was right and it was random. Maybe someone had come in to steal stuff and Horatio had gotten in the way. Tried to stop them and they'd grabbed one of his tools and stabbed him. If it was his tool. But a random robbery and act of violence wasn't usually so . . . vicious. I'd read somewhere that stabbings were the most personal way to kill someone, that they were full of supercharged emotion. Robberies were not personal. And I had no idea if anything of his or anyone else's was even missing.

But if it wasn't a robbery, that meant someone had murdered him with intent. But why? Business? His dating life? What if Lila had lost it? What if I had been on time for our appointment? Would she have thought we were having a clandestine meeting and killed me too? I felt sick. "I'm worried about Katia," I said. "I had to tell them I saw her arguing with him."

"That doesn't mean anything," Josie said. "I'm sure he argued with a million people a day. That's what happens at these things." At the look on my face, she squeezed my arm. "Maybe you should go home. I have no idea when or if they'll open today anyway."

"I can't go home. I don't want to talk about this with Fiona all day." I glanced over at Cali's tarot table. Still empty. "Have you seen her?"

Josie shook her head. "She hasn't been here at all."

That was odd. Could she have heard already? If

she had been onsite already, it was highly likely. So then where was she? His problems with Lila had been more obvious, but his current relationship could have also had its problems. Cali could've been upset about Lila. Or the secret-keeping could have become overwhelming. What if it had all come to a head and they'd fought? Could Cali have been mad enough to kill him? But a witch wouldn't kill a mortal, especially like that.

Would she?

CHAPTER TWENTY-FIVE

I had to find Cali. I told myself it was because I wanted to see if she was okay. It was, mostly. But I also wanted to see if I could get a sense about what happened. As I made my way through the crowd, I saw a familiar face. Two, actually. Serenity and Alan from the Magickal Council. They were standing near one of the booths, but speaking to each other in low tones. They were so engrossed in their conversation that they didn't see me. They didn't appear to be shopping, either.

What were they doing here?

I tried to keep some heads between us so they wouldn't notice me as I walked past. I didn't know council members came to things like this. I made a mental note to ask Fiona.

There were a lot of whispers around me as I walked over to where some of the fair officials were gathered. Avilyn stood near the giant fake rainbow with the pot of gold where the raffle tickets were being collected. She was crying into her notebook. Two security guards—mortal ones—stood near her, looking solemn. I hadn't seen any of the leprechauns yet. Maybe they'd wanted to stay out of the fray. Mortal murders probably weren't their thing.

"Excuse me. Hi. Sorry to interrupt," I said.

Avilyn looked up, her eyes watery and red-rimmed. Purple smears from her eyeshadow made her look like a punk rocker gone bad. "Violet. Hey," she said in a choked voice. "I heard . . . I'm so sorry."

I didn't really want to get into this with an audience. I concentrated really hard on getting the security guards to go away. I'd intended for them to physically walk away; however, they suddenly vanished. Like, poof. Shoot. What had I done with them? I really needed to get the hang of this.

Avilyn stared at the spot where they'd been. She blinked, then rubbed her eyes. Hopefully she chalked it up to her emotional distress.

"I'm sorry too," I said, trying to act like nothing had happened. "Are they going to close the fair down today?"

"I think we're going to open but I'm not sure when. The police asked us to wait until they've talked to whoever was here this morning. So many people are depending on us to open. And I know Horatio would want it that way." She started to cry again. "This fair was his pride and joy. He was so dedicated to it. He really wanted to make it better."

That word again. "Better? What was wrong with it? Was he planning to change things up?"

Avilyn shrugged. "I know he thought we could make it bigger, get more sponsors, maybe do a couple more events for other occasions, like a Solstice fair or something. He was worried about it getting stale. He had some ideas that he'd brought to the board. He was already making such a difference." She sniffled and pressed a tissue to her face. "I'm so . . . sad."

"I'm sorry, Avilyn. I really am. I didn't know him well, but I'd hoped that with the opportunity to meet him here that I might be able to work with him. I'm sad too."

"Did you really see his body? That's what people are saying. That you were there."

"I was meeting him. I was late and when I got there . . ." I broke off and looked away. "Yes, I found him. It was horrible."

She reached out and squeezed my hand. I squeezed hers back. When I let go, I said, "I'm trying to find Calliope Diamond. Have you seen her?"

Avilyn closed her eyes briefly. "Poor thing. She's not here. I called her. When I heard. She deserved better than to hear it through the grapevine, you know? She's just devastated. She wanted to come, but I told her to wait. It's so crazy here, she doesn't need that."

"So you knew they were together?"

Avilyn nodded. "I did. She told me. Horatio didn't want people to know. Didn't want any sense of impropriety with her being a vendor. I think he was being overly cautious, but it was his choice." She shrugged. "But I don't think Cali was happy pretending she barely knew him."

Interesting that Horatio had told me the complete opposite of this story. "She told me the day I met her that she was seeing him," I said.

Avilyn smiled a little. "She is kind of a rebel."

"So who was his next of kin, then? Who would the police contact to tell about his death?" I asked. I knew his cell phone had been at the scene and wondered if they would have used that to find an emergency contact.

"The police just asked me that. I had to go look it up. He still has his ex-wife listed." She wrinkled her nose.

"That's an interesting choice, considering they don't seem to get along," I said.

Avilyn sighed. "No, but they still worked together."

I stared at her. "They did?"

She nodded. "She handles a lot of administrative stuff for him. Weird setup, but hey." She shrugged as if to say, *What do I know?*

"Have they reached her yet, do you know?"

"I don't know. I just gave them the info."

"Do you know where Cali is staying?" I asked. "I thought maybe I'd go talk to her. She shouldn't be alone, you know?" I felt kind of guilty misleading Avilyn, but what other choice did I have?

"Oh, you are too sweet. That's a lovely thing to do, Violet. She's staying at Gray House."

*   *   *

Gray House was a newish B&B not far from the amphitheater. It was a converted house that was, unsurprisingly, gray. I went to grab my coat and bag from our booth and told Josie I'd be back. I hurried outside to my car and drove the half mile to the hotel. Too late I realized I could've just magically appeared—Cali was a witch, after all. I had to remember to stop wasting time like this.

When I got inside, I hurried to the front desk. The smiling man at the counter immediately rubbed me the wrong way, mostly because there wasn't much to smile about today. "I'm looking for Calliope Diamond," I said in response to his inquiry about how he could help.

He nodded and punched a few keys on his computer. "I'll call her room. Whom shall I say is calling?"

"Violet Mooney." I hoped she'd see me.

He spoke softly into the phone, then hung up. "She would like you to go upstairs. Room 414. The elevator is that way." He pointed to the left.

"Thanks." I hurried over to it and jabbed the button for the fourth floor.

Cali waited at the door. She wasn't crying, but she looked pale and shaken—kind of out of it. Nothing like her tarot persona. She wore a green bandanna over her head and a faded University of Rhode Island sweatshirt over a pair of black leggings. And she looked really surprised to see me.

"Violet. What are you doing here?" she asked.

"I came to see how you were. Avilyn said she told you."

"Yeah. At least someone did." Her tone was resentful. "She didn't have details, though. Do *you* know?"

So Avilyn must not have heard about me until after she'd made the call. "Can I, um, come in?"

She stepped back, making room for me to pass, and closed the door behind me.

I paused in the doorway. The room was small, but chic and modern, with black, white, and metal furniture. A depressing view of rusty railroad tracks was visible through the narrow space in the window where she hadn't covered it with the blinds.

"I'm so sorry," I said. "I don't even know what to say."

She hesitated a minute, then started to cry. "I feel so useless," she said. "No one even knew how close we were. Except for a few people that I made a point of telling. That crazy ex-wife of his was still the one the police called to tell he was dead!" She buried her face in her hands, sobbing in earnest now.

Her tears kind of freaked me out. I didn't know her well enough to really comfort her, and I wasn't sure she'd want my comfort anyway. But I did have to tell her I'd found him. I wondered what she'd think of that, given that I'd also found her cousin in an equally dire position.

I gave her a moment. Gave myself a moment, really, then took a breath. "Cali. I found him."

She raised her head from her hands, disbelief shocking the tears right out of her eyes. "What?"

"I had a meeting with him. He wanted to show me some moldavite he had. I've been looking for some and no one else . . . never mind. That's not important. Anyway, I had a meeting scheduled with him at ten this morning. I was late. When I got there, he was dead. Someone stabbed him."

I thought she was going to throw up at this news. Her face actually turned pale, then green, then back to white. I jumped up and went to the little refrigerator. There were mini water bottles inside. I grabbed one and opened it, then handed it to her.

She drank some, taking a moment to breathe. When she'd regained her composure, she said, "Do they know who?"

I shook my head. "No. Do you know if he had tools with him?"

She looked blankly at me. "Tools?"

"Like, mining tools. I know sometimes he used them in talks."

"Oh. Yeah, actually. He was scheduled to do a class about mining on Thursday. So he had tools for a demo with him. Why?"

"Someone killed him with . . . one of the tools. I'm guessing it was his."

She sat slowly down on the bed. "What tool?"

"An axe."

At this, she looked horrified.

"Cali, do you have any idea who would do this to him?"

"No," she said sharply, and a little too quickly. "No, of course I don't. I don't understand how anyone could do this. I mean, he was beloved on that circuit." She looked up at me. "Did a mortal do it?"

The question took me by surprise. It could've been my naivete or just my mother's vehement and constant reminders that witches shouldn't interfere with mortals, but I wondered why that was even a question. "I presume so. I mean, obviously I don't know who did it," I said uncertainly. "Why would a witch kill him? Can witches even do that to mortals? Did he know other witches? Did he know *you* were a witch?" It was a lot of questions to throw at her, but my mind was working on overdrive trying to make some sense of this.

"He didn't know about me. And don't judge me. I bet there are a lot of people who you haven't told yet about you."

I held up my hands. "No judgment. Trust me. But why would you think a witch did it, then?"

"I don't. I was just asking." She didn't look at me, though.

I wasn't sure I believed her, but I didn't push. "What about Lila?"

But Cali looked uncertain. "She was crazy but not that bad. At least I don't think."

"You know they still worked together, right?"

I could see from her face that she hadn't, but she covered it up well. "Of course. It was just temporary."

"Uh-huh. Your friend whose reputation was in danger. Was it Horatio?"

She hesitated. "Yeah," she said finally. "Just stupid people who were jealous of him."

"Like who? Did he tell you?"

"He was kind of vague, but he said there was this woman. Another supplier. She's dragging his name through the mud. She's from around here. Katie or something?"

My heart sank. "Not . . . Katia?" I asked.

"That's it."

"Do you know what she was saying about him?"

Cali shook her head slowly. "I heard bits and pieces. She was trying to say he was using some of the same sourcing practices he spoke out against. Said she had evidence. I don't know the details, but he was pretty upset. Said she didn't know anything and she needed to shut up or she was going to screw it all up."

That sounded ominous. But in this version, it would seem Horatio had motive to kill her instead of the other way around. "Do you think it was true?" I asked gently. "I heard her tell him she was going public with something."

"Of course it wasn't true. I mean, I didn't get involved in his work at all, but he was so passionate about what he did. I can't imagine . . ." she trailed off, shook her head. "She tried to talk to the podcaster. I don't know what ever came of it. Horatio went to Rand about it. Tried to get her kicked out of the fair. Rand wouldn't do it, which really upset Horatio. They haven't been getting along either. Rand thinks Horatio is trying to take over the fair. This thing . . . there are so many politics." She studied me. "Why are you playing detective right now, anyway?"

"I'm not playing detective," I said. "I just . . . I found him, so I feel kind of invested, you know?" I didn't want to add that I was worried about Katia. I didn't think it was wise right now to tell Cali we were friends. That would shut her down. I was also a little irrationally terrified they were going to come back and blame me because I was there and I knew about the axe. But she was actually giving me good information that I could take back to Gabe.

"You seem to have a knack for that," she said. "You found my cousin too."

There it was. "I'm also trying to do whatever I can to help her."

We eyed each other for a moment. I guessed Cali didn't completely trust me, no matter how well we'd hit it off that first day of the fair. No matter what Ginny said.

Finally she looked away. "I'd like to be alone now."

"Okay. Let me know if you need anything," I said.

She didn't respond.

CHAPTER TWENTY-SIX

As I left Gray House my phone dinged, signaling a text. It was a group vendor text from Avilyn, telling us the police were letting the fair open at two p.m. It was almost one thirty now. I couldn't believe the last three hours of this day had even happened. I really just wanted to go home, but since I couldn't go to my home it didn't seem as appealing.

I pulled into the parking lot and called Gabe. His phone went to voicemail. I was sure they were busy. And he probably couldn't tell me anything anyway. I stuck my phone back in my bag and eyed the building. I was so not ready to go in there, but I couldn't just keep dumping everything on Josie. With a sigh, I got out of the car and breathed in the fresh air deeply, feeling it in my lungs. Cold enough to clear my head a bit. I headed past the crowd that was lined up waiting to get in. I wondered what they were telling all these poor people who had been waiting all morning to get in, *Hey, sorry for the opening delay today, but one of our organizers was stabbed with an axe. Have a pleasant day at the fair! Spend lots of money.*

As I approached the entrance, I spotted another familiar face waiting in line. Alan Black from the council. The third council member I'd seen. I'd had no idea that this would be an outing of choice for my fellow witches. He didn't see me, though, engrossed as he was in conversation with a woman wearing a hat overflowing with flowers.

I slowed as I reached the door. Burton was out front with his little drink machine and tray full of paper cups, but he wasn't pushing his product. He was deep in conversation with Detective Briggs.

I gave my name to the cop guarding the door. He checked some list and then gave me a nod. I pushed past him and went inside. Avilyn was at the door. She'd made some effort to put herself back together, but she still looked haggard and sad.

When she saw me, she lifted her hand in a wave. "You find Cali?"

I nodded.

"How is she?"

"Upset," I said. "How's it going here?"

She sighed. "They've talked to like, everyone. Some people twice. I don't know if they found out anything though."

"Yeah. Detective Briggs is outside with Burton right now." I jerked my thumb in the direction of the door.

"Burton Jillette? Yeah I heard he was still outside." She shook her head and smiled. "He's a character."

"I heard he and Horatio had a problem," I said. "That he wouldn't let him exhibit."

"Yeah. Horatio was pretty adamant about how it wouldn't be up to standards if he let him in without the right paperwork, or something. He and Rand actually argued about it, but Horatio stood his ground. Burton and Rand go way back, you know, to when Rand's mother died. He was so young, and I guess Burton really helped raise him." She looked at me. "Why are they talking to him?" Then her hand flew to her mouth. "Oh God. They don't think Burton . . . do they? He's so sweet! He would never hurt anyone." She looked horrified at the thought.

"I don't know," I said. I patted her arm and went over to my booth. Josie wasn't there, but Gabe was.

When he saw me coming, he straightened, a look of relief on his face. When I reached him, he pulled me behind the booth and out of earshot.

"Good. I needed to talk to you anyway," I said. "But what's going on? Did you find out anything?"

"First, you doing okay?" he asked.

"I'm fine. But why were you waiting for me?"

"They had me go track down the next of kin. Who was his ex-wife. She says they still have a business relationship."

"Yeah. Avilyn just told me that. One of the fair people," I said at his questioning look.

"She says she travels with him and takes care of all the scheduling, does research for him, kind of like a personal assistant. She handed over her computer willingly with all her work and her correspondence with him. We're looking into it. But she's . . . an interesting character."

"Interesting how? Do you suspect her?"

"We're definitely looking at her, but he was her bread and butter. He was paying her a lot of money to do this job. I did get the sense she thought it might get them back together, sure, but my gut says she wouldn't kill the guy who was basically paying her bills." He hesitated. "But I'm a little worried that she's obsessed with you."

I stared at him. "With me? Gabe, please don't tell me this woman still thinks—"

He held up a hand. "She does. She wanted to know when we were arresting you, actually. She said—dead serious—that she knew he wanted to come back to her but you were standing in his way. She said he had probably told you he was leaving you and that's why you killed him."

I wasn't usually speechless, but this was definitely one of those times. "Me?" It came out as an indignant screech and I cleared my throat, trying to regain my calm. "Is she serious?" I guessed Horatio hadn't set her straight the other day. Although he'd never actually answered my question about that, just said she wouldn't be bothering me anymore.

"She sounded serious," Gabe said. "Anyway, this is an unofficial conversation. I just wanted to tell you to be careful. This woman seems . . . a bit unstable. I'm also not so convinced she has a great alibi. Alone in the hotel room working isn't what we want to hear from persons of interest in a murder, so we're still trying to find someone who had eyes on her."

"Great," I said. "Just what I need. Another lunatic on my tail."

He looked at me, his eyes narrowing. "What?"

"Nothing," I said quickly. "Where is she staying?"

"The North Harbor Inn, right down the street."

So she could've gotten to the amphitheater and back pretty quickly without anyone knowing, especially if she used a back door. "I do need to tell you something. I just went to see the girlfriend."

"You did? Vi, why didn't you call me?"

"I'm sorry. I was just thinking of how she must be feeling."

He sighed. "What did she say?"

"She said a lot of things, actually. Oddly, she doesn't think the ex-wife is crazy enough to kill him."

Gabe frowned. "What else?"

I told him what I'd learned about Katia from Cali. "Katia's one of my suppliers, but she's also a friend. She's not a killer, Gabe. And she also said something about Rand thinking Horatio was trying to take over the fair so they've been squabbling."

"Okay. I'll go talk to her. Cali, you said?"

"Calliope Diamond. She's staying at Gray House."

"Thanks. Be careful, okay? I'll check on you tomorrow."

CHAPTER TWENTY-SEVEN

There was more gossiping going on than shopping at the fair that day. Every fairgoer had heard about the murder and apparently that made the fair even more desirable than it usually was. Kind of like the whole car wreck that you couldn't look away from. And to make it worse, people were starting to talk about me being the one who had found the victim. I put on as much of a brave face as I could, but after a few hours I had to get out of there.

"Go, go," Josie said. "I don't know why you came back at all. This was a rough day, especially for you."

"Thanks," I said, grateful to her for being such a good friend. "I'll see you tomorrow." I grabbed my bag and coat and slipped out, virtually unnoticed. Burton wasn't out front. Had he gone home? Been sent away? Brought in for formal questioning?

I hurried to my car, not sure what to do next. I really wanted to go crawl into bed, but that didn't seem possible. I turned the heat up and sat there, trying to find a moment of zen. I hated to admit it, but Gabe's warning about Lila had unnerved me. Was I in greater danger from her than from the bad witches and genies? At this rate there didn't seem to be anywhere in the universe where I was safe.

I drove out of the lot and realized I had no particular destination in mind. There was way too much going on in my brain and I was having a hard time focusing. *One thing at a time, Violet.* I should stop by the store to see Syd. Then I could figure out what was next. Because there was way too much going on in both worlds to go to Fiona's and hide in my childhood bedroom.

I drove to the shop and parked out back. When I got in, the store was crowded with customers so I jumped in and helped Syd until the store emptied out. When we were finally alone, she came over and gave me a hug.

"Josie told me the news." Syd gazed at me, her eyes big. "I can't believe it. Are you okay?"

"I don't know. I mean, I haven't had a second to process it yet. It's been nonstop today."

"I can't believe they opened the fair," Syd said.

"Yeah, well, murder is good for business."

"Do they have any suspects?"

"I think they're looking at a few people." I wondered if I should warn Syd about Lila Hale. What if she came here looking for me? Or worse, decided to take her angst out on someone I loved? Syd was an obvious, and accessible, choice.

"Hey. Listen. I don't want to freak you out, but Horatio's ex-wife Lila is . . . potentially a problem." I explained how she thought we'd been dating, and Gabe's warning before I left the fair.

When I was done, her face had completely drained of color. "This is crazy," she said. "Do you think you need protection or something?"

"I can ask Gabe to have some patrols going by the store," I said.

"No, I mean for you. I'm not worried about me."

"Well, I am. I couldn't take it if something happened to you, Syd."

She hugged me. "I'm fine. And unless she's been in here eating my food, nothing suspect has happened at the store."

"Your food? What do you mean?"

"It's not a big deal. I put food in the fridge this morning and it was gone when I went to get it. Also I could've only thought I brought it, because I've been preoccupied lately. In a good way. With Pete." She blushed just saying his name, her face taking on a dreamy look.

But I was still concerned. "That is weird. Maybe Josie?"

"She hasn't been here at all. Honestly, I'm probably just losing it," she said with a laugh. "Maybe I ate it and didn't remember."

I doubted that, but I didn't want to freak her out by pushing the issue. I made a note to ask Gabe about sending someone to the store periodically, then told Syd to call me if she needed me.

And then I ducked into the alley and teleported to Blake's office. I think I'd known all along that

I'd end up there today. It was the only place I could think of to go right now. Okay, if I were being honest with myself, he was the only person I felt truly safe with these days. I figured I'd drop in on him and see how his first day managing multiple police forces had gone, and if he had any new intel about the investigation. The other investigation, since now it seemed I was embroiled in two. I had no idea from a GPS perspective where Blake's office actually was, but I envisioned the room in my mind where we'd gone after we found Mac.

It was the weirdest thing. Just as I landed it felt like a door was closing, almost like directionally I had to detour. I hit the ground and looked around. I stood in the hallway outside of an office. It looked familiar, so I assumed it was the right office. Maybe my intention was just off. I thought of the other night when I'd landed in his lap. I'd certainly been off then. I went to knock on the door, but as I raised my fist, the door opened.

And Ember Wolfbane waltzed out, wearing a short, tight white dress almost the same color as her hair, white pumps, and a white coat, her black owl sitting on her shoulder. She cocked her head at me and gave me a tight smile. "Violet. Hello. Good to see you."

"Hi, Ember." This morning I'd felt pretty good in my dress. Now I felt like a frumpy housewife next to her.

She started walking away, then turned back. "We should catch up soon. With all this craziness, we've not had a chance to spend any time together. As colleagues."

"Oh. Yes. That would be great," I said. "Thanks," I added, then felt stupid doing so.

"Excellent." She turned and strolled down the hallway. As she reached the elevator bank, she simply disappeared. Unlike Fiona, or even Blake, she left behind no trace that she'd even been here at all.

CHAPTER TWENTY-EIGHT

I turned back to the office door. Blake stood there, holding it open.

"You wanted to see me?" he said with a small smile.

I followed him into the office. "Did I mess up my landing or did you . . . do something to keep me out?"

"I was in the middle of a meeting," he said. "I closed the door."

That kind of stung. I tried not to take it personally. "How did you know I was coming?" I didn't know it worked that way.

He smiled. "Practice, Violet. Have a seat. Everything okay?"

I sat, still frowning. "What were you guys meeting about?"

The levitating coffee service floated over to me

and poured me a cup. I took the coffee and sipped. It was delicious—nice and strong.

Blake leaned back in his chair, his fingers steepled together, and regarded me with that perpetual look of amusement he seemed to have when it came to me. "Some council stuff. Why? Is there some reason I shouldn't be meeting with Ember?" His tone was teasing, and it reminded me of how infuriating he could be. He probably wasn't even interested in me at all. I'd let myself get caught up in Syd's and Zoe's innuendo and hints about Blake, and I had started to think about him differently, but who was I kidding? He probably had loads of women. Maybe he was even with Ember. She hadn't looked amused when I'd landed in his lap at the council meeting, come to think of it. But at the time, I'd been so focused on Posey and her nasty comments that I hadn't thought much about it.

"Not at all. Just curious," I said coolly. "I thought I'd come by and see how your day went. If there was any news. I was also wondering why so many of my fellow council members were at the fair, and if that was normal."

He studied me for a long minute, not speaking. "What's wrong?" he asked finally. "I know you, and something's up."

I stared at him incredulously. "Of course something's up. A lot of things are up. You know that. And everything is getting worse, not better." I felt tears stinging my eyes and tried to blink them away before he saw.

"Nope. Not buying it. What else is bothering you, Vi?"

I sighed and looked away. "Today, I went to meet

a famous crystal supplier to look at some stock before the fair. He was dead. Someone stabbed him
with a crystal mining axe. And since I found him
the cops are probably suspicious because I knew
what kind of axe it was and they tried to arrest me
before. And Mazzy's cousin was dating him, and
his ex-wife thought I was dating him, and now
Gabe thinks she's stalking me." I was pretty sure I
wasn't even making sense by the end of this rant.

Blake was up and around his desk in a flash. He
reached up and pulled a glass of water seemingly
out of thin air. "Drink," he said, his voice gentle.

I did, then leaned back and closed my eyes. The
tiredness I felt was bone deep. My brain finally
started to fizzle out and I just wanted to curl up in
a bed—any bed at this point—and sleep for days.

He gave me a moment, then squeezed my hand.
"Better?"

"Sure," I said. It seemed like too much effort to
tell the truth.

"Good." He leaned against the desk. Our knees
were almost touching, and I was hyper aware of it.
"I'm so sorry this happened, Violet. Do they have
any idea who did it?"

"I don't know. I mean, there are suspects, sure.
But I don't know who's really a suspect and who
isn't."

"And you said Mazzy's cousin is involved?"

I nodded. "Calliope is—was—dating Horatio."

"That's right. You mentioned she was in the
booth next to yours. Horatio is the dead man?"

I nodded.

"Was he a witch?"

"No."

"Did he know *she* is a witch?"

"She said he didn't."

"Do you know if Mazzy and her cousin were close?"

"She said they were like sisters."

He was silent for a moment. "How did you end up with this booth again?"

"They draw vendors in a lottery. Someone backed out last minute and my name came up."

"And you're sure it was random."

"Well, yeah." Wasn't it? That's what Horatio had told Josie. I looked at Blake. "What are you thinking?"

"I'm not thinking anything. Trying to put this all together. It seems like a bit of a coincidence. Do you think she had anything to do with the murder?" Blake asked.

"I have no idea what to think. She sounded happy with him, but no one knew they were together. Because he wanted it that way, according to her. But he told me *she* wanted it that way." Then I remembered the piece of our conversation that had struck me as odd. "She did ask me if a mortal had killed him. I asked her why she thought it would be someone—something—else and she brushed me off."

"I see," Blake said slowly. "I'm going to mention this to the investigative team. Just to make sure all the bases are covered."

"Great." I slumped back down. "So are you dating Ember?" The words were out before I even realized I was going to say them, and I wished I could take them back.

He almost dropped the pen he was fiddling with. "I'm sorry?"

I shrugged. "Just curious."

He closed his eyes briefly. When he opened them, his were serious. "Violet. I am not dating Ember."

"Why not? She's hot. Sexy. Probably smart. Even her owl is sexy. Why wouldn't you?"

He gave me a strange look. "What owl?"

I rolled my eyes. "The one always on her shoulder. Although if you're too busy looking at her face, I guess you wouldn't notice."

He still looked confused, but shook his head. "I wouldn't date her because I'm not interested in her. Besides." One side of his lips lifted in a smile. "I dated her once, a long time ago. For a short time. She is very smart. But she's not my type."

"What's a long time ago?"

"When we were in law school," he said.

"You've known her that long?" I wondered why that made me feel kind of jealous. They had a real history together. And Ember seemed like the type to go after what she wanted.

Blake nodded. There was something in his eyes I couldn't quite read.

"So is she a lawyer now?"

"She is." He didn't offer up any more information.

"Does she work here? With you?" I realized I didn't know much about Blake's work, other than in the most general sense. He was a lawyer and he was the Magickal Council's legal counsel. I knew he was big into advocacy work, and he'd done a lot of good for the witch community. Otherwise, I was kind of fuzzy on the details. And I knew nothing about Ember and her life outside of the council. That was true for all of them, actually.

"She does not."

I waited for more, but it didn't come. "You're certainly a wealth of information."

He smiled. "I didn't know you were that interested. Ember works for herself. She's more of a . . . legal consultant these days."

"Who does she consult with?"

He shrugged. "Big organizations, mostly. Universities, banks, other large companies. Sometimes government agencies. More coffee?"

"Please." The coffee set floated over to me again and refreshed my cup. "Government agencies, huh? Like what?"

"Law enforcement, for one. She was here because she's interested in consulting with the genie task force."

Great. So she could help solve this case and look like a hero. And that way she could work next to him every day. I took a sip and decided I didn't want to talk about Ember anymore. "So you haven't told me how your day was."

"No, I guess I haven't." Blake raked a hand through his hair and stood up, moving back around to his side of the desk. "It was a lot of getting organized. Pulling all the pieces of the investigation together and then figuring out who will move which piece forward."

"But no progress?" I was feeling so impatient about all this. It seemed like all anyone did was plan and think. But Mazzy and Mac were still gone.

"Lots of progress. But it's not as easy as it sounds. Can't just wave a wand and make it happen, unfortunately."

I kind of wanted to ask what the point was of being a witch if you couldn't do that, but I didn't.

"They're taking some extreme measures that I'm not thrilled about," he went on. "Chief Bell is planning to announce limits on genies across the board. Curfews, not allowing them in certain places. They want to make it so anyone in partnership of any kind with a genie—business or otherwise—is monitored until this is handled."

"What?" I was stunned. "But that's so . . . discriminatory."

He nodded. "It is. And it's terrible for the majority of the species that hasn't done anything and is just trying to live with the shadow of their ancestors' war looming over them. But they do have two of the Fernsbys under surveillance."

"That's good, right?"

"If they're the right two, yes. That's why they're waiting a couple of days to announce the limits. They're hoping they can get them on something suspicious before then. Otherwise they might go underground."

"Hopefully it doesn't get out since they told the whole council about it."

Blake grimaced. "Fiona made that clear. She got everyone on a call this morning."

"Oh. She didn't tell me."

"She knew you had the fair. She also knows you wouldn't tell anyone."

"Was there a specific reason you and Fiona pulled the plug on the committee? Or was it just out of caution?"

Blake thought about how to answer that. "Caution, but also we're trying to limit any Sageblood knowledge of what they're doing, given the circumstances."

"So it's about Oscar."

"No. He's not the only Sageblood on the council."

I was surprised. "He's not?"

"No. Gordon is a distant relative. And Serenity married into the family. Jet isn't related, but he is closely aligned. Been in business with the family for years."

I thought about this. "But Gordon seems so . . . sweet."

"He may be," Blake said. "But the truth is, we just don't know."

"One could argue you have ties too," I pointed out.

"One could. But anyone would be hard pressed to suggest I even speak to anyone in my family, let alone conspire with them."

I thought about what Pete had told me and realized I wanted to know more. I knew how hard it was to be cut off from parts of your family. Maybe we could help each other. I screwed up my courage. "So your parents," I began, but he cut me off.

"Look. I have some work to finish up. How about we touch base tomorrow night? At Potions?"

"Sure," I said, not wanting to push the issue. "Tomorrow."

"Thanks." He gave me a brief smile, then tapped his computer. It opened, and he focused on the screen. I'd lost him.

CHAPTER TWENTY-NINE

Wednesday
Four days before the full moon

My sleep that night was broken and full of dreams of platinum-haired women, leprechauns in bottles, and trying desperately to get to Blake but not being able to reach him. After waking up multiple times before four a.m., I finally just got out of bed and stopped fighting it. I really needed a sleep spell.

I wondered why Blake had shut me down last night. I knew the subject of his family made him uncomfortable. He knew it had been a point of contention for me. Or maybe he just didn't want to confide in me. That made me sad. I wondered if it was because he thought I wouldn't understand because I really knew nothing about this world. It wasn't the first time lately I'd had this thought. I needed to learn more about my history. All of our history. I'd used the excuse that life was crazy right now, but maybe learning this stuff would give me a better perspective on everything crazy that was happening. Either way, it was time I took responsibility for figuring some of these things out.

But first, I had a parade to attend.

I wasn't in the mood. But it was a huge part of our community, and this year, it was an extension of the fair. The St. Patrick's Day parade had been marching down my street every year for, well, a lot of years before I got here. People had already started setting up chairs along the sidewalk to save their spots. The smart ones had blankets, because even in March when the warmer weather started to tease, it never stayed long and it could get cold really quick. Then they wandered inside the shops and restaurants to get warm. We'd be busy, and I needed to be on my game.

When I got to the shop, I saw they'd painted shamrocks along the street for today's celebration. Three in a row, every few feet. I felt so disconnected from my neighborhood. I hadn't even known they were painting. Between spending the last three days at the fair and moving into Fiona's temporarily I had a lot of FOMO for my regular life.

Syd was at the store and she had Presley with her. Pete was there too, and so were his special shamrock lattes he'd brought for all of us, the sight of which gave me huge relief.

"Morning," I said, genuinely happy for the friends and the company.

"Morning," Pete said. "Trying out a new delivery service and figured you could be my guinea pig."

"You figured right," I said. "Syd, would you be mad if I told Pete I loved him right now?"

She ran over and threw her arms around me. "Of course not. How are you holding up?"

I hugged her back. "I'm fine. I mean, you know." Other than never being able to look at a mining tool in the same way again.

"Hi, Auntie Violet!" Presley piped up, waving at me from where she sat on the floor cradling a fluorite free-form stone. She was wearing a green dress for the occasion, and her hair was in two little braids with green ribbons.

"Hi, sweetie," I said, relieved to stop talking about Horatio. "That's a pretty stone. Did you pick it?"

Presley nodded proudly.

"I hope it's okay," Syd said. "I told her if she breaks it that you won't ever let her come back."

"Syd! Don't tell her that. She's fine." I admired the way Presley was carefully holding the stone, looking at it from every angle. When it caught the light and shimmered, she would squeal with glee.

Syd shrugged. "She can be rough with things. Hey, this was outside this morning." She handed me a package.

I took it and examined it. It was heavy for a manilla envelope and had no postage on it, so it had clearly been dropped off, but there was no return address. "Huh. Thanks. Are you excited for the parade?" I asked, refocusing on Presley, tucking the envelope under my arm.

"Yeah," she said in that typical, distracted-by-something, four-year-old way.

"Oh, come on. You've been talking about this for weeks! This is going to be so fun." Syd knelt next to Presley and smoothed her hair, which had started to take on Syd's wild curls. "We might even see a leprechaun! Right, Vi?"

I blanched—visibly, apparently, from the way Syd's smile faded.

"What's wrong? You don't like leprechauns?" she asked. "But they're so cute and they have pots of gold."

I could feel Pete's eyes on me. "Of course I like them. I just . . . they're kind of cliche, that's all. I mean, St. Patrick's Day was about more than *leprechauns.*"

"Yeah, snakes," Syd said, making a face. "I'd rather see leprechauns any day. Right baby?"

"Leprechauns!" Presley nodded vehemently. "I already saw one."

"You did?" Syd pretended to be enthralled. "Where? Out on the street?"

"Here! In the store."

I felt my entire body chill. What was she talking about? I looked at Pete. He shrugged imperceptibly.

Syd, completely oblivious, laughed. "Wow! I missed him. When did you see him?"

"When I was having my snack last night. I gave him some. He didn't have his hat on, though." I presumed she was thinking about the top hats that the cartoon leprechauns wore. Presley reached for her juice and took a long sip. "Can I have my muffin now?"

Still smiling, Syd reached for the pastry bag and took out a muffin, breaking it in half and handing it to Presley. "I brought her back with me last night to refill some jewelry," she said to me. "I think she's been caught up in too much St. Paddy's Day fever. She was wandering around entertaining herself. She's a good storyteller."

"Must be," I murmured. "I'll be right back." I hurried out to the back room, ostensibly to deposit my coat and bag, but really I needed to catch my breath for a moment. What was Presley talking about, she'd seen a leprechaun? Had Mac's people been here? But why would they come here? He wasn't genied here.

I deposited my stuff, including the envelope, on my desk and stood very still, trying to tune in to the space to feel if anyone else had been inside. But leprechaun PIs were, according to Blake and Fiona, incredibly stealthy, so it was likely I'd never know if they'd been back.

Pete came in a moment later. "You okay?" he asked.

"What do you think Presley meant about seeing a leprechaun?" I asked. "I mean, that's a little coincidental."

"It's St. Patrick's Day," he said. "There are probably people dressed as leprechauns all over, Vi. Maybe she saw one outside and just misremembered. She's a kid. They see things a whole lot differently than we do."

"Maybe someone was here. Mac's team is looking for him. Maybe they're looking for things to connect his case and Mazzy's."

Pete didn't look convinced. "They would have to tell you. I mean, how would they even get in?"

"I don't know! Do leprechauns have powers?"

"Of course they have powers, but they're not like witches' powers."

I heard Presley's voice getting closer, so I changed the subject. "Have you seen Todd?"

"I haven't," Pete said. "Still nothing, huh?"

"No. No one's heard from him either. Ginny asked me about him too."

Presley hurled herself through the curtain. "Pete! It's starting! Can I sit on your shoulders?"

He laughed and scooped her up. "Of course you can." He settled the little girl on his shoulders like he'd been doing it forever, winked at me, and carried her into the shop.

I knew I should follow, but instead I sat down at my desk. Xander appeared next to me, startling me, then I laughed. "Well, I guess now I know for sure that you're magick, since Fiona's house isn't two doors down like mine."

Xander purred.

I rubbed his head. He settled down on the desk and proceeded to take a nap. When I went back out front, Syd, Pete, and Presley had already gone outside to watch the festivities. I could hear the music getting closer, the people clapping, the stomp of feet on the pavement as the band marched in sync.

The crowd on the sidelines had tripled, and the mood seemed light and joyful. I grabbed my coat and went to stand on the sidewalk. The Irish step dancers were passing by, and I watched their perfectly in-sync movements with some envy. I'd never had much rhythm so had always avoided dancing of any kind.

As the parade wound its way down the street, I scanned the crowd. In the past, Todd was a sponsor of the parade, with a float and everything. I had missed the first few floats, but I didn't see anything relating to the bar in the rest of it. I decided to go over to the bar today and ask around.

I also saw some familiar faces from the fair. Some had joined the parade; others were on the street watching, showing their support to their friends and colleagues. There were police too, a larger presence than usual. While the crowd was festive, I could sense a cloud hanging in the air—likely due to Horatio's murder. He'd been such a larger-than-life presence at the fair that, love him or hate him, his absence was felt pretty acutely.

I felt sick thinking of him again, and abruptly turned to go back into the store for a moment alone.

And bumped right into Rand Gallagher, who stood in front of my door.

CHAPTER THIRTY

"Rand, hey," I said, pressing a hand to my pounding heart. Man, I was a little too jumpy for my own good.

"Sorry about that," he said. "I didn't mean to startle you."

"No problem. How are you doing?" He looked kind of terrible, actually, long hair pulled back into a disheveled ponytail, face unshaven, bruised half-moons under his eyes. He wasn't even wearing a coat, just a green-and-black plaid flannel shirt.

Rand shrugged, looking down the street at the disappearing step dancers, but I had a feeling he wasn't really seeing them. "I'm okay. I mean, I feel like I'm dreaming. It seems surreal, you know? Horatio was larger than life and he lived for this stuff. I keep expecting him to show up in the middle of the parade or something and tell everyone it was just a big joke."

"Yeah." The awful picture of the axe, the blood, swam in my head. I shoved it away. "Do you want to come in for a minute? I can make some tea. I need to get out of the crowd. Plus, you look cold."

He looked down at himself and seemed surprised at what he saw. "Good idea. I am chilly. And I'm feeling a little claustrophobic in this crowd myself." He followed me into the store and I closed the door behind us, then flipped the lock. We weren't opening until the parade was over.

"I have a lavender rose tea," I said. "That okay?"

"Lovely," Rand agreed.

I went out back to heat the water. I was on high alert for any kind of presence that might be back there, leprechaun or otherwise, but there was nothing. Not even Xander. I wondered where he'd taken off to. When I went back out with the two mugs of tea, Rand was browsing my various displays.

"You have a great selection," he said, waving a tower stone at me. "Is this astrophyllite from North America, or Russia?"

I handed him the mug of tea and motioned to the two chairs in the back where I did my crystal consults. "Neither, actually," I said as we sat. "This particular shipment was sourced in Norway." Astrophyllite was a unique, rare stone that was mainly sourced from Russia, but could also be found in certain places in the United States, Canada, Norway, and Greenland. I cocked my head at him, curious. "How did you know where astrophyllite is found?"

He shrugged. "I'm a little familiar with crystals."

I hadn't known this. But why would I? I realized I had no idea what Rand did aside from the fair. "Do you work with crystals too? Or was it just from hanging around Horatio so much?"

"I don't work with crystals," he said, still studying the stone as if transfixed by it. "My mother did. She sold them for a while, many years ago. But she taught me a few things." Finally he placed it back on the shelf, focused on the tea, and took a sip. "Thank you. This is good. It's still cold outside."

"It is," I agreed. "I can't wait for spring. It's been a long winter."

We sipped in the awkward silence that followed. "So you don't work with crystals, but what do you do outside of the fairs?" I asked finally.

He smiled a little. "The fairs are it. I'm the only full-time employee. These things are a ton of work. For a while I was the only chairperson, but then when we began expanding further across the east coast and the fair kept growing, the board thought I needed some help. They wanted me to appoint co-chairs. So for the past four years, I've chosen co-chairs on a rotating basis. Two-year maximum appointment."

I did a quick calculation in my head. "So was this Horatio's second year?"

Rand nodded. "He actually wanted to stay on. Said he had a ton of ideas. He was campaigning for a full-time position."

"Would the board have let him?"

"I don't know." Rand's shoulders drooped. "He

hadn't gotten very far in the process. He was going to focus on it after the event."

"How long have you worked for the fair?" I asked. I couldn't quite figure out how old Rand was. I got the sense he was pretty young, perhaps around my age.

"For the past ten years. I grew up here. It was my second job out of college."

"Wow. That's a long time. You must love it."

"I do. It's my family. I don't have much family," he added. "My parents are gone, and I have no siblings."

That was sad. I knew how that felt, for sure. I'd been alone until Fiona and Zoe had shown up. We both fell silent again. Rand drank more tea. I studied him, trying not to let him notice. I wanted a sense of his aura but I felt guilty for doing it without his permission. Just a little peek, I promised myself. Right away I saw beige. Lots of it. Which made sense. Beige was all about predictability and dependability. That certainly seemed right. But I also saw some green. When it was bright, green meant nurturing and abundance. This green was darker, which typically meant either jealousy or selfishness. I thought about what Avilyn had said, about Horatio's new ideas, and wondered just how Rand had been threatened by them. Threatened enough to kill his competitor?

I suddenly realized we were alone in here, despite scores of people being out on the street, and shivered a little.

As if he was reading my thoughts, he cleared his

throat. "Have you heard anything else? About . . . the case?"

"I haven't. You were close to Horatio. You guys ran in the same circles. Who could've done this? Anyone stand out in your mind?"

He shook his head slowly. "I don't know. The cops asked the same thing. I wish I could tell them something more. But I wasn't as tight with him as you might think. We ran the fair together, but we weren't . . ." he looked away. "We weren't real close. Like outside friends. He was having issues with Katia Leclerc, though. I didn't know much about it, but he was quite unhappy."

I nodded. "I saw them fighting the other day."

"In public?" He frowned.

"Outside the amphitheater," I said, not sure why that mattered now. "But do you know what it was about? She was publicly going after him."

"I don't."

"Did you know he was dating Calliope Diamond?" I asked.

"I didn't. I mean, I'd heard of her because she's a vendor, but I didn't know they were dating. I found out yesterday. But he had no reason to tell me. We weren't sharing our love lives with each other."

"What about Burton? He had some negative things to say about Horatio." I didn't want to get Avilyn in trouble by saying I'd heard Rand and Horatio argued about that, so I waited to see if he'd mention it.

"Ah, Burton." Rand sighed. "I do feel bad for

him. He has been part of the fair for so long, and to be shut out—well, I can see how he'd be upset."

"Didn't you have any say in that?" I asked. "He said you two go way back."

Rand shifted in his chair. "I wish I did. But Horatio was very adamant about the updated rules. He got the board to sign off. Unfortunately I couldn't do anything about it."

I studied Rand's face. I got the sense he didn't agree with this approach, but either he'd made peace with it or he'd decided he wasn't going to talk poorly about a dead man. "Can I ask you a question? How did I get picked to fill in for the woman who got sick?"

The change of subject seemed to surprise him. "You were drawn from the lottery," he said.

"So is it like a bunch of names in a hat? Randomizer online? How does it work?"

He was back to drumming his fingers. "I don't know exactly. There's a whole system. Horatio and some of the volunteers overhauled it last year. He actually did the honors of choosing vendors."

Horatio had been in charge of picking me. Now Blake was in my head and I wondered exactly how random their system was, at least in this case. The shop door opened and Sydney came in with Presley, who was clearly pouting.

"What's up with her?" I asked Syd when Presley stormed out back.

"She's mad because I wouldn't let her go talk to the leprechauns," Syd said, rolling her eyes. "She said she wanted to see if one of the leprechauns in the parade was her new friend."

Rand laughed. "Adorable. Children's imaginations are so rich. Anyway, nice to see you, Violet. I'll see you at the fair in a bit. Thanks for the tea." He stood and headed for the door.

Once he was gone, I turned back to Syd. "So, leprechauns, huh?"

"I swear. She's obsessed. Who was that?"

"He's the co-organizer of the fair. He worked with Horatio."

"Oh, wow," Syd said sympathetically. "He must be devastated."

"Yeah, he is."

"I better go see what she's up to," Syd said, and hurried out back after Presley.

I picked up our mugs to bring them out back to wash. Presley was sitting in the corner, refusing to talk to Sydney. I put the mugs in the sink and went to my desk. The package that Syd had handed me earlier was sitting there. I grabbed it and went out front, sliding my finger under the tape to rip it open as I walked. Pausing at my desk, I pulled out a heavy, bubble-wrapped object. I pulled the wrap away to find a pyrite stone. Pyrites were the stone of riches, symbolizing abundance as well as protection and security. I checked the envelope again. Nothing else.

"You sure you don't know anything about where this came from?" I asked Syd when she returned.

"No. It was propped up against the door. What is it?"

"A pyrite."

"Huh. Why would someone leave you a crystal?

Maybe it's one of the sellers and they want to show you the quality of their stuff?"

"Then why wouldn't they leave a card?" I asked.

"Good point. No idea, Vi. Hey, I'm going to go drop her off before we open. Mind sticking around until I get back, then you can head over to the fair?"

"No, that's perfect. I'm going to pack up some new things for today anyway."

She and Presley left. I kept the closed sign up, welcoming the few minutes of peace and quiet before I had to go back out into the world and deal with whatever was next.

CHAPTER THIRTY-ONE

I brought the pyrite with me to the fair when I headed over an hour later. Josie, bless her, was already there when I arrived and she had our display set up.

"I had stuff in my car," she said, giving me a hug. "How are you this morning? How was the parade?" Josie wasn't much of a parade person.

"It was fine. A lot of leprechauns," I said with a grimace.

Josie smiled gently. "Vi, they've always been there. You're just noticing them more now." She squeezed my arm and took the box I carried. "Let's get going. People are going to be excited to come in, with all the parade vibes."

That was true. "Hey, question for you." I pulled the pyrite out of my bag. "Someone left this at our door."

Josie took the stone and examined it. "It's a nice stone. Looks like good quality," she said. "Who left it?"

"That's the thing. No return address. It was dropped off, no postage on the envelope. No note."

"Odd," she said. "Any thoughts?"

"None," I admitted.

"Well, maybe you have a secret admirer."

That made me think of Lila. I changed the subject. "Are you still friendly with Ember?"

Josie nodded. "We stay in touch. Last time I talked to her was when I asked her about that issue you had about the stone getting hot after that woman touched it. She checks in every few weeks, always asks about you. Why?"

"Really? She never even talks to me, but she's asking about me?"

"I think she's interested in knowing how you're acclimating, that's all."

"Anyway, when I went to see Blake at his office last night she was there. They were having a *meeting.*" I used air quotes. "The door was shut. But it was late at night."

"Did you ask Blake?"

"I did. He said she dropped by to talk about council stuff. He also said they dated a long time ago."

"Oh that's right," Josie said. "I'd forgotten about that. It was way back in the day. Around the time your grandmother was mentoring the law students. It didn't last long."

"Wait. My grandmother?" I was confused. What did she mean, mentoring the law students?

"Yeah. Abby was a lawyer, an activist, and a mentor to students studying witch law. Back in her heyday, of course." Then her eyes widened as it dawned on her that I had no idea what she was talking about. "Oh, Violet. I'm sorry. You didn't know that. Shoot. I keep forgetting there are things . . ."

"Things I don't know. Right. Apparently a lot of them." I turned this over and over in my mind. Grandma Abby? A lawyer? I was ashamed to realize I'd never really thought of my grandmother having a career. My sweet, tea-drinking, crystal-loving grandma out fighting for justice. Seemed every time I turned around I learned something new about my family. "So she mentored Blake and Ember," I said slowly.

"And lots of other students, yes."

"Did she like Ember? Were they close?"

"They were for a while. I know Abby helped her get some jobs, kept mentoring her well into her career. Then I guess they drifted apart. They weren't close the last seven, eight years. I don't know why."

"But my grandmother and Blake stayed close," I confirmed.

Josie nodded. "Really close. He was one of her star students. Ember too, actually."

"He never told me," I said. That bothered me.

"He loved Abigail a lot, Vi. I think he might still be processing. And I bet he doesn't want to cause you any sadness either by talking about it."

"Maybe." I didn't want to talk about that anymore.

"Anyway, that was how long ago they dated," Josie said, obviously also wanting to change the subject. "It's like, not even worth mentioning."

"That's what he said when I asked."

"You asked?" Josie laughed out loud. "Good for you, girl."

"I don't know if it was good," I protested. "He kind of took pleasure in thinking I was jealous."

"Well, are you?"

"No! I don't know. Maybe a little."

She spread her arms wide in an exaggerated gesture. "Hallelujah! I thought you were never going to admit that you liked him. You have since you met him."

"Not true. He was annoying when I first met him. Still kind of is, actually."

"You did so. And you'll be much better off when you admit it to him. You might even get him to make another move, if that's what you're waiting for."

"I don't know, Jose. It's complicated right now. And he hasn't even tried to kiss me yet." I was kind of embarrassed to admit that.

"Maybe he's giving you some time. He knows this Todd thing was a shock, and you're right, there is a lot going on. Maybe he's afraid of overwhelming you."

"Maybe Ember wants him back," I countered.

Josie made a dismissive gesture. "I doubt it. And Ember doesn't stand a chance against you."

"What are you talking about? She's beautiful."

"Beauty has nothing to do with it. Ember is . . . intense. You're much more his type." She grinned and punched me lightly on the shoulder. "Now you just need to show him that you're interested."

"How do you know I'm really his type? He's so . . . put together, you know? And I'm just this newbie who's trying to figure all this stuff out. I have a target on my back, I have a crazy family—"

"And he doesn't?" Josie snorted with laughter. "He's part Sageblood. They're not only crazy, they want to bring the world back to what it was two hundred years ago. I think he'd be more than happy to have you in his life. Plus, you're smart too. And you have yourself together, no matter how much you think you don't. Look at what you've built with your store. You're a loved and valued part of this community, and you've adjusted to your new life incredibly well given all the challenges that have accompanied it. You need to stop being so hard on yourself, kiddo. And you need to recognize that you are worthy of a man who worships the ground you walk on, treats you like an equal, and really sees you. Blake sees you. And from what I've seen, he treats you like an equal. So now, you need to let him worship the ground you walk on. Try it," she suggested. "I have a feeling you'll really like it once you have a taste of it."

I tried not to react with my knee-jerk response, *Right, but this isn't a Hallmark movie. That crap doesn't happen in real life.* "I get what you're saying and it sounds great, but I feel like it's a little more complicated than that." I clasped and unclasped my hands, trying to figure out how to put into words what my sleep-deprived brain hadn't even processed yet. "I haven't even had any closure with Todd—he's pretty much vanished—and that doesn't bode well for starting something new, right? You're not supposed to rebound, and all that." It sounded reasonable. Didn't it?

But she wasn't having it. "Violet, it's time to wash that dude out of your hair once and for all. I'm serious. He was never good for you and clearly there's a reason for that—he was messing around with you from the start. So forget about closure. Write him off and move forward. In fact, that's the last time I want to even hear his name. *Capisci?*"

I had to laugh at Josie's bad Italian imitation. She didn't.

"I'm serious," she said again.

"Okay, okay. I get it. Thank you."

"Doors opening in five!" Avilyn's voice came over the sound system.

I looked around. Cali's booth remained empty. No sign of her. "Have you seen our neighbor?" I asked Josie.

"No. But Oscar Sageblood is here. With Jet from the council. I know you're not a fan."

I stared at her. "You're kidding. I've seen a few others, too. Why are they all coming to this? Is it normal? Or are they . . . here for some other reason?"

"I think it's normal," Josie said. "I mean, there are a lot of magickal beings congregating here so it might be on their radar to just come and get a sense of what's going on in the community."

Her explanation made sense, but it still made me feel unsettled. Maybe it was just that I wasn't used to them being in what I'd always deemed "my turf." Also, seeing Oscar here was a reminder that the Sagebloods—and anyone else with questionable intent—could easily walk among us without anyone realizing.

CHAPTER THIRTY-TWO

After we were set up, I took the pyrite and walked to Katia's booth at the other end of the exhibit hall. She was alone at the booth, for which I was grateful. She was also not doing anything. Just sitting, staring into the distance.

"Morning," I said as I walked up.

She glanced up at me, and I felt my smile fade. She looked terrible. Her hair, usually sleek and shiny, was flat. Her eyes were dark and ominous. "Good morning."

"Did you leave a pyrite at my shop?" I asked, holding up the stone.

She peered at it, disinterested. "Why would I do that?"

I shrugged. "Someone did. In an envelope with no return address and no note. I thought it was weird."

"It is weird," she agreed. "But it was not me."

"I didn't get a chance to talk to you yesterday. How are you doing? With . . . everything?"

"How am I doing?" she repeated. "Did you tell the police I was fighting with Horatio? That I was . . . a killer?"

"No! I mean, I told them about your argument but I figured I wasn't the only one who saw it," I said. "But no, I don't think you're a killer." *Please don't be a killer.* "I actually told them the opposite. That if you were questioning his reputation, he would have more motive to kill you, right?" It sounded bad when I said it out loud but I swore I meant it as a good thing.

"And who told you I was questioning his reputation?"

I gave her a look. "I overheard your argument the other day. And his girlfriend confirmed it." I could tell she hadn't even thought of Cali. "Look. The police asked me if I knew of any conflicts he was having. It sure looked like a conflict. So what were you arguing about?"

She stood so we were eye to eye. Even though we were the same height, I felt very small under her intense gaze. "Why are you involved in this?"

I stared at her. "Because I found him! Because I looked up to him. And because regardless of whatever professional dispute you were having, what happened to him is . . . unforgivable."

"I agree," she said. "Unfortunately the police seem to now be convinced I am their likeliest suspect."

"But can't you just tell them where you were yesterday morning?" I asked.

"Yes. Unfortunately, I was here."

"Well, of course you were here. Probably a lot of vendors were."

"They don't seem to care about a lot of vendors."

"Did you see him yesterday morning?"

"I did not. I was here, setting up."

"Did you go to the back building?"

She hesitated.

"Katia."

"I did, but to see someone else."

"Who?"

She didn't answer.

"How do you know you're their likeliest suspect?"

She said nothing. I sighed. "I'm your friend, Katia. I want to help. I do," I said at her skeptical look. "Look. I found his body. That was traumatic, okay? And I know how traumatic it is to be a suspect for something like this. So tell me what was going on and maybe I can help."

She was silent for so long I thought she just wasn't going to speak to me anymore. Finally she said, "There are people out in New Mexico running illegal mining operations under the cover of legitimate mines. I've been doing a lot of research on mines around the country," she said at my questioning look. "I'm going for my PhD in environmental studies. My final research paper is all about gemstone mining."

"Wow. I had no idea," I said. "You never mentioned this."

"I didn't want my clients to think I wasn't going to be as dedicated," she said.

I wondered if that was why she'd been unable to hunt down my moldavite. "Go on."

"I've been taking trips out there every couple of months to get the lay of the land, talk to people, gather information, and get a feel for the work. In my travels, I've met people who know this has been going on and have tried to stop it. There have been whistleblowers, but nothing has come of it. Someone powerful is in their pocket. And recently, someone died in an accident. A Native American to whom they were paying pennies for the work." She looked disgusted. "And on my last trip there, I saw Horatio. With the very people I've been told are the minds behind the operation, the ones greasing the pockets of the local environmental officials. It took everything I had to not confront him then."

"*What?*" She had to be mistaken. "When was this?"

"Last month. So I asked around. Turns out he's been colluding with them for ages."

"Did he see you? Did you talk to him about it?"

"Not at first. I didn't know him well enough to just confront him out of the blue. But when we came here . . ." she shook her head. "I couldn't hold back any longer. It was wrong." She looked straight into my eyes. "People trust him to do the right thing. And he only cares about his pockets.

That is something I saw a lot of in my country, and I can't just look past it. That's how everything becomes wrong." She looked away from me. Around us, people continued to file out of the hall and head to their cars, background noise to the serious conversation we were having.

I didn't know what to believe. I felt betrayed too at the thought that Horatio had been talking out of both sides of his mouth. "Are you sure? Did anyone else know about this?"

"I have been talking to Lorelai about it. I pitched a series based on my research when it's done."

"And she's going to do it?"

"She hasn't committed yet. She was also very wary about using Horatio's name. She wanted to look into it herself." Now Katia just looked disgusted. "He has made it so people are afraid to cross him. *Oh, he would never*, they say. But I will prove it. Even if he's gone, he should be brought to justice." Those gray eyes were back on me, boring into my head. "But if you think I killed him, you are wrong. That would be letting him off easy. He wouldn't have to face his followers and confess what he did."

That, at least, rang true with me. Katia definitely seemed like the flogging-in-public sort. "Okay. But maybe it's good she's looking into it. There could be another explanation. Sometimes things aren't what they seem." Something I knew all too well.

Katia narrowed her eyes at me. "I know what I saw."

"Fine. But again, all of this speaks to him going after you, not the other way around. The police have to see that, yes?"

"The police see that they have to make an arrest." She looked at me again and her eyes were wet. "I did not kill him, Violet. But I'm afraid that I am their best guess at the moment."

CHAPTER THIRTY-THREE

Despite the busy afternoon in front of me, I couldn't concentrate. I was worried about Katia. I tried calling Gabe, but he didn't answer and just sent me a short text saying he was busy. I really wanted to know if she was as high on the suspect list as she thought she was.

But I had a ton of customers and then Lorelai invited me to do some podcast recordings, so the next few hours passed in a blur of podcasting and selling. I really wanted to get her alone to talk about the series Katia had pitched, but every time I tried to grab her she had someone to interview. I finally had to give up and leave, but I promised myself I'd corner her tomorrow.

Back in my room at Fiona's, I closed the door and sat on the bed. Monty was curled up in a ball in the middle. I lay down next to him, stroking his chubby cheeks. He opened one eye, purred, then went back to sleep.

"You miss your tree, huh," I said to him. Monty had a cat tree in my living room. He loved to split his time between that and his window bed, watching over the town below him. Here, he had only the views of suburbia and I wasn't sure he knew quite what to do with that yet. He hadn't caught on that there were squirrels and birds and other fun things to look at out the windows so he was spending most of his time sleeping. Plus, I think he was a little afraid of Fiona. I made a mental note to get him a new cat tree. I wondered if I had to actually go to a store or if I could just conjure one up. So many questions.

I looked around for Xander but he was nowhere in sight. I wondered if he was in the house somewhere, or off doing something that witch familiars do, though I wasn't sure what that might be.

I tried to focus and do some work. I had to send some website updates to my web guy, and I had a bunch of inquiries about stones that had come in that I needed to get to. But my mind kept drifting back to Horatio. I didn't have a great sense of Horatio's career at the time of his death. I'd been a little out of touch given recent events and hadn't been keeping up with all the news in my circles. Was he focusing more on selling or on activism? Something told me the latter. His supplier business pretty much ran itself, and he had employees for the parts that didn't. No, activism was what kept his name at the top of the field, and from what I could tell from simply following his work for so long, what really lit him up.

I grabbed my laptop, kicked off my combat boots, and fluffed up my pillows so I could lean against them. And then I Googled his name.

The first hit was the news about his death, not surprisingly. A murder made it newsworthy even though he wasn't well known outside of our metaphysical circles. Then came his website, links to some of his more popular talks and videos, his social media accounts. His Wikipedia page, which had his whole biography. His real name (Horace von Haller), his place of birth (Little Rock, Arkansas), his degree in geology and his career history. He'd worked in mining during his college years and for a couple of years after, which gave him that initial credibility when he started speaking out about bad practices and he really earned his chops as an environmental activist in places like New Mexico, Tennessee, and Texas. Most notably, he had pushed for reform at a mine in Texas that had resulted in a large-scale corruption investigation when he was only twenty-five years old, bringing down some powerful people who had been covering up environmental issues that were polluting water supplies.

I pulled up Instagram and scrolled through Horatio's most recent posts. They were all about the fair—the weeks leading up to it, opening day, photos and musings from the first two days. No new videos, no recent exposés, nothing controversial that I could see. I checked Lorelai's website and social too, in case she was hinting at an upcoming episode or series that might involve him. Her accounts were chock full of fair content and some snippets of the Horatio tribute she was putting together, but nothing else. Next, I went to Katia's Instagram page. Nothing personal on there, just business. I scrolled through photos of crystals. There was some pyrite, but there was no way I could tell if it was similar to the piece that had been left at my shop.

I turned back to my computer and typed in Rand's name and the fair. He came up immediately on the fair website. Randall Patrick Gallagher. I read his bio. It lined up with what he'd told me, about how he'd worked at the fair mostly for his whole career, rising through the ranks to his current position. Someone—probably a fair junkie—had done a Wikipedia page on him. It was short, but the primary details were there. Born and raised in New Mexico. I'd been right about his age. He was two years older than me. His mother, Selena Gallagher, had died when he was only ten. Suicide, the entry said, which was interesting. He hadn't mentioned that to me, although I supposed that wasn't something you mentioned in passing to a stranger. No father was noted. Rand had gone to a community college in Albuquerque, then he'd pursued a career in law enforcement, which surprised me. I couldn't picture mild-mannered Rand a cop. Apparently he couldn't either, because it didn't last long. He'd left the force three years after joining and took a job with the fair, working his way up from assembling booths to being the show warehouse supervisor, to finally running the place.

And then Horatio had come in and, from the sounds of it, started to take over. That must have been tough.

But still, it didn't mean anything by itself. I sighed and shut the laptop. I wanted to keep going, keep searching, but really what I needed was a brain break. Some time in nature, like the time Grandma Abby and I used to spend up in the woods behind the house. I decided to go up there and meditate, maybe try to tune in to her and get some spiritual guidance.

I'd just started gathering my crystals and some other supplies when I was startled by a crack of what sounded like thunder. As I watched in amazement, a cat tree dropped seemingly out of nowhere and landed in front of the window. Monty jerked awake, leapt off the bed, and scrambled for cover.

"What the . . ." I crawled off the bed for a closer look. The tree was nice—a lot nicer than the one I had at home. And it had a toy hanging off one of the platforms, right in front of the little cubby, that a kitty could bat around if he or she was feeling feisty.

I looked around, a smile breaking out over my face. Fiona, in her typical dramatic fashion, was trying to help. I appreciated it.

CHAPTER THIRTY-FOUR

I slipped out of my room armed with a small bag of crystals, a candle, a cozy blanket, and Grandma Abby's spell book. Grandma Abby had created the book for me—I'd found it in this very room when I'd come here searching for some kind of peace and direction after Fiona came to town. But I hadn't been able to open it until I'd accepted that I was a witch and committed to the path. The cool thing was, new pages kept appearing the more I learned and practiced. I hoped she was watching over me now and the book was about to impart some words of wisdom.

I went out the back door and followed the yard way up into the back, a path I'd watched my grandmother walk for years from my own window. Halfway there, I heard a rustling and turned to find Xander trotting along beside me. I grinned.

"Thanks for joining me, buddy," I said.

He meowed at me and raced ahead.

I reached the clearing high in the woods. There were still patches of snow and wet leaves on the ground. I made a sweeping motion with my hand to clear myself a dry spot and spread my blanket out on the ground, placing the book carefully on top of it, then set up my crystals around it in a grid design. I'd brought blue kyanite, amethyst, blue lace agate, clear quartz and angelite, some of my favorite stones for connecting and receiving divine messages.

Finally, I lit the candle with the lighter I'd brought with me. I'd seen Fiona light candles with her fingertip before but that was one I hadn't been able to do yet. She'd told me it was because I probably had some fear of fire I had to clear from my vibration before I could.

As I lit my candle I recited:

> *I am clear, my mind is free*
> *Earth and air provide clarity*
> *My next steps unfold with ease*
> *As naturally as waves upon the seas.*

I sat for a moment, pulling my wrap tighter around me against the chilly night air, letting the quiet sink in. Xander had curled up in a little ball next to the candle, absorbing the warmth from the flame. I could hear the wind, the leaves skittering along the ground as the air picked them up and sent them further along their journey, the soft rustle of squirrels and other forest creatures going about their business. I could see why my grandmother had loved it here. It was peaceful. It felt miles away from the bustling neighborhood in which she'd set up house, as if she were sitting high above everything and observing. Of course it was literally higher up—technically this spot was at the top of a hill, but also figuratively it felt that way. I wondered how it had been for her, really been, to have turned her back on living a full life in the only world she'd ever known, just for me. I wondered if part of her resented me or my father for the duplicity she'd had to introduce into her daily routine, for the things she'd missed, for the power she'd probably given up.

According to what Josie had told me about my past, since Fiona didn't talk about it much, my father had refused to raise me as a witch, which prompted the nasty breakup. Despite the fact that he was part witch, he hadn't wanted that for me. My mother couldn't accept it, and when things went sideways my Grandma Abby stepped in. She declared that I would be staying with her and my dad and she put a spell on a necklace that she made me promise to always wear. The spell prevented Fiona from even contacting me. So when Fiona left when I was five, she couldn't reach me until the day I broke the spell by breaking the necklace—by accident, of course.

My Grandma Abby was dead now, and I couldn't ask her to explain. I know she and my father both did it for me, that my father truly believed that I would be better off without this world and she supported him even though she didn't agree.

What I couldn't figure out was why she hadn't just let my father and me go off and do our thing. Why had she decided to be part of it, especially because she still remained with one foot in the witch world, still interacting with Fiona almost daily, and as part of the Magickal Council? Maybe she'd worried that without her constant oversight, Fiona would find a way past her spell. But at some point, my father should have taken responsibility for the choices he'd made and let her off the hook.

I closed my eyes, picturing her face in my mind, and silently asked her to show me the way. There were too many puzzles and problems to solve and it was all starting to feel hopeless. Mazzy would be lost forever in a few days. It didn't seem like anyone was any closer to finding out who had done this to her or to Mac. Todd had vanished. My family remained a mystery to me—both sides. Horatio was dead, and his girlfriend was Mazzy's cousin. I truly hoped that I was not a contender for the murderer title, but there was a part of me that wouldn't rest until they arrested someone.

I picked up the spell book and started flipping through the pages, startled when two dark feathers flew out of it. Cautiously, I picked them up and examined them. I couldn't tell what they were from—birds weren't my thing. Or maybe they hadn't come out of the book and had just blown onto my lap. It was a little windy out here. I tucked them into my bag anyway and went back to the book.

I wasn't sure exactly what I was looking for, but usually the book provided me exactly what I needed at the right time. But tonight, nothing was jumping out at me. No new pages had appeared either. And I was so tired. Maybe I needed to clear my head with a power nap, just ten minutes. I curled up next to Xander, said a protection spell that I hoped would keep anything away from us since we were out in the open, and closed my eyes. I fell asleep immediately.

Disparate images and faces filled my dreams. Sunlight glinting off crystals. Bottles filled with rainbows. Gold spilling out of cauldrons. A snowy owl sitting high above me in a tree. An axe covered in glitter. I woke with a start when I felt something on my arm, a pressure that wasn't supposed to be there. In my half asleep haze, it reminded me of the time I'd been locked into some kind of battle with a being that came to me in a scrying mirror and clearly wanted to hold onto me, probably to suck my soul away or something. With a gasp, I tried to pull away, trying not to look in case they could grab me with their eyes and keep me there.

Then through my panicked haze I heard a voice that I vaguely recognized. "Violet. It's just me."

I opened my eyes, blinked, and tried to focus. And saw . . . Blake, his hand wrapped around my arm, probably trying to wake me.

I jerked upright. "What are you doing out here?" Xander was still with me, sitting upright also, those bright eyes trained on me as if waiting for my cue.

"Looking for you. Sorry to startle you. You didn't show for our date." He smiled a little as he tried the word on.

Now I was really confused. A date? Seriously? Then I remembered—we were supposed to meet tonight at Potions. "Shoot. What time is it?" I started to get up but he held onto my arm.

"Relax. You don't need to meet me, I'm right here. You must have been tired." He nodded at the nearly melted candle. I'd apparently been asleep for a while.

I tucked my legs under me. "Yeah. I was. It's been a long week. I'm sorry I stood you up. How did you know I was up here?"

"Fiona. She saw you sneaking off. Nothing gets by her."

Of course it didn't. "Yeah. And here I thought I'd escaped those teenage years of sneaking out without my mother noticing."

Blake laughed. "Hey, the offer still stands. I'm happy to babysit at your place."

I frowned. "Babysit? Seriously? You sure know how to sweet-talk a girl." I blew out the candle and started gathering my things, trying not to show the disappointment I was definitely feeling. I'd just about gotten up the courage to let him know how I felt, but what if I was really just a project for him? Not exactly how I wanted to be thought of by a guy I had gone and fallen for.

Apparently the spell I needed most was the one to get my judgment back, because when it came to guys, mine had long since hit the road.

But Blake grasped my arm again. "Vi, I was kidding."

I made a noncommittal noise. "So what were we supposed to talk about tonight?" I asked, pulling away and tucking my stones back into my bag. "I'm tired, but if it's quick—"

He grasped both my arms, holding me mere inches from him, eyes glued to mine. "Listen to me. I know exactly what you're thinking right now, and you've got it wrong."

"Oh, do you? I didn't know mind-reading was one of your skills."

"When it comes to you, I've gotten pretty good at it."

He smelled of that smoky, faintly sweet scent that I'd come to recognize as his and his alone, a scent that sometimes stopped me in my tracks when I smelled it. And he looked good. So good. I wondered how, in the midst of all these crises, he could continue to look like he'd just left a modeling job when I probably looked like I'd just gotten through a particularly hairy battle with a mortal enemy, complete with leaves in my hair from sleeping in the woods.

I tried to forget all of that. "I sincerely doubt it."

"I'm not just here because of your mother. Or your grandmother. So get all that out of your head."

"Then why are you here, Blake? You have a job. And a missing leprechaun to find. You don't have time for a side gig. Especially one as high maintenance as me." I tried halfheartedly to pull away again, but he wasn't budging.

He held on, those smokey eyes boring into mine for what felt like an eternity. And then he leaned forward and I thought, *Finally. He's finally going to kiss me.*

And then I heard my name being shouted up the hill, carried by the wind.

CHAPTER THIRTY-FIVE

"Violet!"

Blake let go—reluctantly, I thought, and pulled me to my feet. I could see Zoe hurrying up the path, her skirt dragging through the brush.

"What's wrong?" I asked when she had finally reached us.

She paused for a moment to catch her breath. "Why are you out here? It's cold." She looked at Blake, her sharp eyes taking in the scene. "Having a romantic picnic? I hope you used a temperature control spell for yourselves."

"Zoe," I said impatiently, "what do you want?"

"Sydney is at the house. She's looking for you. Said it's kind of important."

I'd left my phone in my room. "Is she okay?" With a snap of my fingers, all the remaining supplies packed themselves up. The blanket gave itself a shake to remove all the leaves and twigs, folded itself, and settled on top of my bag.

"She looks . . . frazzled. But she didn't say. I don't think she knows what to make of me," Zoe said, smiling a little.

"Thanks," I said. Blake picked up my bag and motioned for me to go. He followed us down the hill.

I went in through the back door and found Syd perched stiffly on the purple velvet couch Fiona had installed where Grandma Abby's old, comfy couch had been. Fiona sat across from her, watching her with an amused look on her face.

Syd jumped up when she saw me, relief spreading across her face. "There you are. Thank goodness. I've been calling."

"Sorry, I went out for a walk. Is everything okay?" When Syd hesitated, clearly unsure about speaking in front of such a big audience, I said, "Want to come upstairs?"

"Yes," she said with relief.

"Come on. Blake, I'm sorry I missed our meeting. Can I . . . call you tomorrow?"

He nodded. I got the sense he wanted to know what was up, but I left no room for discussion by taking Syd's hand and pulling her upstairs and into my room.

"This was your childhood room?" she asked, looking around.

I nodded.

"Nice." She sat on the bed and petted Monty, who had still not gone near the cat tree Fiona had delivered. "Presley misses you," she told him.

Monty yawned and flicked his tail.

"So what's going on?" I asked Syd. "Are you okay?"

"I'm fine. But . . . someone's been in your shop, Vi. I think someone broke in but I haven't figured out how they did it."

I felt cold all of a sudden as my mind tried to process this. "Broke in? But how . . . did you see someone?"

"No. I thought I heard something out back, so I went to look. I didn't see anything, but it felt kind of weird. I know that sounds woo-woo." She laughed a little. "What is happening to me? I never used to be like this. But maybe it won't sound so crazy to you."

"It doesn't sound crazy at all," I said slowly.

"Some things were out of place. And remember I said there was food missing? It happened again. I had some sushi in the fridge, and when I came back in at the end of the day, it was gone. I know no one else was out back. You and Josie didn't come back today. Anyway, I wasn't sure if I should call the police, but what would I say? Someone stole my half-eaten sushi and left all the crystals? So I wanted to get your opinion."

"I'm going to go over there," I said.

She grabbed my arm. "You can't do that. What if it isn't safe?"

"You were there alone," I pointed out. "And I'm sorry about that. It's my store, and you shouldn't be putting yourself in any jeopardy."

"Should we call the police?"

"No," I said. "I want to check it out first." Besides, if anyone had been in there, I was ninety-nine percent sure it wasn't a mortal, unless Lila

Hale had found a way to mess with me. I wondered if genies could hurt a mortal. The last thing I could stand was if one of my friends got hurt. Especially one who had no ties at all to this life.

"Then I'll go back with you," Syd said. "I can show you what I thought was out of place. In case I'm imagining it and you or Josie had done it, you know? Before we get all carried away. But with the Horatio thing . . ." she trailed off. Of course everyone in town was on edge. There had been a murder, in our holistic circle no less. It was a lot to take in.

"No. You should go home to Presley," I said.

"Pete is watching her. It's fine. Come on," she said. "I don't want to let it go too long in case it is something, you know?"

"Okay." I grabbed my coat off the chair I'd tossed it onto earlier. "Let's go."

I stuck my head into the living room before we left. Only Zoe remained, watching *The Sopranos*. "Did Blake leave?"

"No. Kitchen," she said without looking away from where Tony was beating the snot out of someone.

I stuck my head into the kitchen. Blake and Fiona were talking in low voices, and stopped as soon as I came in. "Syd needs help with something. I'll be back," I said as casually as possible.

"Everything okay?" Blake asked.

"Yeah, fine. The store." It wasn't really a lie.

"I'll catch up with you tomorrow," he said.

"Be careful, darling," Fiona said. "Bad things are happening even to mortals out there."

Like I needed the reminder.

I followed Syd back to North Harbor. The ten-minute ride felt like hours. I parked and looked around before getting out of the car. St. Paddy's Day celebrations were still in full swing, judging by the sounds drifting up the street from the bars and restaurants, but this block was fairly quiet. Syd had left some lights on in the store, thankfully, so it didn't look as black and unwelcoming as I'd imagined.

I parked behind her and went to her car window. "You can wait here," I told her again, but she shook her head firmly.

"Let's do this," she said.

I led the way, pausing at the front door before unlocking it. Everything looked normal, nothing disturbed. With a deep breath, I opened the door and listened. Nothing.

I went in, flicking on the rest of the lights as I went. The front of the store felt normal, the energies of my crystals enveloping the space with peace.

Syd watched me. "Out here is fine," she said. "It was out back."

I moved toward the curtain that separated the backroom from the storefront, pausing before I shoved it aside. Syd was so close I could feel her breathing behind me. We both stood stock still. Nothing moved, there were no sounds, but I could feel it. There was some kind of energy out here that didn't belong to either of us.

"What is it?" she murmured.

"I don't know," I said, afraid to move.

"But you feel it too," she confirmed.

"Yeah. Stay here." I stepped forward. "Who's

there?" It came out kind of squeaky. I cleared my throat and repeated it, trying to sound forbidding as I peered into the shadows at the back of the room. The black curtains that hung in front of one of my supply areas were moving, and the shadow behind them was definitely too large to be Xander.

Syd was holding onto my arm. Without even thinking about it I shook her off, strode forward and yanked the curtains back.

And stared.

It couldn't be. Could it?

"Mac?" I said, when I'd finally found my voice. "Omigod. Is it really . . ."

I'd never been happier to see the sullen little leprechaun face staring back at me. "Well, who were you expecting, the genies?" he snapped.

"Kind of, yeah." He couldn't really be here, could he? But he seemed to be, and I'd never thought I could be so happy to see a cranky leprechaun in my life. I felt like hugging him. "But what—"

"Vi?" Syd's voice came from right behind me.

I spun and stepped in front of Mac, trying lamely to hide him from her gaze, but she was staring straight at him. "Who is *that*?"

"Uh, he's a friend of my mother's," I said. "I'm so sorry he freaked you out. Right, Mac?" I turned and gave him a look.

He frowned back at me and said nothing.

But Syd moved closer, still staring. "Presley was telling the truth," she said, her tone full of wonder. "She really did see a leprechaun. But why are you still here? Parade's over. Don't you have to give your costume back? Well, I guess you aren't really wearing one." She took in his hoodie and jeans. "Why are you hiding behind the curtain?"

Mac rolled his eyes. "Is she for real?" he said to me. "Look. We need to talk."

"Can you give me a minute," I said through gritted teeth. "Syd, come with me." I grabbed her arm and pulled her away from the scene, out into the front of the shop.

"Hey." She yanked her arm out of my grasp. "Stop. What's going on? Why is that guy here?"

"Listen. It's a very long story and I don't even know all of it. But I need you to forget you saw him. Okay? Syd." I grabbed her arm and looked her in the eyes. "I'm serious. You have to promise me you won't say anything to anyone, not even Pete."

"I promise." She tried to look over my shoulder again.

"Why don't you go home while I get this straightened out, okay?"

"Go home?" She stared at me, incredulous. "And leave you with him? Did he break in? Is he dangerous?"

"No. He's not dangerous. I promise. I'll find out what he's doing here and how he got in. Thank you so much for being so aware and telling me about this. I'll see you tomorrow, okay?"

"Fine, sure. Just be careful," she said. "There has to be a reason he was hiding, right?" She gave me a quick hug, then left, closing and locking the door behind her. I realized I was going to have to come clean with Syd sooner rather than later, or risk alienating her if things like this were going to keep happening.

But that was a problem for tomorrow. Right now I had to see where Mac had been since Saturday night and what he was doing hiding in my curtains.

I took a deep breath and headed out back.

CHAPTER THIRTY-SIX

Mac had moved out from behind the curtains and now sat at my desk. His tiny legs were propped up on the edge as he leaned back in my chair. "Feels good to stretch. Been cooped up. But I guess it's better than being in a bottle."

I pulled over another chair and dropped into it. "Mac. I can't believe you're really here. What happened? Why didn't you tell someone you were okay? People are frantic."

Mac regarded me with incredulity. "You're kidding, right?"

I flushed. I reminded myself that, in addition to his naturally cranky state, he'd narrowly escaped a harrowing fate and I needed to be patient. "Not really. I mean, I'd have been happy to have you—"

He let his feet fall off the desk. I think he was hoping for a dramatic thunk but, being a leprechaun, his legs were too short to reach the floor.

"You really think I wanted to hang out in this dusty room behind a pair of cheap curtains?"

"Hey. Those aren't cheap. My grandmother made those," I protested. "And if you hate hiding in my back room, then why the heck are you?"

Mac let out a loud sigh. "I had to come here. Safer than my office."

That made no sense to me. I gave him a blank look. "How is it safer? Someone got genied here too."

"You really need to brush up on your non-mortal crimes," he said. "It's almost physically impossible to genie someone in the same place twice. I'd explain the science to you, but I feel like it might be a waste of time. But since this place and my office are the sites of the only two genieings in this century and my office is kind of a busy place, I came here."

"I see," I said slowly, trying to take in all this information.

"While you're thinking about that, you got anything to eat? You don't keep enough food in this place. And your friend doesn't leave enough leftovers from her lunch during the day. That little kid was feeding me crackers, but that's not enough to sustain me."

I hid a smile. Presley had been telling the truth all along. "Sure," I said, and closed my eyes. When I opened them, a spread of food had appeared on my desk. I admired it. I wasn't sure what leprechauns ate, so I added a bit of all the things I liked. Tacos, lasagna, French fries, more sushi. Food was definitely my specialty.

Mac's eyes widened at the feast and he dug in

without another word, eating like he hadn't in days. Which maybe he hadn't. I was starting to feel sorry for him.

"You know, if you'd told me you were here, I could've brought you some food," I said, taking some sushi myself. I hadn't eaten dinner tonight either. I hadn't been hungry thinking about all the problems that I felt like I needed to solve. "Have you only been eating Syd's leftovers?" At least it explained the mystery of the missing food.

"That's pretty much it," he said. "Slim pickings if you ask me."

We ate in silence for a bit, then finally Mac let out a loud burp and sat back.

"Hey, Mac?" I asked after a minute.

"Yeah."

"Who *did* get genied?"

A long pause, then he looked up at me. "Goldie," he said, and darn if that gruff little voice didn't wobble.

"Oh, Mac. I'm sorry. What happened, exactly?"

"I was on my way to the office to meet you and my DetectEvil went off."

"Your . . ." I cleared my throat. "Your what now?"

"My evil-energy detector," he said, amazingly without the condescension I'd come to expect. "My team and I created it for dangerous jobs where energy takes on different forms and tries to separate so it's undetectable."

I sat up straighter. "Wow. That's amazing. Can I get one?"

He stared at me. "No."

I frowned. "Why?"

"No," he repeated. "It's not a product you can

just buy. If it was, don't you think everyone would have one?"

"I don't know. Why can't they?"

"Because most beings have no clue how to handle evil spirits unless they've been specially trained," Mac said. "My team and I have been through extensive trainings with the most accredited experts on evil beings in the land. They helped us create a limited number of these detectors for the highest-risk jobs. If we gave one to every idiot unicorn and shapeshifter who wanted one, they'd think they were some supernatural superhero and try to chase the evil spirits. They'd be wiped out in five seconds flat. It's happened before, trust me."

I did. And I didn't really want the details right now. "Okay. So your DetectEvil alerted you. What happened then?"

"I aborted," Mac said. "I immediately went dark. And I called Goldie and Shiloh to tell them the office was off-limits. But I was too late. Goldie was working and he'd gone to the office to get some equipment. They thought it was me." He swallowed hard, and his cranky little face contorted.

I realized he was trying to hold back tears. Without even thinking about it, I reached over and squeezed his little hand.

He looked down at where my fingers grasped his. For a minute I forgot about our differences—his dry, not-quite-human feeling skin, his surly attitude, the fact that he'd been hiding out in my shop for days freaking out my best friend—and we just became two beings who'd both experienced trauma and tragedy. His eyes met mine and that understanding passed between us before he let go and took a deep breath.

"I'm going to get him back," he said quietly. "Shiloh and I are the only ones who know. If they find out, they'll destroy Goldie's bottle and there will be no getting him back. So I have to stay super hidden and quiet while I work on this." He looked at me. "That's why I'm here. I didn't mean to intrude."

I tried not to let my surprise at his civility show and smiled. "You aren't intruding, Mac. If you're safer here, by all means, please stay. Maybe I should get Blake—"

"No!" He jumped up so fast he scared the crap out of me and knocked a pile of papers off my desk in the process.

"Jeez. Why not?" Now he was scaring me.

"Because I can't trust anyone right now."

"Not even Blake? You trusted him enough to tell him to bring me to you for some big reveal."

We both glared at each other—a standoff.

Then Mac shook his head. "Look. It's not that I don't trust *him*. I don't trust the institution right now. I shouldn't even be trusting you, but that human kept sniffing around in here like a bloodhound. It was either show myself to you and threaten you to keep your mouth shut or put some kind of spell on her."

"Leprechauns can spell cast?" I asked. I was genuinely curious.

"No. But I have friends."

I sighed. "Mac, what do you mean *the institution*? Blake isn't an institution."

"He's part of the council. The legal part."

"I'm part of the council too," I pointed out.

"Yeah, but you're clueless. No offense," he added. "But Blake's the lawman. At some point, his allegiance has to be with the governing body. It's his job. And as for you, if you tell anyone, what happens next is all on you."

That was enough to get me to swear to keep my mouth shut. I already had enough guilt about all the bad things that had occurred so far. I didn't need more.

But he was freaking me out.

"What do you mean about the council? Who don't you trust?" I asked.

"All of them. I'm not sure how deep this runs."

"How deep *what* runs? Is this about what you were going to tell us the night we were supposed to meet you?"

Mac was quiet for a long moment, just watching me. I couldn't tell if he was assessing me to see how much he could tell me, or merely thinking about how stupid he thought I was. Finally he said, "Yes. I didn't have everything, but I had some pretty good leads. And the fact that the genieing happened that night tells me I was on the right track. They didn't want me to get to you."

I felt my stomach do a long, slow flip and I clutched the sides of my chair. "Go on."

"Your grandmother hired me. About six months before she died."

I frowned. "Grandma Abby? Why?" Picturing my grandmother in serious conversation with a leprechaun wasn't something that came easily to me.

"Because she was being blackmailed out of her powers."

"*What?* How?"

"She had been getting correspondence. Anonymous at first, threatening you unless she gave up her powers."

I tried to wrap my mind around what he was saying. "Threatening me?"

Mac nodded. "It was easy to threaten you with all kinds of black magick because you were a witch but you had no clue. She was worried about your safety. They knew everything about you."

"Because they'd been watching me," I said slowly. "That's what Mazzy found out."

Mac nodded. "Abby and I didn't know that yet, of course. It took a while to get there. But anyway, the initial demands were small, so she thought that she could keep it at bay without it having too much of an effect on her. She tried to look into it herself, but wasn't getting anywhere."

"But wait," I said. "What do you mean, give up her powers?"

Mac shrugged. "Your father did it. There's a specific way to renounce powers. If you do it, you can't get them back. Like I said, she started small, but the demands grew. That's when she hired me—when she realized their ultimate goal was to strip her of everything so they could . . . get rid of her. But it was already kind of late. She couldn't get back what she'd already lost, so she wanted to try to stop them from going after you and even Fiona after she was gone."

"And she did this willingly?" I tried to comprehend this. "You're saying that my grandmother died because she gave up her powers to save me?" I felt that choking sensation in my throat that meant I was about to cry.

Mac watched me, and darn if there wasn't some compassion on that sour little face. "Yes, Violet. That's exactly what she did."

CHAPTER THIRTY-SEVEN

I got up and walked around the room, trying to breathe, but it was harder and harder to get the air into my lungs. All of this was because of me. Mazzy, Goldie, and my grandmother. My precious grandmother. For the first time, I understood Fiona and her fierce nature. If this was the kind of thing she was up against, I didn't blame her.

Mac watched me. "Violet?" he said finally.

I refocused on him, remembering there was more to his story I had yet to hear. "Yeah. Sorry. Please, go on." I sat back down. "So what did you find out? Who was doing this?"

"Well, that's the thing. I traced the actual black-mailer to some wizard-for-hire. From there, I tracked the source back to the council. Unsurprisingly, a Sageblood. His name was Hugo."

I frowned. "There's no one on the council by that name."

"You're correct. It's because he's been banished. This all happened about three months before you came. Chief Bell stripped him of his powers and turned him over to the Black Magick Oversight Board. Jet inherited his seat."

Jet hadn't been as outwardly hostile as Oscar, but I wondered if he was also plotting my demise.

"The thing is," Mac said, "I'm not sure we had the right guy."

"What do you mean?"

"It was all a little too convenient. Council technology was used to contact Abigail. That's just sloppy. And Hugo isn't one of the hardcore Sagebloods. We—and by *we* I mean my team, the police, the Squad, lots of different groups—keep files on all of them. That family is always underground working against the government, trying to rally believers, gain the majority, the usual tricks. They're also usually involved in some kind of underhanded deals. Hugo hasn't been involved in much. Even stopped participating in family events in recent years."

"To throw everyone off his trail?"

"Possibly. Or he was really trying to distance himself. Bell acted quickly, though. Too quickly. Scooped Hugo up and that was that. Abigail and I both thought it was premature. And it let them know we were on to them. I would've preferred seeing who else this led us to."

"So you're saying he may have been set up," I said.

Mac nodded. "That was our working theory. It did have Sageblood written all over it but we thought there might be another motive and perhaps another player."

"And?"

"And then Abigail died."

My heart sank. "So you stopped."

Mac shook his head slowly. "No. We agreed I would keep going, no matter what. She wanted you safe, Violet. And I would've done it anyway. I was . . . very fond of Abigail." He looked away for a minute, then back at me. "And I started to narrow down my list. At the same time, Mazzy uncovered the surveillance scandal, and we know what happened after that. I gotta say, that was some decent investigative reporting. I still think she's trouble, but at least she's a decent detective."

"Mac," I said impatiently.

"Right. Anyway, Mazzy's biggest mistake is the one that actually gave me my best lead," Mac said. "She went to someone for help. And I think that was her fatal choice."

"How do you know all this? Were you working with her?" I asked.

"No. I hacked her files," he said matter-of-factly. "I was monitoring your name and when it started coming up in her research, I kept on it. Tapped into all her correspondence from that point on."

"So who did she go to?"

"Well, here's where I'm still putting the pieces together, but this name started to become a common thread. Mazzy went to a source she'd used before for stories and background. A trusted voice in witch law who has had a very successful career. Figured it was a safe bet. But I'm thinking it's what cost her her soul. Potentially," he added at the look on my face. "Unless we can confirm my theory."

I was starting to feel terrified that he was going to tell me she'd gone to Blake. "Just tell me who," I snapped.

"Ember Wolfbane."

I was so relieved he hadn't said Blake's name that it took me a second to process the name he did say. I blinked at him. "Ember?"

Mac nodded.

And then I remembered what Josie had told me. About Ember's history with my grandmother. "Grandma Abby mentored her," I said. "They were close. And they fell out of contact in recent years— right?"

"Exactly," Mac said. "She, Blake, and another Sageblood cousin were Abigail's star students. When I started pushing Abigail to think about any enemies, she was reluctant to put Ember in that category. They've had a cordial relationship on the council, but seems things were simmering underneath, at least on Ember's side. Abigail finally admitted that Ember had started to cross some lines. She apparently convinced herself that she was some kind of heir to Abigail given that you weren't in the picture, at least in this realm."

"Which meant Ember thought she had a lot to lose if I came back," I said.

"Bingo," Mac said. "It apparently all blew up when your grandmother publicly went against Ember's mother—who is also a lawyer, but with a reputation for helping bad witches—and her mother told her to make a choice. Thinking she had bet-

ter chances for getting ahead with Abigail, Ember
chose her. Then when she realized Abigail had no
intention of naming her as a successor . . ." he
shrugged. "Sounds like she lost it."

Chills were starting to run through my body.
"Did Ember . . . kill my grandmother?"

Mac chewed on his lip. "I'm still working on
proving that. I don't have enough yet because I
can't physically connect her to anything. But I'm
trying to connect her to the Fernsbys. If I can do
that . . ." he trailed off.

"Does my mother know about this?" I asked.

Mac shook his head. "Abigail was my client. And
I didn't want anyone to know about the real reason why Hugo was pulled off the council. It
would've complicated things with Fiona. So I gave
Bell a story."

"But Fiona hired you too."

"She hired me to figure out Mazzy's genieing.
Since I haven't precisely tied it to Abigail's case, I
haven't told her yet. But there's one other interesting connection that I found. Despite my situation." He waved at our surroundings with a
grimace.

"Tell me."

"The guy who got killed? Your rock friend? He
didn't invite you to that fair by accident," Mac said.
"He was sent to you."

I felt that chill again, remembering Blake's questions about Horatio. "What does Horatio Hale
have to do with anything? He's not even a witch!"

"He's not, but he had some contacts. That girlfriend of his. The other Diamond," he said with a
grimace. "Calliope. Looks like she made contact

with Horatio not long after Mazzy's genieing. Someone orchestrated it. Got her to cozy up to him. I
don't think he knew why or what the plan was. He
was just a puppet too."

"How is it connected?" I asked.

"Ember reached out to Calliope. I was able to
find that out pretty easily. Mazzy thought Ember
was a friend, remember. So she played the card of
helping Mazzy, that one of her contacts had a contact, et cetera, who said that if she would do this to
get close to you, there was a chance of getting
Mazzy back."

"And Cali played into this even though Ember is
part of the council? Wouldn't she have realized it
sounded sketchy?"

Mac scoffed. "Why would she care about that?
Every government is corrupt. Even magickal ones.
It's not surprising."

"So then what? They killed him?" I was still having a hard time putting it together.

"I don't know who killed him. Doesn't seem like
that would fit into the plan, but I'm not completely sure what their plan was, aside from getting
close to you." Mac said. "Your girl Cali helped get
rid of that vendor whose place you took at the
fair."

I gasped. "No. Someone got sick! That poor
woman ended up in the hospital, they said."

"Yeah, well." Mac shrugged. "Collateral damage."

"Isn't it really bad for a witch to kill a mortal?" I
asked.

He gave me that look I was getting used to.
"Sure. Just like it's really bad to genie someone."

Touché.

"We have to tell someone. That Stalker Squad guy. Someone who can get her. She can't get away with this."

"You cannot tell anyone now," Mac said sternly. "Do you hear me? You'll get me thrown in a bottle faster than you can say *genie*. There is definitely law enforcement involved in this. Possibly Bell. I'm not taking chances until I know everything."

I tried not to scream in frustration. "So what's the plan? You can't hide behind my curtains forever!"

"No kidding. I'd starve to death. Look, I'm doing my best to keep going on my investigation from here. I have to be really careful and I don't have access to a lot of my stuff, so it's slow. But I need a little more proof that she was the one blackmailing Abigail and using Hugo to do it, and I still need to tie her to the Fernsbys. If I don't have that, nothing will stick anyway."

"So what are we going to do?"

He gave me another look. "*We* are not going to do anything. You're going to sit tight and wait to hear from me. And remember, don't tell anyone you saw me."

"No." I was already shaking my head. "Absolutely not. I want in."

"You want in on what, exactly?"

"I want in on taking her down. Look, Mac, you need me." I leaned forward earnestly. "I can be your boots on the ground. I can help."

"You're a PI now?" His tone was skeptical, but he was studying me in a way that suggested he hadn't completely rejected the idea out of hand. He must really be desperate.

"No, but it doesn't seem like you have a lot of choices," I said. His silence told me I was right, so I went on. "Everyone's been telling me that I'm this powerful witch and I have this heritage to step into. Well, let me see what I've got. Someone killed my grandmother, and they need to go down for it."

We stared at each other. I was determined not to break eye contact first.

Finally he nodded slowly. "Fair enough. But you get yourself genied, it's not my problem."

I bit back a grin. Mac was starting to grow on me. "I know someone who can help."

"No," he said immediately, but I held up a hand. "Hear me out. Solomon, the Witch Web specialist. You know him?"

"Solomon Ash?" Mac's eyes almost popped out of his head. "How do you know Solomon?"

I shrugged, trying to sound casual, even though I didn't even know that was his last name. Zoe had been light on details when she introduced us. "He's been helping me too. I think if we put our heads together, we're going to be able to get there faster. And Solomon is pretty hardcore. He knows how to be discreet."

"Believe me, I know. Can you get me to him?" Mac asked. If I didn't know better, I'd say Mac was a little starstruck. And a lot impressed that I knew Solomon.

I resisted doing a fist pump. I was in. "You bet. As long as you agree not to try to cut me out."

"Hey, I'm fine with you helping. I did mean it though—I take no responsibility if you get ge-nied."

"Fine. Let's go so you can stop hiding out in my curtains. Hold on to me and I'll get you there." As he rose to go, I said, "Can I ask you something?"

He made a *go ahead* gesture.

"How did you get in here?"

"When Fiona hired me, she gave me some pow-ers to use while I was working on this case. One was the ability to get into places. You know, with-out using the door. Definitely came in handy a few times."

I had to laugh. Leave it to Fiona.

CHAPTER THIRTY-EIGHT

I felt empowered as I grabbed Mac's hand and teleported us to Solomon's. My decision to stop letting myself be sidelined felt right. And then Grandma Abby's voice came into my head, clear as if she was in the room with me: *You can do anything you put your mind to, Violet.* I knew she'd be with me, helping me, pointing me to the person or people who had harmed her.

And it gave me confidence. Last week I would have agonized over showing up on Solomon's doorstep without Zoe's intervention but now I just closed my eyes, imagined myself in that beautiful room with all the hovering computers, and took the liberty of going straight there. I supposed if he didn't want me he'd do what Blake had done and slam the door.

But he didn't.

In fact, he appeared to be expecting me. When

he saw Mac, he didn't even raise an eyebrow. "Violet," he said with a nod. "I was wondering when you'd come back." He looked just as I remembered—dressed in all black, his waist-length hair in a ponytail. The silver skull ring on his finger gleamed in the light of the nearly full moon.

His greeting was a relief. "I wasn't sure if I should. I don't know the protocol for this," I said.

He smiled a little. "No protocol." He turned to Mac. "Mac Finnegan. Heard your name a lot lately. I have to say I'm surprised to see you, but glad."

Mac nodded. "Long story. Violet offered to bring me here."

"He was hiding in my shop. I'll let him explain."

"As I said, I'm glad you came. Come into my office. We can talk there," Solomon said.

We followed him down the hall. Tonight, there were no computers hovering around the space as there had been on my previous visits. It was late, and his people must be done working for the day. But the computers in Solomon's office were still whirring. There were two hovering above the desk, both busily working, keys clicking. He slid into his chair. "There's been some excitement since I saw you last," he said.

"That's putting it mildly." I sank into the comfy chair in the room. It felt like a cloud and I wanted to stay in it forever. "Mac? Fill him in."

Mac ran through his version of Saturday night's events. Solomon listened without comment until he was done. "So one of your partners is the real victim but they don't know that."

Mac nodded. "That's why I was hiding out at Violet's."

"Smart," Solomon said. "They can't genie you there. But you'll be safe here. My estate is . . . quite protected, given my line of work."

Mac let out a relieved breath. "Thank you."

Solomon nodded. "Of course. Just so you're aware, Dewin Mallor brought me in on his unofficial investigation. Not to be confused with the task force."

I didn't know a Witch Web expert collaborated with magickal law enforcement. When I asked, he nodded. "It's definitely common. I can be a resource to them. I just don't advertise it. And I don't work with just anyone."

"I know, no one can be trusted." It was a common refrain. "You must know Blake, then."

"I know that he's the lawyer Dewin is also working with. We have not worked together directly."

I glanced at Mac. "Mac doesn't want Blake to know that he's okay. Said his loyalty will need to be with the council."

I appreciated Solomon's thoughtfulness before he responded. He actually looked like he was considering this theory for a moment, then he shook his head. "Mac, I understand your hesitation, but with all due respect, my sources tell me Blake Alexander is trustworthy. But if you feel that strongly, I'm happy to withhold that tidbit."

"If they find out it's not me, they'll destroy Goldie," Mac said. "I can't take the chance."

"Fair enough," Solomon said. "So we should get him rescued and put all this to bed."

It sounded good to me. "We thought if the three of us put our heads together we would figure this out faster," I said. "Because I'm starting to question whether this task force is really competent."

Solomon threw his head back and laughed. "They told me you were sassy." He turned to Mac. "Fill me in and then we can come up with a plan."

Mac launched into his findings up through Saturday night. At Ember's name, Solomon's eyes sharpened. "I had her noted as someone to look further into. After what I found out when I compiled Abigail's dossier."

"You have a dossier on my grandmother?" I asked.

"I've been collecting information on the council members since the first time you came to see me, especially since that's where Mazzy Diamond's inquiries were directed when she was genied," Solomon said. He turned to the keyboard, fingers flying over the keys. A printer on his desk started churning out pages. They separated themselves into piles and bound themselves together, then landed in a neat stack on his desk.

"What did you find out?" I asked.

"After your grandmother's and Ember's public falling out, Ember's choice of companions became a bit questionable," Solomon said. "She started taking on some cases that her mother would've been proud of. Not so many that people would notice unless they were looking, but enough that she was . . . opening herself up to a new circle of people. She actually got in trouble once too, which had never happened to her before this. She used a dirty spell to get a witness to cooperate. Got suspended and everything."

"How did she get on the council?" I asked.

"A vote," Mac and Solomon said together. Solomon smiled. "It was the reason she'd hoped your grandmother would pull strings, give her a permanent seat. But she didn't. And Ember needs to be reelected every four years. She's up for reelection this year."

I pondered that as he went on.

"The story Mazzy Diamond was working on. About the illicit surveillance on you. It seemed that request originated from someone on the council. I was still trying to figure out who."

"I got stuck there too," Mac said. "It was a lot easier to trace Abigail's blackmailer, which is why I think it was a setup."

"I agree with you," Solomon said. "I don't think Hugo was anything more than a scapegoat born into the wrong family."

I wondered why they weren't mentioning the one person who seemed like the likeliest choice in all this. "Isn't it obvious who the mastermind is?" At their blank looks, I sighed. "Oscar. It has to be. I've always thought it was him."

"Too easy," Mac said.

"Easy? He hates my family. And me. And doesn't try to hide it."

"Like I said. Too easy."

But I was more interested in Solomon's reaction. Or rather, the lack thereof. I started to get a weird feeling. He snapped his fingers and the pile of papers flew into my hands. He didn't offer commentary. "You should read Oscar's file," he said instead.

I stared at the stack of pages. There had to be hundreds, between all of the council members. I shuffled through until I found Oscar's packet. "Does this have information on his extended family too?" I asked, thinking of Todd.

"As much as I've gotten so far," he said. "The only thing I ask is that these documents don't leave here. I am happy for you to stay as well. I have plenty of room."

"I'm in," I said without hesitation.

He nodded. "I will make us some tea." He rose, then paused. "But Violet, when you read Oscar's dossier, there's one thing to which I immediately want to draw your attention. I am still corroborating, but I presume it's something about which you'll have a lot of questions. If you want to read that now while I get your tea, I'm happy to discuss it with you."

I frowned. "Come on, don't leave me in suspense. There are a lot of pages."

"Page fifty-six," he said, then left the room.

Curious now, I found the pile with Oscar's name and flipped to that page. And read it twice. Then a third time, still not sure I was comprehending. It couldn't be. Solomon was mistaken, simple as that. Or whoever on his team had allegedly done this research. "No," I said softly.

Mac came and peered over my shoulder. "Oh. That. Did he confirm it? I was trying to verify the rumor when . . . well."

I stared at him. "You knew this? You left it out of your version?"

"Didn't want to report on something I wasn't

one hundred percent sure of. But see what I mean about it being too easy? I feel like he's using hostility as a diversion."

I turned furiously to Solomon as he came back into the room. "I'm sorry, but this can't be right."

He smiled ruefully. "I had a feeling you'd say that. I'm ninety-nine percent confident that I'm not mistaken. Believe me, I'm running all the traps to be one hundred and ten percent sure. But all evidence right now points to Oscar Sageblood being Zoe's father."

CHAPTER THIRTY-NINE

I shook my head, trying to make what he was saying go away. How could that be? Oscar hated us. Fiona seemed to hate Oscar. And what about Zoe? Did she know?

Solomon pressed the mug into my hand. "Drink," he said gently. "And try to suspend your judgment until you know the whole story."

I clenched the mug so tightly I felt it burn my hand. I felt the room spinning around me and forced myself to get a grip and hear him out. "Suspend my judgment? Oscar wants to see me go down for these crimes. He's never been anything but horrible to me. And my mother has lied to me this whole time." I was furious. "What is she doing? Why did she really come back to me?"

Solomon sat next to me. "You need the whole story," he repeated. "I have some of it in my documentation. Some of it is history that is common knowledge. Like Oscar's father, Rune, who is a very dangerous witch. And his grandfather, Kadir, named for his father, Oscar's great-grandfather, who was destroyed by a coven of female witches during the genie wars." Solomon's eyes bored directly into mine. "Those witches were led by the Ravenstars. There were Moonstones involved, but the Ravenstars led the charge. And the Sagebloods have never forgiven."

Pete had told me some of this. "Did Oscar ever threaten my grandmother? Have you tracked him to any contact with her?"

"Outside of the council, no," Solomon said. "As a matter of fact, he had come to her defense a couple of times."

I snorted. "An act, I'm sure."

"Perhaps," Solomon agreed. "But perhaps not. He's not terribly shy about sharing his feelings."

"Are he and my mother . . . do they hate each other? Was it a long time ago, like a one-time thing? Or were they . . . are they . . ." I couldn't even finish the thought.

"It's been very well hidden, but my team's surveillance tells me your mother and Oscar have been in a relationship for many years," Solomon said quietly. "They meet in very specific places. Their conversations are protected, so I can't even get close."

I tried to absorb that, but it just wasn't computing. "Then why is he so rude to my mother if they're such . . ." I swallowed, "good friends?"

"That could be the act," Mac said. "It would be more dangerous for him to be seen aligning with a

Ravenstar." He looked to Solomon for confirmation. Solomon nodded.

We were quiet as I took this in. "Does Zoe know about Oscar?"

"I don't believe so."

I sat back and drank my tea, trying to digest all this. "Tell me everything you know," I said finally.

Solomon took a moment to gather his thoughts. "The patriarchy of the witch world is not much different than the patriarchy of your mortal world," he began finally. "The long-standing male elders are feeling more and more like things are out of their control, with female witches leading and their heirs filling council seats, giving them an undefeatable majority. The female witches had to take drastic actions after the genie wars. Those wars were a result of a contingency of male witches, the ones feeling threatened, who empowered the bad genies, thinking they could show their force while still keeping them under control. That backfired. It caused a lot of destruction and heartache. Witches like Fiona's grandmother and Abigail's mother were the ones to put the world back to rights, hence securing their standing and their heirs' standings. But they took a vow also to make sure their heirs were aligned with their responsibilities. They had the power to remove them from the council lineage if they felt they couldn't uphold what was of the highest good for the land."

"But Solomon, all of this just reinforces why Oscar hates us all. And why do you think this wouldn't mean he's behind it? He has the perfect solution—install Zoe as the Sageblood heir. It's the perfect way to tear the family apart." I felt sick as I said it.

"Ah, but as Mac said, we must be on the lookout for things that seem too easy," he said with a small smile. "There are many pieces to this puzzle. And that's what we're here to figure out."

"So what's next, then? Where do we go from here?" I asked.

"Your mortal murder," Mac said, and we both turned to him. I'd almost forgotten about Horatio and the potential that he was connected.

"Mortal murder?" Solomon asked.

I nodded. "Horatio Hale. Possibly connected to Mazzy." We took turns filling in what we knew.

When we finished, Solomon pulled one of the computers over and keyed in a few things. "That's where you can be most effective to start, Violet. If you can get Calliope Diamond to give us Ember as the witch who wanted her to connect with Horatio—and if she killed him—it will be much easier to connect her to the other crimes."

So not a huge deal at all. I smiled, trying to infuse confidence into it even though I had no idea how to go about this. "On it."

CHAPTER FORTY

Thursday
Three days before the full moon

I landed back in North Harbor with both a renewed sense of purpose and a sick feeling in my stomach. It felt good to take some action. It also felt good to know Fiona was probably wondering where I'd been last night, too. But she wasn't the only one who could keep secrets. The Oscar Sageblood revelation had thrown me for a loop. I was fine letting Solomon and Mac work on that piece, honestly. They'd do it with less emotion than I would. Part of me had been convinced from day one that Oscar was the enemy here, and I didn't want to let my bias color the information.

No, I was fine focusing on Horatio. Especially if Katia was still a suspect. If someone from my world was responsible for this . . . well, I wasn't sure how that would work. I didn't suppose they could arrest a witch. But that part wasn't my problem. I just needed to figure out who had done it. Which meant I needed Cali to talk to me. She needed to know she was a pawn and that there was never a plan to trade Mazzy back. Maybe if she realized that, she'd tell me who had set her up.

I was almost to the store before I remembered my other problem: Syd. Who knew what she would be thinking, after last night. I wondered if she'd told anyone. Or if she was upset with me for not explaining. One thing was for sure—Mac's reveal had pushed me to take the step I'd been needing to take for a while. She deserved the truth.

I changed course and headed down the street to Pete's, not only to get a good cup of coffee but also to tell him that I was telling Syd. At the end of the block, I paused. There was some activity outside Luck o' the Irish, Todd's bar. Beer delivery, from the looks of the truck parked halfway in the middle of the street. A guy stood outside the bar holding the door open, waiting for the beer truck guy to finish stacking up the dolly. I looked more closely at him. He was short, not much taller than Mac, actually, but he didn't have the look of a leprechaun (was I really saying that now?). Balding. Overall unattractive. But there was something about him . . .

Curious, I moved closer. The beer guy threw one last case onto the stack on the dolly. "Need help with that?" I heard him yell down.

The short guy waved him off and started backing the dolly into the bar, struggling under the weight and height of it. The beer guy watched for a moment, then shook his head and began stacking another dolly. As I reached them, the short guy saw me and stopped short. The dolly caught on an uneven sidewalk brick and the cases shifted, the top one falling to the ground. He cursed, loudly.

That voice. I knew it well. I stepped right up, searching his face. "Who are you?" I asked.

He shook his head and brushed past me to pick up the case of beer. But when he picked it up, liquid gushed out of the box from the broken cans inside.

"Dude. Seriously?" The delivery guy said from inside the truck. "You've gotta pay for that."

"I said, who are you?" I repeated. "Where's Todd? Are you related to him?"

"Leave me alone." He didn't look at me as he said it. "Just go away, Violet."

I froze. How did this stranger know my name? Unless . . . I grabbed him by the collar and pulled him up to standing. He didn't fight me, just let me haul him up and take a closer look at his face. And here it was—the little mole on his chin, the one that was shaped almost like a star.

"Holy Goddess." I said it softly, but he still winced. "Todd, I know it's you. What happened?"

Finally he looked right at me. "What happened?" he asked with a laugh of disbelief. "Are you serious? Your mother happened."

Shocked, I stepped back. "What do you mean, my mother? The last I saw you, you vanished from . . ." I lowered my voice. "From that cluster at Mac's office. Which you shouldn't have done, by the way. And now you want to blame my *mother*?"

The delivery guy came down the ramp with the other dolly. "I don't have all day," he reminded Todd.

Todd wordlessly opened the door for the guy, who pulled the dolly inside. He turned back to me. "I did vanish Saturday night. I was freaked out. I called on my father for help. He pulled me out of there and brought me home. To my parents' house. I didn't know he was going to do that," he said at my expression. "It was a knee-jerk reaction."

"Did you tell that reporter? That I was there that night?" I demanded.

Todd's eyes widened. "Of course not. Why would I do that?"

"To screw me over, of course. It was all over the newspapers . . . over there. People now think I'm part of this because I was connected to two genieings."

He winced. "I'm sorry. No, of course I didn't. My father brought me home, but I didn't stay. I . . . hadn't seen them in a long time and I wasn't comfortable. So I came home. Here. Fiona was waiting for me. She did this." He looked down at himself with disgust. "Said this was the last time I would use my charming good looks to be dishonest and hurt someone. I haven't been plugged in to anything that's happened since."

I couldn't find words. I wasn't even sure he was telling the truth. One thing I'd learned in my adventures over the past few months was not to take anything at face value. This could all be a ruse.

But my gut was telling me it wasn't. Or at least, that this really was Todd. And I didn't know my mother well yet after twenty-seven years apart, but I knew enough to recognize that at her core, she could be vindictive. I had no doubt Fiona was not above down and dirty revenge, especially if someone had wronged a family member.

"Todd. I don't . . . I don't know what to say. I'm sure it's reversible. I'll talk to her."

"Don't bother. It's a time-delayed spell combined with an appearance-altering spell. And, because she's Fiona, she topped it off with a nonreversible spell. It's only going to get worse from here. I know. I looked it up." He paused as the beer guy came out, grabbed the other dolly, and dragged that inside as well. "Listen. I deserve it. I didn't understand the assignment—I still don't—but the truth is, I was complicit. I agreed to set it up so I met you and started dating you. Truth was, it was easy. I . . . I did fall in love with you, Violet. And since you weren't doing anything with your powers and had no clue you were a witch, most of the time I convinced myself that I wasn't really doing anything wrong. I'd just met you in a duplicitous way, but I figured that the end would justify the means. I'd convinced myself that we could go about a mortal life and be happy. It's what I wanted anyway. I don't want any part of . . . my other life. But then Fiona showed up and things started happening and . . . you know the rest." He finally met my eyes, and his were wet. "I'm sorry."

The delivery guy came out, clanging the dolly to show his agitation. "You want to replace the broken case?" he asked.

Todd shrugged. "Whatever."

The guy shook his head. "Where's Todd? Crap like this doesn't happen when he's managing the deliveries."

I watched Todd's whole face fall.

The guy went inside the truck and returned with a case, tossed it to Todd. He had to lunge forward and still, he barely caught it. "I'll add it to your bill," the driver said, then closed up the back, went around to the front, and drove away.

We remained on the sidewalk alone, a leaking case of beer lying on the sidewalk between us. "What *was* the assignment?" I asked, because I had this need to hear it from him.

"I was supposed to keep an eye on you. See if you started exploring your powers. For a while it was easy. Because you didn't." He shook his head, looking away again. "I know. I was a jerk. But you have to believe me. I really didn't think—"

"Who gave you this assignment?" I asked.

"My father made me do it. Said I owed it to him after basically removing myself from the family. He was pretty adamant. But I know he got orders from someone else. I'm just not sure who."

"So you were just never going to reach out to me to even explain yourself?" I felt angry tears welling up in my eyes, clogging my throat so I had to swallow just to be able to say those few words. "Even if my mother hadn't showed up. You were going to vanish."

He looked away. "I didn't know what to say to you. I was clueless, but that's no excuse. I should've known there was something off about the ask. But ignorance is bliss, right? So I went with it. And now," he shrugged, "now I guess I can say I'm Todd's cousin who he sent in his place to manage the bar so he could travel the world to get over his broken heart." He looked back at me with the saddest eyes I'd ever seen. "It's true. I do have a broken heart."

A group of teenagers came around the corner, laughing loudly, shoving each other. I could hear the music blasting out of their AirPods as they passed us, barely sparing us a glance. After they'd passed, Todd turned back to me.

"I'm sorry, Violet," he said again. "I really am." And he moved slowly into the bar, leaving the broken bottles spilling out onto the sidewalk. The door slammed shut behind him.

CHAPTER FORTY-ONE

I stood on the sidewalk for a few minutes, shell-shocked into stillness. I was so mad at Fiona I couldn't even see straight. I appreciated that she was trying to look out for me, but at the same time there had to be a better way. Didn't there? She couldn't stoop to Todd's level.

A car drove past, music blasting, pulling me out of my reverie. I turned and hurried to Pete's. He was behind the counter when I burst through the door. A bunch of heads, his included, turned toward me. Pete said something to the other barista, picked up a cup, and crooked his finger for me to follow him. I did, out to the break room, where he handed me the cup. "Irish cream latte. Been keeping it hot for you. I figured you'd be here earlier."

"Thank you. Yeah, I got . . . sidetracked this morning."

"What's wrong?" he asked.

I couldn't even sip my coffee. I put it down on the table and paced the small room. "I don't even know what to do. I just saw Todd."

His eyes widened. "Where?"

"Outside of the bar. But Pete. He . . . looks different."

He gave me a funny look. "What do you mean?"

"Short. Bald. Really ugly, honestly. But it was him. He told me . . . he told me Fiona did this to him."

"Wait. What? Slow down, Vi." He pulled out a chair and indicated that I should sit.

I did, finally sipping the coffee. Delicious. "He said Fiona put a spell on him. To change his appearance, then make him age prematurely or something."

"The Obscene Transformer Spell," Pete said, almost to himself.

I stared at him. "Not even gonna ask. But I didn't get a chance to confront Fiona about it yet. Is there a reversal?"

"Do you have proof Fiona did it?"

We both turned at the familiar voice. Blake stood in the doorway, leaning against the frame. But his eyes glittered with anger, belying his casual appearance.

"Hey man," Pete said, his eyes shifting from Blake to me and back, obviously reading the room.

"Hey," Blake said, but his eyes stayed on me. "Well? You have proof she did it?" His tone had an edge to it that I'd never heard before, at least not directed at me.

What was wrong with him? "No, not aside from him telling me. You're right. I probably shouldn't believe a word he says. Although, do you think she wouldn't do something like that? She hates Todd."

"So do I," he said. "Doesn't mean I put a spell on him. I know we joked about it, but doing it is completely different. Even if I did, I wouldn't do it so blatantly. You know we aren't supposed to use our powers for evil, even if it just seems like cosmetic mischief. How did he know it was her?"

"He said she was waiting for him Saturday night. You were right, about his father pulling him away." I glanced at Pete, figuring it was okay to say all this in front of him since the cat was already out of the bag about me being at Mac's the night of the genieing.

"Waiting for him?" Blake frowned.

"Yeah. When he came back here after leaving his father's." I tried to remember the words he'd used. "She said he wasn't going to use his good looks to be dishonest anymore, or something like that."

"And you think that sounds like something Fiona would say?" He didn't try to hide the skepticism in his voice.

"I don't know. I guess so." But would she? Had Fiona even thought Todd *was* good-looking?

"Your mother rules the magickal world, Violet. This is black magick. Something we swear on the council not to practice."

I tried to read between the lines. "So you're saying this is a crime. Not as bad as genieing—"

"I believe you all would call it a misdemeanor here," he said. "So no, not nearly in the same league. But like I said, we took a vow."

"So he said it was her to stir up trouble? Wouldn't it be easy to prove she didn't?"

Now Blake just looked troubled. "I don't know. You think she'd take the time to go tell Todd all this in person? Do I think Fiona would care that she vowed not to use this kind of magick? Probably not if she was angry enough. But think about her brand. This seems . . . petty. And not a headliner. Fiona would always go for the headliner, yes? This is clunky and quite frankly, small potatoes. Do I think he's lying? Probably not. But perhaps he was supposed to think it was Fiona and it wasn't."

Now I really wasn't following. "Are you saying . . . someone impersonated her?"

"I'm just telling you my gut. That it wasn't Fiona. And yeah, people can assume characteristics of other witches. Usually they can't completely clone them, but if they're good, they can get close enough that someone under stress wouldn't notice any discrepancy. And Todd would have definitely been under stress."

I suddenly felt very cold and hugged myself to ward it off. "So what happens now? Is there any cure?" I looked at Pete, who had been silently listening this whole time, eyes moving between us like someone watching a particularly engrossing game of tennis.

"I don't know," Blake said. "First we'd have to

figure out if that was really the spell, and who cast it. But before we can do that," he came over and pulled out a chair at the little table, scraping it mercilessly along the floor, "where the hell were you last night?"

I stared at him. "Excuse me?"

"Fiona said you didn't come home. And she couldn't tune in to where you were. She thought something had happened to you, Violet."

"I was with a friend," I said defensively.

"I should get back," Pete began, but I shook my head.

"Stay. I need to talk to you anyway."

Pete looked uncertainly at Blake, but stayed where he was.

"With a friend," Blake repeated, not even looking at Pete. "Are you kidding me?"

"No. I'm not. Look, I appreciate what you and Fiona are trying to do, but I'm done with sitting in the corner like a little kid while the adults figure this out. I've got a stake in this game too. And since it seems like all of this might be tied to my mortal murder, you bet I'm going to step up and start doing what I should have been doing all along." I stood, feeling calmer and more in control than I'd felt since Fiona came to town.

"Which is what?"

"Which is figuring out my history. My powers. Not just making my hair look pretty. How I can help put all of this back to rights. And if you don't agree with that, I'm sorry, but that's the way it's going to be." I crossed my arms over my chest defiantly, waiting for him to freak out and tell me all the reasons why this was a terrible idea. The room was frozen for a long moment, then Blake smiled.

"Well," he said. "It's about time."

Chapter Forty-two

That wasn't the reaction I was expecting. From the look on Pete's face, he wasn't either.

"I'm sorry?" I asked.

Blake shrugged. "I said, it's about time."

I knew that should have made me feel better. But it didn't. In fact, it was insulting. "Are you kidding me? You've spent this whole time telling me how I need to *not* get involved, and how dangerous it is, and how all you big strong witches would take care of things. Now you're acting like I was wussing out all along?"

"No, I'm saying that if you feel confident enough to see how your powers can work here, then I can get behind that. Fiona won't be so easy to convince, but personally, I like this side of you." Now he grinned.

Infuriating. That was the only word I could come

up with to describe him. I think he knew I was
about to tell him exactly what I thought of him because he abruptly stood. "Come to my office later.
We'll figure out where to go from here. Pete, sorry
to intrude, mate." And he was gone.

Pete stifled a laugh at the look on my face.

"Can you believe that guy?" I slid back into my
seat. "Anyway. Forget him. The other reason I
came this morning is because . . . I need to tell
her."

Pete was clearly trying to keep up with my train
of thought. "Tell who what?" he said.

"Sydney. About . . . me. Fiona. Everything."

He paused for a moment, then nodded slowly.
"I see. I think that's a good idea, Violet."

"You do? Really?"

"I do."

"You're probably going to have to tell her too."

"I know. It's okay. I want to." He took a deep
breath, and I could see him mentally preparing.
"That way, if she runs screaming from the building, I won't be in too deep yet, right?"

It was false bravado, I knew. Pete was already in
way deep with Syd, even if they'd only been dating
less than a week. He'd been crazy about her for a
long time. I said a silent prayer to whoever might
be listening that for his sake, she took this news in
stride.

"Seriously, I think it's good," he said. "I'm not a
fan of keeping things from my significant other. I
like her, Vi. A lot. I want to see this keep moving in
the right direction. And I don't want our begin-
nings to be built on lies."

I thought of Todd and felt my eyes well up. Our whole beginning—and everything else apparently—had been lies. Look how well that had turned out for us. For him. "You're right. I'm ashamed of myself for lying in the first place. I kind of dragged you into this. I'm going to tell her today."

"Hold on," he interrupted. "I'm not trying to shame you, or tell you that you did something wrong. You did the best you could with a crazy situation that got sprung on you. And now you've had some time to digest it and you're ready. It's good, Vi."

He was way too generous. I leaned over and gave him a hug. "You're a good guy, Pete. You know that?"

He nodded, one side of his mouth lifting in a smile. "I sure do. Let's go get some coffee and muffins to bring to her. Maybe it will soften the blow."

When I got to the store a few minutes later, Syd wasn't there yet. "Dammit," I muttered, and threw my bag on the desk.

"What's wrong?" Josie emerged from out back.

"Oh, hey. Nothing, I just hoped Syd was here. I'm telling her today, Jose."

"Telling her what?"

"About me. Us. I can't do this anymore. Is that okay with you?"

Josie studied me, smiling a little. "Yeah. That's perfectly fine with me. I think it's a good thing."

Well, she and Pete were at least on the same page. "She might not want you to be Presley's nanny anymore."

Josie waved that off. "I seriously doubt that."

"Okay. I'm glad you're so confident." I moved to my desk, and frowned when I saw another package on it. "Another one?"

"Yeah. It was in the door. Still no idea who those are from?"

"No." I grabbed it and tore it open. This time, a blue chrysocolla stone. I studied it. Chrysocolla was all about peace, intuition, patience, and unconditional love. It was also known as a healing stone for physical illness among Native American cultures. I checked the envelope. No note.

Was this a good omen from someone? Perhaps it was a fellow crystal lover who knew some of the things I was going through and was trying to leave me positive messages anonymously. *It could be as simple as that, Vi,* I told myself. *You don't need to let paranoia take over every aspect of your life.*

But I wasn't feeling it.

Josie watched me. "No note again?"

"Nope." I put the stone on my desk, next to the other one, and turned back to her. "Hey. Would you be open to Syd working the fair today for a change of pace?"

"I think that's a great idea," she said. "It'll give you two a chance to talk."

"Yeah. And if we're in public maybe she won't freak out," I said.

I heard the key in the lock then, and we both

turned as Syd walked in. She paused when she saw us both staring at her. "Hey," she said. "What's up?"

I turned my most dazzling smile on her. "Pete sent you some coffee and a muffin. Also, want to work the fair with me today?"

She brightened. "I'd love to! I've been dying to get over there." Her hand flew to her mouth, horrified. "Bad choice of words. Sorry."

"It's fine," I said, forcing a laugh. "It does make you think about the words we all use so callously though, right?"

"God, it does. I'm so insensitive." She shook her head.

"Why don't you two take my car?" Josie said. "I've already got a bunch of stuff in it. Vi, there are a few other boxes out back that I put aside that you might want to bring. One has all the new animal crystals."

I'd ordered a bunch of animal-shaped stones, everything from foxes to owls to dragons in all kinds of stones, from jasper to obsidian to amethyst. They were going to be a huge hit and I couldn't wait to display them. "Great. I'll grab them." I hurried out back.

Syd followed. "I'll grab a box," she said.

Our eyes met and I knew she was thinking about last night. She didn't mention it, though, for which I was grateful. "Yeah. Fine. You can grab that one." I pointed. "I'll be right out."

After she left I pulled out my phone and texted Gabe. "Any updates?" I waited for the "I'm texting" dots to appear, but nothing.

I wondered if that was a good sign or a bad one. Not that there was any real good outcome at this point. But I was also worried that if Horatio's killer was a witch, they would never know that and go ahead and pin it on a mortal anyway. So that meant it was up to me to find that out.

CHAPTER FORTY-THREE

On the way to the amphitheater, Syd was focused on her coffee and muffin. I concentrated on driving and creating a script in my head to tell her the whole story. I mentally wrote it, crossed out and started again, trying to imagine all the different reactions she could have. My heart was pounding so hard I felt like it might fly right out of my chest and I felt kind of dizzy. I couldn't bear it if Syd disowned me as her best friend. It would be catastrophic, mostly because I didn't have a lot of other friends at this point and I certainly wasn't making them in the witch world. But more than that, Syd was the person I'd felt closest to next to Grandma Abby and Josie. Since I'd lost my grandma I'd felt so empty, and without Syd things would be unbearable.

"Vi?"

I glanced over at Syd. She held out a piece of

muffin. I hadn't even heard her speaking to me, I was so engrossed in the dialogue in my own head. "Sorry. Thank you." I took it, even though I wasn't hungry.

She sighed. "Are you mad at me or something? About last night?"

"Mad at you? Why on earth would I be?"

"I don't know. That whole thing was just . . . weird." She looked out the window. "That little man," she began, but luckily we had arrived at the amphitheater and I cut her off.

"Wow," I said, forcing some enthusiasm into my voice. "Lots of people here already."

"Yeah," she said, and I could tell she was forcing the same enthusiasm. "Can't wait."

I was such a chicken. I parked and we grabbed our boxes. I led the way inside, greeting Avilyn at the door. The room was already lively and bustling with all the vendors floating around talking to each other, or setting up their wares. I wondered if the cops were going to be back today. It had already been forty-eight hours since Horatio's death. I hadn't heard anything about where they were in their investigation.

I headed to our table, Syd on my heels, and set the box down. It wasn't until I went to stash my purse that I noticed something to my right was very different.

I stared at the spot where Cali Diamond's tarot card booth had been. Burton Jillette waved frantically at me from inside three walls painted like heaven—or like an angel had thrown up. There were literal clouds floating around above his head. A giant pot of some sort bubbled behind him, and there was a sign that listed all the tincture flavors available. Despite the fair not being open yet, other vendors were clamoring around him, trying samples and *oohing* and *ahhing* over his creative display.

I couldn't help but gape as I waved back. Where was Cali?

"I'll be right back," I said to Syd, and hurried over to Avilyn.

She was helping someone whose vendor badge wasn't working. I waited impatiently until she was done and turned to me. Her smile was back, if not a bit subdued. "Hey, Vi. What's up?"

"Where's Cali Diamond?" I asked. "Her booth is gone."

"I know. She sent me a note that she couldn't come back after . . . what happened. I totally get it. I know Horatio didn't want Burton here, but, well, Rand asked me to offer him the space. He felt bad after what had happened."

So Cali had bailed. Or had she been forced out? Then an even more sinister thought struck me. What if something had happened to her? What if some bad witch had killed Horatio and decided she was too much of a liability, so they had to kill her too? Or what if Horatio dying hadn't been part of the plan, and now she was in some sort of trouble with the witches? That meant it had been a mortal murder. Or maybe she'd vanished because now they needed a different plot to get to me and she was taking part?

"Vi?" Avilyn stared at me. "You okay?"

I shook all my potential theories off. "Yeah. Do you know if she's still in town?"

"I really don't know. We don't do hotel arrangements; we just tell the vendors where we got deals. I wouldn't know if she checked out, but I guess I don't really expect her to stick around. I'm sure it's painful."

"I'm sure. Thanks, Avilyn." I turned to walk away, then paused. "Hey, when you said Rand and Burton go way back to Rand's mother, what did you mean by that?"

"Oh sorry, I forgot you haven't been around to really know all the stories. Rand's mum died when he was really young. She and Burton were good friends. He looked out for Rand after his mum died, because he didn't have a dad. Burton kind of helped him get into this field." Avilyn smiled. "This community is kind of incestuous. Anyway, let me know how Cali is doing if you track her down, okay?"

I told her I would and went back to my booth. When Burton caught my eye again, he pointed to the paper cups on his table then flashed me a thumbs up.

"Vi?"

I realized Syd was talking to me. I put my questions about Burton on hold and turned to her. "Yeah. Sorry. Let's set up."

Syd and I worked in companionable silence setting up the space. Being a retailer herself, she had an eye for displays. And even though crystals hadn't been her thing until recently, we were pretty in sync with how things should look. I checked my phone. We still had about thirty minutes until the doors opened. No one was paying any attention to us.

It's go time, Vi.

"Hey, Syd. I have something to tell you."

"Hmm?" She looked up from where she'd created a little Noah's Ark line of our crystal animals. "I wish I had a little boat. That would be so cute. Sorry. What's up? Is this about what happened last night?"

"Kind of." I took a deep breath, not really sure where to start. "So, here's the thing. You remember when my mother showed up out of nowhere a couple of months ago?"

Syd nodded. "Of course. I know it's been rough on you."

I shook my head impatiently. "No. Well, yes, it has, but that's not the point." I took a deep breath. "You know my mother left me when I was a kid. I blamed her for a long time, but I found out recently it was because she was forced to. My father didn't want me to grow up like her, and my grandmother supported him. Which meant keeping my mother away."

"Oh my gosh, Vi." Syd reached over and squeezed my hand. "I'm so sorry. That's awful."

"Well, there was a reason for it. My mother is a witch."

A sympathetic look passed over Syd's face. "I mean, she seems a little intense, but that's just how some people are, Vi. She's not that bad. And I'm sure it wasn't bad enough that she needed to be kept away from you."

Oh jeez. She wasn't getting it. "No," I said, leaning forward earnestly. "You don't understand. She's really a—"

"Violet!"

We both turned as Burton Jillette came over, holding two steaming cups of his tinctures. "So lovely to see you. But I'm disappointed." He clucked his tongue, nodding at my abandoned coffee cup. "It appears we still have some work to do with you. So here is a special tincture for you. An energy one. And one for your lovely friend. Hello, gorgeous. I'm Burton." He beamed at Syd.

Syd smiled, clearly already charmed by him, whereas I wanted to strangle him. It was hard enough trying to get this out without being interrupted. And it looked like this was going to take a lot of explaining. Perhaps I'd been too simplistic in how I'd thought it would go.

"Thank you!" Syd accepted the cup and sipped, eyes widening as the liquid hit her taste buds. "This is amazing! What is it?"

"It's a special tincture made of very special herbs and flowers, all anointed by the angels. The archangels, more specifically, so it's very powerful. It's meant to remove the devilish effects of caffeine and bestow the energy and health of the angels upon you." He swept an arm at his booth and the floating clouds. "Isn't it heavenly?"

Syd sipped again, savoring the beverage. "Wow. This could be the best thing I've ever tasted. And it might get me to give up coffee, which could be a bad thing for my relationship with Pete." She smiled, a little flirtatiously, I thought. "I must get your card, Burton. I'm Sydney, by the way. I work with Violet."

"Of course, my love. It's wonderful to meet you." He handed her a card. "We need to work on Miss Violet here," he added with a wink. "She's resistant to my charms. She's holding a grudge because I made her spill her coffee when we met."

"Ouch," Syd said, glancing at me. "She takes her coffee seriously."

"Which is exactly what we need to fix!" He turned to me. "You need a tincture," he said in a singsong voice. "And soon you'll earn your wings!"

I was so not in the mood. "My what?"

"Your wings." He pointed at the angel wings suspended over his booth. "Once you join my monthly club, you get your own pair. They come divinely blessed by an angel of your choice." He observed me critically. "I'd ask for Archangel Michael, if I were you. He's got healing powers. He can heal that addiction of yours."

"Terrific. I've always wanted angel wings." I took the cup. I wanted to talk to Burton more about Horatio, but I was in the middle of this thing with Syd so I let it go for now.

He waggled his fingers at us and floated away.

Syd glanced at me, her smile fading. "He's charming! Why don't you like his stuff?"

"I do like his stuff. I just hate being lectured every five minutes about coffee. It's not like it's cocaine, for crying out loud."

Syd's eyes went wide. "Okay. You're right. You sure you're okay today? I know you've been under a lot of stress lately."

"I'm fine. But I really need to talk to you."

"About your mother? Okay, I'm listening." Syd sipped her drink, eyes intent on me.

"It's not just about my mother. It's about me, my mother, my grandmother, Zoe . . . we're all the same, Syd. We're all witches."

Now Syd looked concerned. "Vi, everyone has problems with their family. But if you're feeling that strongly about it, maybe you should see a therapist. I can give you a name. I started seeing one after everything that happened with Presley's dad and his family and it's really helped." She pulled out her phone. "I'll text her name to you. She's great."

My phone dinged with the contact, and hers rang at the same time. "It's Pete. Mind if I grab this before we get rolling?" She squeezed my hand, then hurried off with the phone pressed to her ear.

I stared after her, wondering how exactly I'd managed to screw that up.

"Didn't go so well, eh?" a voice said near my ear.

CHAPTER FORTY-FOUR

I spun around, startled. Ginny Reinhardt stood behind me, a sympathetic smile on her face.

"Sorry. I wasn't eavesdropping, but I heard the tail end of that. You have to admit, it's kind of funny."

When I didn't laugh, she sobered up. "Okay, it's not. Sorry."

"It's not your fault, Ginny." I sighed and sat down. "It's mine, for waiting so long. I'll figure it out. Anyway, what's going on? Are the doors open already?" I checked my watch. I hadn't heard the announcement.

"No. I'm helping out one of the food vendors today. The gluten-free bakery. I know her from the deli and she offered me the gig because she's shorthanded."

"Cool." Then I sat up straight, realizing that she

might be able to help me. "Hey, have you seen Cali?"

Ginny's gaze slid over to where her booth should have been and she did a double take at what was there instead. "What the . . . no. Where is she?"

"Gone. Avilyn said she pulled out, but I'm curious."

"Hmm." Ginny frowned. "It's not crazy to think she didn't want to stay where her boyfriend was killed, though." A cloud came over her face and I knew she was thinking not only of Mazzy but her other friend, Nicole, who was killed recently.

"It's not, but there was . . . possibly some weirdness related to Horatio and her relationship with him. Something to do with witches."

"What?" Ginny frowned. "I didn't think he was a witch."

"He wasn't. But I have a hunch that someone put her up to bringing him and me together. And I need to find her, but I have no idea where to look. You're friends, right?"

"Yeah. I mean, kind of. I haven't seen her since . . . Mazzy. But yeah, we used to hang out."

"Do you think you could track her down? It's important, Ginny. I need her, like, today."

"Sure thing. I'll let you know what I find out."

"I appreciate it."

"No problem," she said as Avilyn's voice came over the sound system, announcing that they were opening the doors. "Hey, Syd."

Syd walked up and slipped her phone in her bag, smiling stupidly. "Hi, Ginny. That was Pete," she said to me with that dreamy-eyed look.

"Yeah, you said that." I was feeling crabby. I had half a mind to call Pete and tell him he'd just screwed up my best efforts to come clean with Syd, and now I had to try again. Thankfully, customers were approaching so I had some time to regroup.

A woman approached the table with two teenagers. "Hi there. We came to your store yesterday and loved it so much, my daughters wanted to meet you."

Syd brightened. "Yes! Hello! This is Violet," she said, tugging me forward. "They couldn't wait to talk to you in person. They wanted to book consults," she told me.

"Oh, how lovely. It's so nice to meet you," I said. "I'm booking consults for next week when I'm back in the store. Is that okay?"

The girls nodded excitedly. I reached into my bag for my scheduling book and when I glanced up, noticed a familiar face standing behind them. Gordon Magnum, one of my fellow council members, with his ferret curled around his neck like a scarf, watched me. I was starting to get creeped out. I managed a fake smile and wave and then refocused on my customers. After they'd booked appointments and picked out bracelets, they thanked me and walked off, comparing their purchases.

Gordon walked up. "Hi there, Violet," he said.

"Hey. What are you doing here?" I flushed as soon as I said it, realizing it sounded rude.

"I heard about this event from Fiona and thought I'd check it out. It's quite a show," he remarked, looking around, reaching up to absently stroke the ferret's nose.

"It is," I said. "What's his name?" I nodded at the ferret.

He smiled. "Jimmy."

"That's cute. Hi, Jimmy," I said, reaching out a finger for him to sniff.

"Hey, I noticed the leprechauns," Gordon said. "They look official. Do you think they have anything to do with Mac?"

"Um, I really have no idea," I said. "I think they're security of some sort. Listen, Gordon, I have a couple things I need to do—"

"Go, go," he said, waving me away. "I know you must be busy. Just wanted to say hello. But maybe you could tell me, are there any tarot readers here? I thought I heard there were."

I felt a chill spreading through my center. Was he looking for Cali? Had he been involved?

"There was but she left. There might be others, though. If you go to the front, there's a woman who can tell you. Her name is Avilyn," I said, trying to make my voice sound normal.

He saluted me. "Great. Thanks very much."

I watched him walk away, my mind running through multiple scenarios. Had he been the one who had been working with Cali, and now he was looking for her because things had gone wrong?

I was so deep in thought I didn't see Gabe coming until he waved a hand in front of my face.

"Vi. Got a sec?"

"I texted you earlier," I said.

"I know. I was tied up. Can Syd cover for a minute?"

I started to feel a tingle of dread. "Yeah. Syd, be right back," I said.

"Of course," she said, shooting a curious look at Gabe.

I led Gabe to a spot away from the booths. "What's going on? Did you find who killed Horatio?"

"We'll talk about that later. We got a call from your building manager. They caught Lila Hale trying to get into your apartment. We have her in custody."

I felt the room start to spin around me and forced myself to breathe until it righted itself. "What was she doing at my place? Did she have . . . a weapon or anything?"

Gabe shook his head, lips pursed. "She had nothing on her. Insists she just wanted to talk to you."

"Why? Did she kill Horatio, Gabe? Was she coming after me too?"

But he was shaking his head slowly. "She didn't do it, Vi."

"How do you know?"

He sighed. "I hate to have to tell you this, but she was sitting on your building the morning Horatio was killed."

Definitely not what I was expecting. "What do you mean, sitting on my building?"

"Staking you out. She got inside, like she did today. Your building manager verified seeing her there. When they caught on that she was just lurking in the lobby and didn't belong there they asked her to leave. We have her on camera. Today, she got in behind someone with a key. One of your neighbors noticed her in your hallway, trying to get into your place. When they asked her who she was, she said she was your sister."

"Mrs. Owens," I guessed. Mrs. Owens was our resident building busybody. She knew everything about everyone, and if she didn't, she'd go to great lengths to find out. In the past she'd annoyed me, but today I was grateful.

Gabe nodded. "Yeah. And since she's seen Zoe, she knew it wasn't your sister. So she alerted the authorities."

I couldn't believe this. "So she hadn't actually gotten in?"

"No. She was using a credit card to try and pick the lock."

Seriously? She had to have been pretty intent on getting in. What was she going to do when she did? I shook my head, not really believing what I was hearing. "This is all so weird. Was she your primary suspect in the murder?" I asked.

"Actually, no. We're about to make an arrest. Although you didn't hear that from me."

My heart dropped. "Who? Not Katia." I didn't want it to be her because she was my friend—but I also didn't want it to be her because I wanted it to be Ember. So I could help get her on the other stuff. Like my grandmother.

"I can't talk about it yet. But Vi, you have to decide if you're going to press charges against Lila. We can get her on stalking, harassment, attempted breaking and entering." He ticked them off on his fingers.

I pressed a hand to my temples. That headache that had been around for the past three months or so was back. "Do you think I should?" I asked.

"It's really up to you."

"I don't think she should go to jail. I mean, if she really didn't kill him. As long as she wasn't planning to kill me. She'd probably get out on bail anyway, right?"

"As long as there's someone to post bail."

"Okay, say there is. Then she'd just be mad. What if she comes back? Should I file a restraining order instead?"

"You could," Gabe said.

"There's no way to prove it wasn't me seeing him, huh?"

"Not unless the girlfriend wants to tell her the truth," Gabe said. "But we'd have to find her first. She seems to have skipped town. Which normally would make me suspicious, but there's no evidence that points to her. Or motive, really."

If he only knew. "Yeah. Fine. No charges. Can you get her to leave town? She lives out of state."

Gabe nodded. "Maine. I can tell her we won't press charges as long as she leaves, but I can't guarantee she'll go. You're sure, Vi?"

I nodded, hoping I was making the right call. "I'm sure." I had more to worry about with the bad witches and genies, but I didn't tell him that.

CHAPTER FORTY-FIVE

"**W**ant to grab a quick drink with me?" I asked Syd when the doors closed for the day. "I didn't get to tell you about Gabe's visit." Plus, I was determined to tell her about me and have it stick this time. And then I was heading back to Solomon's. I had a lot of reading to do. Fiona was probably livid by now, and maybe I should check in, but the revelation about Oscar and Zoe was really throwing me for a loop and I didn't know what I would even say to her. And if Oscar was guilty and he was really Zoe's father, that was a whole other drama that would unfold. But I was getting ahead of myself.

Syd checked her watch. "Sure, I can do that. Presley's grandpa isn't expecting me until nine."

"Plenty of time. If you want to grab the car, I'll pack this up. I can be quick." I had thought about mind-packing in front of her, but figured that

would be like hitting her over the head with everything. I packed everything up, keeping one eye on
Burton's booth. I still wanted to talk to him, but
he'd stepped away and hadn't returned yet. I lin-
gered as long as I could, but he didn't come back
and I couldn't keep Syd waiting.

Fifteen minutes later, we were sitting at the bar
at Evarito's, one of our favorite restaurants near
the shop.

"That was fun. Thanks for bringing me." Syd
sipped her margarita and popped a handful of
peanuts into her mouth from the bowl the bartender had put in front of us. "You want me to
come back tomorrow?" she asked hopefully.

"That would be great. I'll tell Josie."

She grinned. "Cool. So, Gabe?"

"Yeah. Crazy." I filled her in on Lila's visit.

Syd looked horrified. "Trying to get in to your
place? How scary!"

"I know."

"But why didn't you press charges?"

I sighed. "She didn't kill him. They eliminated
her as a suspect." I didn't tell her where she was
that morning. "Honestly, I feel kind of sorry for
her."

"Vi, she sounds nuts." Syd was definitely less forgiving than me.

"I know. But hopefully she goes back to Maine
and forgets she ever met me."

"I hope so."

My phone dinged with a text. I picked it up.
Ginny.

I talked to Cali's mom. She said she took off pretty

abruptly to go stay with a friend. She wasn't sure who. You think she's okay?

I felt that familiar sense of foreboding and really hoped she wasn't next on the genie hit list. I texted back.

Is she sure she went alone?

I set the phone face down on the bar. "Syd." I took a deep breath, swiveling my bar stool so I could face her. "What I said before, about Fiona, it's true."

She sighed and grabbed some more peanuts. "This again?" she said around a mouthful. "Seriously, Vi. You brought me here to berate yourself and your mother?"

"No! Syd, listen to me. I'm not calling my mother names. I'm telling you we are real witches. Like, magic. Spells." Now she was looking at me like I had two heads. I leaned closer to her. "Do you remember that weird memory lapse you had right after she came here? With your apartment?"

"I didn't have a memory lapse," she said dismissively. "I was just stressed out. Had a little bit of an anxiety attack, that's all." But for the first time she looked a little uncertain.

"You had a memory lapse. Because Fiona moved you out of your apartment and moved herself and Zoe in. And then when I protested, she put it all back to rights."

Syd laughed, but the sound was high-pitched and unnatural. "Violet, I'm getting worried about you. Maybe you shouldn't drink that drink. Can I get some water over here?" she asked the bartender. He nodded and went to fill two glasses.

"I'm a witch," I repeated. "My mother is a full witch. My dad was half-witch. My grandmother was also a witch. She was one of the most powerful witches in witch land, and my mother is now the most powerful. My grandmother put a spell on me when I was little so my mother had to stay away. It's kind of a long story, but after she died my mother showed up in my life. After Carla died."

At Carla's name, Syd winced. Her daughter's grandmother was a sore subject for her. "Why are you bringing that up?" she asked. "And why are you saying all this? Is it some weird joke? Are you trying to punk me?" She looked around the bar as if expecting to see people with cameras popping up from under the tables.

Man. I'd been afraid to do the slightest thing in front of her in case she suspected, but I was practically begging her to believe me and she wasn't having it. Looked like I'd have to take drastic measures. It was either that or beat my head against the bar. I looked around. No one was paying attention to us. Once the bartender slid our waters over, I made my move.

I pointed at Syd's margarita glass and watched with satisfaction as it rose and glided right over to hover in front of her.

She stared at it, her face draining of color. She reached for it with an unsteady, jerking hand and instead knocked it over. It slipped and smashed on the bar, spraying lime and salt all over the place. I felt some of it spatter right into my eye. My hand flew up instinctively as my vision blurred in front of me.

The bartender looked at us and shook his head, moving over to wipe away the shards of glass, which Syd stared at like she was in a trance. "I'll get you another," he said, clearly annoyed. He threw the glass pieces into the trashcan behind the bar and grabbed his shaker.

Syd still stared at the place on the bar where the glass had been. Slowly she lifted her eyes to me. "What the . . ."

I wet my napkin and dabbed my eye. The salt burned. "I'm trying to tell you," I said gently. "But you weren't listening. It's not just being able to make things move. It's a whole . . . lifestyle. Crazy things my mother has been showing me. There's a whole government that I'm part of, and there are . . . so many different kinds of beings. That man you saw in my shop. He's a real leprechaun. I didn't believe it either at first," I said with a self-conscious laugh. "But he really is." I was babbling now, but I didn't know how to stop. "And Todd. I just found out Todd is . . . like me. There's a whole story behind it and it's not good, so I don't want to get into that now." I was fidgeting now, clasping and unclasping my hands, rubbing them together nervously. She still hadn't responded. Nothing. Just stared at me like she'd never seen me before. "Syd?" I said. "Please, talk to me."

But she was shaking her head. "Violet. This is crazy. I think . . . I think you need some help. I have to go." She grabbed her coat and bag and almost ran out of the bar.

I stared after her in dismay. That was exactly

what I'd been afraid of. And now I needed to warn Pete. This was a disaster.

But really, what had I expected?

I threw some money on the counter and hurried outside. No sign of Syd. Great. I grabbed my phone and texted Pete.

DISASTER.

He wrote back immediately.

What happened? Come to the cafe.

I hurried down the street. Pete waited at the door. He was closed for the night, but he usually stayed pretty late. I think sometimes he had witch gatherings here or something. But no one was around tonight.

"Tell me," he said, pressing a latte into my hands. It was late for coffee, but there would be no sleep tonight anyway.

"I screwed it all up," I said, swallowing back tears, and launched into my two attempts to tell her the truth, ending with the flying margarita.

Pete listened without comment. "I think you have to be a little patient," he said. "Give her some time to get used to the idea. I mean, it took her a while to come around to even the crystals, right? This is . . . a little bigger than that."

"I know that," I said, more sharply than I'd intended. "But I don't have time. We work together. We're best friends. I mean, what if she comes to you? You won't lie."

"I won't. But I think she probably won't come running to tell me you're a witch."

"No, but she might come running to tell you I need to be committed to a psychiatric ward."

"And if she does, I'll do my best to explain," Pete said.

I glared at him. "Why are you always so chill?"

"Special talent. Look. Leave it be for tonight. We'll see what happens tomorrow and figure it out from there. Okay?"

Easy for him to say.

CHAPTER FORTY-SIX

Ginny texted me again as I was leaving Pete's.
*No luck with Cali. Her mother says she went away
for a few days, not sure where. I tried to tune in to see if I
could get a line on her, but no luck. My powers are not up
to snuff.*

She'd added a sad-faced emoji after that statement.

Crap. I texted back.

Thanks for trying.

I paused on the sidewalk and tried to figure out
what to do next. Then I remembered that Cali had
told me she lived in Rhode Island. At least for her
mortal life. So maybe I could start there.

I was just about to try my hand at teleporting to
her place when Blake appeared on the sidewalk
next to me. "Did you forget about me?"

Shoot. I had. "Not at all. But Cali Diamond has

disappeared and I need to go to her house. Want to go with me?"

To my surprise, he didn't question me. Instead, he nodded. "Her mortal house?"

"Yeah." I didn't say it, but I was hoping Blake would make sure we ended up in the right place.

"Let's go."

He grabbed my hand. I concentrated on Cali's face, saying a silent prayer we'd end up where we were supposed to be.

We landed in the kitchen of a tidy little house that didn't look anything like a witch's place, at least in my opinion.

"Not what you expected?" Blake asked, amused, taking in my expression.

"Not really. See if you can find a computer." I walked through the living room and a guest bedroom before heading upstairs. There, I found what I presumed was her bedroom with an office next door. Here, it looked more like what I'd expect from a tarot/spiritualist who was also a witch. First of all, there were tarot decks galore. The decor reminded me of her booth, all soft colors, flowy fabrics, and tons of plants. And pictures. Of her and her family. Of her and Mazzy. I picked one up and stared at it, surprised by how much alike they looked side by side. Mazzy's eyes twinkled with more mischief.

Blake appeared behind me, holding a laptop. "What are we looking for? I doubt the witches were emailing her."

"No, but I want to know what she was doing with Horatio. Is there a password on that?"

He opened it. "There is, but it's fine." He whispered something and touched a key. The screen immediately flickered and turned to her home screen.

I smiled. "Pretty good."

"Too bad it doesn't work on witch technology." He handed me the computer. "I'll check the office for anything else."

I sat down on the bed and started going through files. She had a lot of files from tarot classes and a bunch of things related to her business. It was there, hidden away in a file marked "Invoices," that I found a folder that simply said "H."

Bingo. I opened it and found pages of research on Horatio Hale, milestones from his career going back as early as his college years. A lot of links to the same videos I'd watched myself. Newspaper articles following his career, the opening of his business, even a list of his clients. Almost like she'd been doing recon on him. Which, it occurred to me, she probably had. Or someone had, in preparation for whatever they were planning to do with him.

I clicked into one of the videos that was in a separate file from all the others. It was a talk he'd done about a copper mine scandal in New Mexico he'd helped unearth. I remembered it vaguely from a seminar I'd gone to about ten years back. I watched Horatio talk for a few minutes, remembering how passionate he'd been, how articulate and knowledgeable about everything he'd been saying. He held a blue stone in one hand—I couldn't quite tell what it was—and a pyrite in the other.

A pyrite. I paused the video and leaned in to see the other stone, but I still couldn't make it out. I turned the video back on and went back to the beginning, listening impatiently until he held each one up. Blue chrysocolla. And pyrite. Two stones that someone had left for me. Cali? But why would she do that?

I sat back, turning the puzzle over in my head. New Mexico. I'd been hearing a lot about New Mexico recently. Katia was doing research there. But there had been something else too. It took me a minute to pull it out of my brain, but then it came to me. Rand's bio—the Wikipedia page. He'd grown up there, been a cop there. What was the connection? Katia had denied leaving me the packages. She could have lied. Or had Rand left them? But again, why?

Blake stuck his head back in the room. "Find anything?"

"A bunch of files on Horatio. Clearly she was doing research on him. For herself or someone else, I have no idea." I really wanted to finish watching the video, but instead I took a screenshot of the link and went back to the files.

Blake sat next to me. "No file on the murderer?"

"I wish." I finished clicking through everything, but there was nothing of any note. Just a collection of all the things that had come up in my Google search last night. "Do you think you can tune into where she went? Ginny couldn't. But Ginny's not really using her powers much, so . . ."

Blake shook his head. "I tried already. I don't think she wants anyone to find her. Which is unfortunate because if the wrong people want to find her, my guess is they'll just override whatever privacy spell she put on herself."

"Can you do that?" I asked, sitting up straight.

"I'm not doing that, Vi. Ethics, remember?"

"But what if she's in danger?"

"What if she isn't? I can't just do that. Our world would be complete chaos if we could all just do whatever we wanted to someone because we thought we had a good reason."

He had a point. But it was still frustrating.

"Any news from today?" I asked.

"They've got one of the Fernsbys in custody."

I stared at him in disbelief. "And you didn't think to mention this earlier? Did he tell them anything? Where's the other one?"

He held up a hand. "They're working on him. The other one went underground. Long story. But it's a good thing that they have him." He checked his watch. "I'm actually going to go check back with Dewin. Are you done for the night?"

"I guess I am." What I didn't tell him was that meant I was going back to Solomon's.

He watched me for a moment, then nodded. "Let's get out of here. I'll drop you at Fiona's."

"I don't need an escort, Blake. But thank you."

I held his gaze until he nodded. "Suit yourself. I'll catch up with you tomorrow." And he was gone.

CHAPTER FORTY-SEVEN

Friday
Two days before the full moon

I'd been impressed that Blake hadn't tried to force me back to Fiona's. I'd arrived back at Solomon's after midnight. Solomon and Mac were still heads-down, unraveling what seemed to be a long line of deceit and treachery. I interrupted by telling them about Cali's unexpected vacation and how a search of her house had yielded nothing of any magickal value, but it was clear that she'd been collecting information on Horatio. I wasn't happy that Cali had used Horatio as a pawn, but if she'd truly done it to help Mazzy, I couldn't blame her. And I didn't want to think of her in trouble either. So I was glad when Mac offered to try and track her to see if she'd left on her own or was coerced. I think secretly he was loving having access to

Solomon's operations—he seemed greatly enamored with the equipment available to him here.

Then I spent the rest of the night reading. I was still focused on Oscar Sageblood, determined to figure out how to connect him to all the bad things that had happened and my grandmother's death. The fact that he could very likely be Zoe's father would just have to take a backseat for now, although I realized that when that came out it would be a whole other drama.

But even as I flipped through Oscar's life, my attention kept returning to Ember. Could it really be her? I pulled out her file. The thing about these packets was that there was no commentary, just straight-up facts. On the surface, she seemed to be just as she'd presented—a legal expert and a competent, driven witch who had earned expertise in many areas.

I also realized that there was a dossier on me. And it wasn't thin, like I would've expected after having only been on the council for a couple of months. No, it was almost as thick as the rest of them. I pulled it out and flipped through, shocked to realize that there was data on me from when I was born. The dossier opened with a short summary on me, my family history, my council legacy—even Xander was noted as my familiar. My childhood. The unraveling of Fiona's marriage to George Moonstone, my father. The story of the necklace that kept Fiona away from me. My father's renouncement of his powers. My grandmother's promise to keep me out of the witch world. And basically my every move after that, as boring as it was as a mortal.

I flipped a few more pages. They knew about Todd approaching me, but there was nothing in there about why his family had orchestrated it or who exactly it had been. The mortal incident that had brought Fiona and Zoe back into my life was noted too. And the powers that I'd begun using, beginning with my aura readings to the healing powers I was able to infuse into my crystals to teleporting and all the little stuff I'd been working on. Even my attempt at erasing Officer Hanlon's memory was in here from two days ago.

I was fascinated. Where did he get this stuff?

And then I sat up straighter, realizing that there had to be notes here on everyone's powers. I went back to the pages where my powers were outlined, hoping it would tell me not only what I could do right now, but what I was able to do as part of who I was, but I didn't see anything.

I grabbed Fiona's packet. In her executive summary, it outlined all her powers. I stared in fascination. Some of them I'd never even fathomed and she'd certainly never told me. It would take me hours to dig into this. I was especially intrigued by something called "chaotic magick," under which there was a long sublist of powers. But the focus seemed to be on something called magickal manipulation, something that was starred and printed in bold. I wondered what, exactly, that meant. She also had magickal immunity, which I thought might be a positive thing, and she apparently had been approved at a young age to study reality warping. Which, at a glance, meant she could change environments around her to suit whatever need she had at the time.

I checked Oscar's. He had a familiar, which I hadn't known because I'd never seen. A wolf, which seemed appropriate. He too had a lot of powers. Necromancy was starred. That sounded a little ominous to me. I scanned for anything about shapeshifting or changing his identity, but I was so green with all this that it was like trying to decipher a different language.

I finally fell asleep at almost four a.m., surrounded by the lives of my fellow council members. I dreamt of my grandmother, and shapeshifters with black feathers, and a barista from Potions Cafe. She was trying to tell me something, but I could barely hear her, and the more I leaned in to listen the farther away she got, until I was finally so frustrated I woke up.

I tried to shake it off and checked my watch. Six ten. Friday morning. Which meant we had only two and a half-ish days left to find the orchestrator of Mazzy's genieing. The full moon was Sunday at 4:54 p.m. I could feel the weight of the ticking clock constantly, hear it in the back of my mind the way we heard it during every episode of *24* as Jack Bauer fought to save the world from whatever danger had presented itself that week. I knew how he felt.

I'd had no business sleeping, even if it was only for two hours. I conjured up an outfit and a cup of coffee and went looking for Solomon.

He was in his office, same place I'd left him last night. I wondered if he'd actually slept.

I knocked on the open door.

"Come in," he said, still looking at the screen.

"Who can shape shift?" I asked without preamble.

He turned to stare at me. "Sorry?"

I held out the dossiers. "Who in the council can shape shift? Like, become someone else? Can Oscar? What's it called?"

He smiled. "Shape shifting, usually. But depending on what you mean, it could be a number of things. Duplication, energetic manipulation. What's the context?"

"Someone put a spell on Todd. Obscene transformer, or something like that? He said it was Fiona. But Blake doesn't think so."

"Replication," Solomon murmured. "Did they speak to him?"

I nodded.

"Then yes, that's what it would be. It's very tricky to get right, especially when you're replicating a witch like Fiona."

"Who?" I demanded impatiently. "Who can do it?"

"Most witches have the ability, Violet. I've only noted in these files what's most used and used well. It might not be called out. Do you think it's connected?"

At this point I wondered if everything was connected. "I don't know. Possibly, if someone is trying to set my mother up to look bad. Hey, one other question. Why didn't you have Ember's familiar recorded in your summary?"

Solomon gave me a funny look. "She doesn't have one. She and your mother are the only two who don't work with familiars."

I shook my head impatiently. "She does. An owl. It's always on her shoulder. Kind of creepy, actually."

He was still looking at me strangely. "I wasn't aware. But I'll certainly look into it."

"Not a big deal," I said. "Gotta go."

CHAPTER FORTY-EIGHT

I headed back to North Harbor. It was the second-to-last day of the fair. And there was still the Horatio mess hanging over me. My gut was telling me this was not a witch's doing, which left me with another mystery on my hands.

The video from Cali's had stuck with me. It couldn't be a coincidence that those two stones Horatio had held in the video had showed up at my door.

As expected, when I arrived at my shop, a package leaned against my door. I didn't need to open it to know it was another stone. Whether or not it would tell me anything was anyone's guess.

I unlocked the door and opened the package while I walked to the back, flicking on lights as I went. Inside, a citrine stone. Joy and creativity. I brought it behind my counter and sat it next to the other two, willing them to tell me their secrets.

I picked up each of them, trying to tune in, willing them to give me the answers. But nothing was coming to me.

Frustrated, I put them back on my desk, knocking the envelope off accidentally. When I picked it up, something fell out that I'd missed the first time. A newspaper clipping, yellowed with age. I picked it up. It was an article about Horatio's work in New Mexico, the same topic as that video Cali had highlighted on her computer. I studied it. There was nothing new in the article. It talked about Horatio and his team and how their whistle-blowing efforts had exposed the players. I just couldn't see how he'd gone from this to a life of deceit, as Katia suggested, although I supposed money was always a good reason. But could it really be that easy to flip someone like Horatio?

I studied the citrine again and then reached for my phone. I couldn't remember where every stone came from so I wanted to check. Citrine was found in many places. It was often mined from the Congo, which immediately told me child labor laws were probably being violated. But it was also a stone that was found in the United States—and New Mexico was one of the places.

I picked up the clipping again. There was a photo of Horatio and some of his team out at one of the sites. He was the only person you could see clearly. I read the caption. I didn't recognize any of the other names . . . until I got to the third from the right.

Selena Gallagher.

The photo was in profile. Her face was mostly covered by long, straight brown hair. She faced away from the camera, shading her eyes, almost alone in the crowd.

I grabbed my phone and pulled up Rand's Wikipedia page to make sure. When I confirmed it, I sat back in my chair, thinking this through. The woman in the photo, on Horatio's team, was Rand's mother. I did some quick calculations. This story was written in 1998—twenty-four years ago. The same year Selena Gallagher had killed herself. Why? And was it related?

I grabbed my phone and called Gabe. Straight to voicemail. I reached for my purse and searched through it until I found the card I'd shoved in there the other day. Lorelai Lewis's card. I'd never gotten to talk to her yesterday, but we needed to talk now. Maybe she'd come across some of this in her research. Maybe she already had Rand Gallagher on her radar. But the fact that his mother had a connection to Horatio was pretty hard to ignore.

As I was punching in her number, the phone rang in my hand. Gabe.

"We made an arrest in the Horatio Hale murder," he said when I clicked over.

I froze. "Who?"

"Burton Jillette. The angel guy. Which feels very disingenuous, considering."

I sat back in my chair, stunned. That, I wasn't expecting. "Are you sure?" I asked. "Because I don't know—"

"He confessed," Gabe interrupted.

"You're kidding." This didn't feel right to me.

"No. Listen, I have to go. Just wanted to let you know it's over. I'll catch up with you soon."

"Gabe, wait." I rose from my chair, about to race over there. "I don't think he did it. This has something to do with Horatio's past. He used to work with Rand Gallagher's mother. I feel like it's connected somehow. Someone's been leaving me crystals and the one today had an article with it—"

"Vi. I'm telling you he confessed. And we found one of his potions there too, at the scene. It took us a while to identify it, that's why we didn't pick him up right away. But it was him."

"A tincture," I said, as Gabe disconnected. "It's a tincture, not a potion." I stared at the phone that had gone silent. Burton hadn't done this. I also didn't think Horatio had been dirty.

And I suspected Lorelai Lewis could help me prove it.

I left a note for Syd to meet me at the fair—if she was still talking to me—grabbed the stones and the article, and rushed out.

CHAPTER FORTY-NINE

I called Lorelai from the car. She answered on the first ring.

"It's Violet Mooney. I need to talk to you."

"I'm at the amphitheater," she said. Her voice sounded kind of flat for her, but it was early.

"Can I come by? They arrested Burton Jillette for Horatio's murder. I think they got it wrong, and I think some of your research can help me."

"I'm at the podcasting table," she said, then the phone went dead.

Odd response—I didn't know her well, but every time I'd spoken to her she'd been energetic and vibrant, and I thought she'd jump at the chance to potentially break a big story like this. But perhaps she was distracted.

I reached the amphitheater in less than ten minutes and pulled up to the front since the parking lot was still nearly empty. It was way too early for most people to be here yet. I swiped my pass at the door and let myself in. Most of the lights were off, but I could see the ones in the back of the room were on. I followed them to the partitioned area where Lorelai had been recording most of the week.

As I rounded the corner of the partition, words already bubbling up to my lips, I stopped short. Lorelai was at her table. She was not alone. But it wasn't one of her producers sitting there with her. It was Rand. My eyes fell to the table. Lorelai's hands were tied together in front of her with some kind of bungee cord. And on the table, a rock pick that matched the axe I'd last seen in Horatio's chest.

He smiled tightly at me. "Come on in. I hear we're having a podcast party."

My eyes met Lorelai's. Hers were terrified.

"Sit," he said to me, and his voice was sharper now. "It's about time you figured it out. Took you long enough."

"Yeah, well, I've been busy," I muttered, sliding into a chair opposite Lorelai. "Rand, what are you doing? Let Lorelai go."

He shook his head. "I'm not going to hurt her. Or you, for that matter. I just want her to record this for posterity. I want you to know the whole story too, since I tried to tell you but you're a bit slow, aren't you? And to ensure Burton doesn't suffer for this. He did nothing wrong, but he should never have butted in and tried to take the blame. So that's all I ask—that you deliver this to the police when I'm gone. Do you promise?"

"You killed Horatio," I said softly. "Was it because he was working with the people covering up the environmental damage in New Mexico? It would've gone against everything your mother believed in, right?" I was kind of grasping because I hadn't put all the pieces together yet, but based on what I knew, that had to be it.

But Rand stared at me in disgust. "Really? I thought you were smarter than that, Violet." He shook his head, then turned to Lorelai. "Are you recording?"

She nodded. "Put the headphones on. The sound will be better."

He obliged, then spoke again. "Katia is smart, but she doesn't look beyond the surface of anything. She stumbled upon an undercover operation Horatio was working on. Came very close to ruining it, although I suppose with his death it's probably ruined anyway. Shame, really." He rubbed his nose, thinking about this. "Anyway, Horatio was too much of an egomaniac to ever flip that way. He wanted to be known as a superhero. It was why my mother fell in love with him."

"Fell in love with him?" I repeated, confused.

He nodded. "Horatio was my father."

I sat stock still, taking that in. "Your father." Mental head smack. Why hadn't I seen the potential for that?

"He didn't want to be, of course," Rand went on. "Which was why my mother ultimately ended up the way she did. She had some problems, of course, that contributed. But having to take care of me when she was making minimum wage and spending most of her time in caves and mines . . ." he shook his head. "It wasn't for her. She got very depressed and couldn't deal with it. He, meanwhile, never looked back. He didn't care about anyone but himself. And he never changed." Rand sighed. "It's too bad, really. But what you see is what you get with him. You just have to look very closely to see the whole story.

"My mother never told me who my father was. Neither did Burton. He looked out for me. He and my mother had grown up together. But it wasn't too difficult to figure out, once I put my mind to it. She'd kept every piece of news, every tidbit ever printed about him. She was obsessed." He looked disgusted by this, and I thought how ironic it was that he didn't recognize that in himself.

"So you sought him out," I said. "That's even why you became a cop, right?"

He nodded, pleased that I'd at least followed that thread. "That's right. Thought if he was going to stick around New Mexico I'd have a chance to bring him down for something. I should have known better. He never stayed in one place that long. My mother learned that the hard way too. In any event, I kept tabs on him for years before I invited him to join the fair. It was my best chance at getting close to him."

"So you've been planning all these years to kill him?" I asked.

He laughed. "Of course not. That makes me sound crazy, Violet. I am not crazy. No, I didn't know exactly what I wanted from him. Some days I thought maybe I'd tell him about me, but I wasn't sure. Really, I just wanted to be close to him, I guess. To try and understand him. I did learn things from him too. He's quite good at what he does." The small smile that had touched his lips faltered. "But then he decided to try and take over the fair. Cut me out of my job and the only family I'd really ever known, outside of Burton."

"He wanted to change things," I said. I had one eye on Lorelai, who sat as still as a statue. I wondered if she was actually recording this, or if she'd been too frozen in fear. I thought about trying to reach for my phone, but I didn't want to trigger Rand to do something stupid.

Rand nodded. "He wanted all the glory here too. I know he was trying to convince the board to let me go and put him in my place. He didn't want a co-chair. He wanted to be the hero. As usual. I saw his sales pitch one day. He'd left it open on his computer. That sealed the deal for me." He reached for the rock pick, caressing the sharp edge. "I saw on his calendar he was meeting you, Violet. I figured that would be the perfect timing. And if the police thought you did it, well, that would've just been easier. But, alas, that didn't happen."

"So what are you going to do? Just give the recording to the police and skip town?"

He shook his head slowly. "I have nowhere to go. No, this is my last stop."

The way he said it sent chills up my spine. He sounded resigned. "Rand, we can get you some help. It doesn't have to be like this."

His eyes flashed. "I killed Horatio. I don't regret it. And by the time the police listen to this, I'll be dead too." He turned to Lorelai. "Give her the recording."

"It's on the cloud." Her voice shook a little. "I

have to email it. And I need my hands." She stood and held her wrists in front of her.

Rand glanced at me, then stood and began unwinding the cord from around her wrists. I calculated his distance from the rock pick then decided I had to take the chance. I grabbed it at the same moment that Lorelai twisted away and dove into the corner, wielding it in both hands like a scythe and praying he didn't have another weapon on him. "Grab my phone out of my bag and call Gabe," I told Lorelai.

"I will, but the cops should be here any second," she said. "I had a live feed going to my producer the whole time."

Rand let out a cry of frustration. I clenched the pick tighter, ready to use it if I had to, but he turned and ran for the back door.

"Come on!" I yelled. We both took off for the front door, figuring we could head him off. I pulled out my phone as we ran and called Gabe.

But I heard his phone ringing as we burst out the front. He was one of the cops standing with a small group, watching two of their colleagues lead Rand from around back to their waiting car.

CHAPTER FIFTY

"That was very smart of you to send the feed to someone who could help," Detective Briggs was saying to Lorelai. She was nodding, but she looked shaken. I felt sorry for her. Briggs glanced at me. "How did you end up in the middle of that?"

"She'd figured out it was him," Lorelai said, glancing at me. "Didn't you?"

"I was leaning that way and wanted to see what you'd found out in your research. But his son?" I shook my head. "Never guessed that piece." I turned to Briggs. "Do you need anything else from me?"

"I don't think so." He'd gotten both of our statements after they'd taken Rand away.

"Burton will go free?"

"Yes, we'll let the angel guy go." Briggs shook his head. "I'll be glad when this fair and its whole nutty lot is out of my town."

* * *

As soon as Briggs gave the word, I raced to my car and drove back to the shop. Something Rand had said had been replaying itself in my brain over and over. *What you see is what you get with him. You just have to look very closely to see the whole story.*

It reminded me of something I'd seen in Grandma Abby's book early on. Not a spell, but a note she'd written to me at the very beginning of the book. I'd read it once, but hadn't paid much attention to it since then. Now it seemed important and I needed to look at it again.

The store was as I had left it—no one else had arrived yet. Good. I raced out back to where I'd tucked the book into one of my shelves at the back of the room and pulled it out, flipping to the very first page. It still gave me a pang to see my grandmother's handwriting, so familiar. I read the short note.

> *My dearest Violet,*
> *If you're reading this, then things did not work out the way your father planned. I told him once he cannot control fate, but he wanted to try. He was always more mortal than witch—Fiona was right about that.*
> *It's a strange but wonderful world you're stepping into, but one not without its dangers. You will need time to learn about all that you are capable of, but I want to offer you one truth for every situation.*
> *You see things in others that not everyone can. You won't understand it at first, and since it can look different depending on the situation, you may*

not realize the extent of your powers. But they are there, inside you, where they've always been despite your father's desire.

Much love, my darling girl. I'm always with you.

I had to blink back the tears as I read the final words again. I missed her so much. But her words were resonating with me more and more. And they'd been here all along, just waiting for me to find them.

It was Ember. I knew it without a doubt, deep in my soul. She was behind all this. And for all of Solomon's detective work, and Mac's tracking, and the police doing whatever they were doing, I had been looking right at the evidence all along.

The first time I'd gone to Potions Cafe, the barista had said she'd heard I could see people's souls. I'd had no idea what it meant at the time. But last night, when I'd been up scouring the factual details on all the council members, I'd noticed that Ember's familiar wasn't listed. When I asked Solomon, he hadn't known what I was talking about. Nor had Blake, when I'd mentioned the owl in his office. The owl that he should've seen, clear as day, just minutes earlier.

No one saw it but me. That was because it was not really there.

Once, I'd taken an animal communication class. We'd learned about different types of animals and what they represented in the spirit world. Black owls were all about shadow work, and also about truth that was protected from those who couldn't understand it.

The black owl was showing me the shadow side of Ember all along. And no one else could see it. Not even witches like Fiona or Oscar or even Blake, whose powers far surpassed mine.

I needed to get to Blake. Hopefully they hadn't actually given Ember the consulting job with the police, because that would mean they could all be in danger if they were getting close to identifying her.

I closed my eyes, touched my grandmother's necklace, and hurtled into Blake's office.

CHAPTER FIFTY-ONE

Blake's office was empty. I bit back a frustrated cry. Where was he? He was always anticipating my next move and showing up before I could even think of it. Today he was distracted?

I had no idea where this mysterious task force was even working. I supposed I could try to teleport there and hope I got to wherever there was. Or maybe I could summon Blake here. I closed my eyes and concentrated on seeing him sitting behind his desk, offering me some of his yummy coffee.

But when I opened my eyes, it wasn't him at his desk.

I stared at Ember, feeling the bile rise in my throat. She smiled lazily at me, propping up one white-heeled foot on Blake's desk. "Nice try, but he's a bit tied up right now," she said. "Not sure you heard, but there's a genie in custody." Her eyes twinkled with black mischief. "He's a bad genie. They're hoping he'll lead them to me, but Alfred Fernsby would rather die with them than die the vicious death I'd have in store for him."

My first instinct was to teleport out of the room, but as I focused on somewhere else—anywhere else—a literal door slammed in my mind.

"Not so fast, sister. We have some things to talk about. Besides, if you go to Blake, that will only mean bad things for him. So don't try it."

My blood literally ran cold at the sound of Blake's name on her lips. "You." Without even thinking about it I used the same energy I'd summoned to shove Oscar Sageblood over a chair at one of my first council meetings and delivered a psychic blow to Ember that sent the chair flying into the wall behind her. She had thought so little of me and my abilities, she hadn't even protected herself.

She looked shocked for a minute, but recovered quickly. Next thing I knew, I was on the floor and my hands were . . . not moving. Neither were my legs. She'd put some kind of paralyzing spell on me.

"What did you do to Blake?" I demanded.

She was on her feet again now, and came to stand over me.

"Nothing. Your boyfriend is fine. But you get in my way and that will change. Don't try me," she warned, leaning down close to me. Hatred twisted her features, and I wondered how I could ever have thought she was pretty at all. I could feel the full force of her fury, the anger that had been building up in her for so many years. She probably didn't even know who she was actually angry at anymore. Just angry at the world that she hadn't gotten what she deemed her fair share.

And she'd killed my grandmother because of it.

The fury of knowing that refocused me. Ember was a pretty powerful witch. She also thought that I was too much of a newbie to know how to do much of anything. She must've figured she could basically wipe the floor with me then send the genies to get me.

Well, she was about to figure out how wrong she was.

"You killed my grandmother," I said. I wanted to get her talking while I concentrated on overriding whatever she'd done to my body. I pictured myself upright, our positions reversed, and said a silent spell, words just flying into my head as if someone was sending them there. And then I felt my fingers tingling, like they'd fallen asleep. Then the feeling flooded down into my feet. I envisioned a force-field of defense around me, so strong that I could literally feel my ancestors coming together from another dimension to give it even greater power.

"I didn't kill Abigail," Ember said coolly. "I just helped her see it was best to let some of her power go. She didn't need it all anymore. Unfortunately that hurried her demise along." She looked away. "I was sorry it had to happen that way. I had been fond of her."

I could sense something in her tone as she said that last bit. Something that told me she had some guilt about my grandmother. Good. Because I had a plan, and it hinged on there being some level of remorse for what she'd done.

"You had Mazzy and Mac genied. And you posed

as my mother and put a spell on Todd. And probably a hundred other horrible things that we haven't even figured out yet. Did you really think no one would figure it out?"

"My, aren't we the busy little detective bee!" Ember said. "I'm impressed. But it doesn't matter. Mazzy's time is almost up, and that leprechaun will never see the light of day again. Besides, the Sagebloods want your families destroyed anyway, so I had plenty of help. They'll never untangle all of this, believe me." She turned to walk back to the chair. Cocky. Too cocky. No clue that I'd circumvented her spell.

I launched myself off the ground and ran straight at her, body slamming her onto the ground face first and landing on top of her. She hit the ground with an unladylike grunt.

"Why did you do this?" I demanded trying to resist the urge to slam her head into the floor repeatedly. "You've hurt so many people. People who cared about you. My grandmother cared about you! And you should have to answer to her."

I closed my eyes and prayed that what I was about to try would work. I'd committed the basics of reality warping to memory after reading about it when I saw it listed in Fiona's file. It seemed like the best way to try and disorient Ember. I envisioned my grandma in all her strong, confident glory standing in the room with me. Then I envisioned multiple Abbys in the room. I opened my eyes and almost cried with relief. I could see them. Six Grandma Abbys in total. I knew they weren't real, but I hoped it would do the trick.

I rolled off Ember and reinforced the defense

spell around me. But she wasn't even paying attention to me. She had come to her knees, and was
staring around the room as one would when one
sees a ghost. Which she was.

"No," she whispered. "No, you're not real." She
pointed at one of the Abbys and muttered something.

I held my breath, hoping my magic would hold,
breathing a sigh of relief when it did. She pointed
at another, tried again. None of my reality-warped
Grandma Abbys had disappeared. I knew it wasn't
the best time for me to feel triumphant, but I did.
My grandma had been right. I could do anything I
set my mind to.

And yeah, I had some pretty awesome powers.

"No, no, no." She looked at me, and the fear in
her eyes was real. "She's not back. She can't be
back."

"Oh, she's back. She's standing right there," I
said. "And she knows you betrayed her, Ember.
She'll never let you rest."

Ember looked terrified now. She'd stopped trying any magick at all and had scrambled as far
back into the corner as she could. I couldn't have
her disappear on me, so I said a quick summoning
spell, asking for Blake, Chief Bell, and anyone else
in law enforcement who could hear me to get over
here now.

Thankfully that magick worked too, and the
room was suddenly filled with people. Two guys
who weren't dressed as cops—Stalker Squad, I presumed—grabbed Ember and disappeared from
the room as fast as they'd come, and then Blake
was there, pulling me to my feet, caught between

trying to see if I was okay to staring at the images of Grandma Abby that were still in the room. "Violet. Are you—how did you—"

"Oh, that," I said. I closed my eyes and reversed the spell. When I opened them, sadly, all the Grandma Abbys were gone. I felt a little like crying. It had felt so real to see her again, even though I knew it wasn't really her. But I knew with absolutely certainty she'd been helping me today.

Blake stared at me. "Did you . . . was that a reality warp?"

I nodded. "I wasn't sure I could pull it off, but I guess it worked."

He laughed, and pulled me into his arms, holding me so tight I couldn't breathe. "You bet it worked," he said into my ear. You basically just saved the world, Violet."

And then he kissed me. Finally.

CHAPTER FIFTY-TWO

Sunday
The full moon

Blake and I sat in Fiona's living room, holding hands, waiting for her to arrive. She'd summoned me there with some big announcement she needed to make. Normally, I would've been stressed about it, but right now I didn't care at all. I was perfectly happy sitting here with Blake. And he'd barely let go of my hand since the showdown between me and Ember in his office on Friday, which had set off a chain of events from which the witch world was still reeling. Personally, I was still reeling from the revelation that Oscar Sageblood was not our enemy, something my family—especially Zoe—would be unpacking for a long time to come.

Fiona had sat Zoe down to tell her last night. I didn't know how she'd taken the news because she'd disappeared. Fiona assured me she was fine, just processing, but once things slowed down I needed to go see if she was okay. That's what big sisters should do, after all.

So while Oscar had not been the bad guy, there were two other council members who'd gone down with Ember—Serenity and Jet. Jet was no surprise. He'd been aligned with the Sagebloods most of his life, and had been an easy sell to get involved with their shenanigans. Serenity was a bit more shocking to Fiona, although she'd tried to hide that. Even though she had married a Sageblood, Fiona felt she knew her well enough that the betrayal stung.

The net around the Sagebloods had been cast far and wide, and there were people even in Oscar's immediate family who had gone down for multiple conspiracies and attempts to overthrow the governing structure, colluding with genies, and practicing black magick that had resulted in the death of a witch.

Finally, there would be justice for Grandma Abby.

Chief Bell had not been part of the coverup. He was just kind of useless. However, Captain Graeme from the Stalker Squad had been protecting the Fernsbys and had even tried to help one of them get away. Dewin, Blake's friend, had been right all along. With Solomon's help, they'd found the evidence to prove it—and gotten him to reveal the location of the bad genie.

Cali had been questioned extensively and ultimately cleared of any wrongdoing. She hadn't known she was helping Ember in her nefarious deeds; she'd just thought she had a shot at helping her cousin. She'd sent me a message apologizing. I didn't think she needed to. We were all victims here.

I'd barely seen Fiona since Friday. She'd been quite busy with the aftermath of this mess, not to mention the Zoe issue. Blake, on the other hand, had been able to step away from the fray while the police sorted everything out. Legal stuff would come later, and then he'd be the man of the hour. But for now, he hadn't left my side.

Mazzy and Goldie had been freed. I hadn't seen Mazzy, but Mac had come to find me to thank me for helping free his friend. And then that sullen little leprechaun had hugged me and told me I could work on his PI team anytime I wanted. The highest praise ever.

And best of all, Syd didn't hate me. She and Pete had come to see me yesterday. She was still digesting everything, but Pete had swooped in and somehow made things better. He'd also told her I was a heroine, which made me kind of squirm. But she'd told me that no matter how weird I was, she still loved me and we'd figure this out.

So all in all, I was feeling pretty good when Fiona finally swept into the room. When she saw us, she smiled. "I like the sight of this," she said, approvingly. "Finally, my daughter comes to her senses." She came over and gave me a hug. She'd told me Friday once she got me alone how proud she was of me. After, of course, she berated me for taking such a huge risk with Ember. But I could tell she saw me in a whole new light.

I think everyone did. Finally, I felt like I was on an even playing field with my counterparts. I belonged.

"Now," she said briskly. "I have an announcement."

"Yep. That's why we're here," I said. Blake bit back a grin.

"I don't want to live here anymore," she said, ignoring us. "I want you to have this house back, Violet. It was your grandmother's, and if you . . ." here she glanced at Blake too, "want to live here, I think you should."

I stared at her, stunned. I'd never thought about moving back here. "But where are you going?" I asked.

She pointed. "Right there."

I followed her gaze left. She was pointing at the Doughertys' house. They'd lived on this street for as long as I could remember. "What? You can't! What about the—"

"The Doughertys have decided to become snowbirds. They'll be much happier in Florida." She beamed at me. "It will work out perfectly. You'll see. Now, I have to get back to meet with Chief Bell." She air-kissed both me and Blake and vanished in a swirl of multicolored glitter.

I looked at Blake. "She's unbelievable. I don't even know what to say to that."

He squeezed me against him. "You don't have to say anything about it today."

"Good. You want to come back to my place?" I asked. "I heard there's a possibility I might still need a babysitter."

He grinned. "You got it. I'll even reduce my rate." He grabbed my hand, but as we were about to teleport there, a figure appeared in the driveway. She turned, shading her eyes against the sun, her multicolored hair unmistakable.

"Mazzy," I breathed.

I ran down the steps and pulled her into a hug. It took her a second, but then she hugged me back, hard and fierce. I finally stepped back and studied her. "You look great," I said, although I wasn't really sure how someone who had spent almost three months in a bottle was supposed to look.

"Thanks. Being bottled up is good for the diet, if nothing else." Then she sobered. "Thank you, Violet. My family told me that you never gave up on me. That . . . means a lot."

We held each other's gaze for a moment, then I nodded. "There's nothing to thank me for. You would've done the same." I grinned. "I think."

She threw her head back and laughed, and the sound filled me with joy. I'd helped save her. I'd used my powers for good and done something huge. Grandma Abby would be proud.

"Hey," she said. "When things settle down, I want to write a story about this. I think this could be my big break. I can see it as, like, a serial, you know? And I think we should write it together. We can pitch it to some really big papers. That *Magickal Minute?* Trash. We can go so much bigger. . . ." She chattered on, and I glanced behind me at Blake. He watched us with a smile, and his gaze filled me with warmth. For the first time, I felt like I was going to be just fine in my new life.

Especially with this hot, sexy witch lawyer by my side.

Visit our website at
KensingtonBooks.com
to sign up for our newsletters, read
more from your favorite authors, see
books by series, view reading group
guides, and more!

BOOK **CLUB**
BETWEEN THE CHAPTERS

Become a Part of Our
Between the Chapters Book Club
Community and Join the Conversation

Betweenthechapters.net